THE

COINCIDENCE

MAKERS

THE
COINCIDENCE
MAKERS

YOAV BLUM

ST. MARTIN'S PRESS NEW YORK

www.stmartins.com

Edited by Rebbeca Hayman and Parrick Lobrutto

Designed by Steven Seighman

Library of Congress Cataloging-in-Publication Data

Names: Blum, Yoav, author.
Title: The coincidence makers / Yoav Blum.
Other titles: Metsarfe ha-miòkrim. English
Description: First edition. | New York : St. Martin's Press, 2018. | Originally published in Hebrew.
Identifiers: LCCN 2017043678 | ISBN 9781250146113 (hardcover) | ISBN 9781250177315 (international) | ISBN 9781250146137 (ebook)
Subjects: LCSH: Coincidence—Fiction. | Life change events—Fiction. | Fate and fatalism—Fiction. | Free will and determinism—Fiction. | Choice (Psychology)—Fiction. | Psychological fiction. | GSAFD: Mystery fiction.
Classification: LCC PJ5055.17.L82 M4713 2018 | DDC 892.43'7—dc23
LC record available at https://lccn.loc.gov/2017043678

Originally published in Hebrew in Israel under the title מצרפי המקרים by Keter Publishing House, edited by Shira Hadad.

First U.S. Edition: March 2018

10 9 8 7 6 5 4 3 2 1

To my parents, who showed me how to find my own path,
and to Rachel, who joined her path with mine

God does not play dice with the universe.

—ALBERT EINSTEIN

Stop telling God what to do with his dice.

—NIELS BOHR

THE

COINCIDENCE

MAKERS

FROM *INTRODUCTION TO COINCIDENCES*
—PART I

Look at the line of time.

Of course, it is only an illusion. Time is a space, not a line.

But for our purposes, look at the line of time.

Watch it. Identify how each event on the line is both a cause and effect. Try to locate its starting point.

You will not succeed, of course.

Every now has a before.

This is probably the main—though not the most obvious— problem you will encounter as coincidence makers.

Therefore, before studying theory and practice, formulas and statistics, before you start to make coincidences, let's start with the simplest exercise.

Look again at the line of time.

Find the correct spot, place a finger on it, and simply decide: "This is the starting point."

1

Here too, like always, timing was everything.

Five hours before painting the southern wall in his apartment for the 250th time, Guy sat at the small café and tried to sip his coffee in a deliberate, calculated way.

His body was tilted back a bit from the table, leaning in a position that was supposed to suggest a calmness engendered by years of self-discipline, with the small coffee cup gently cradled between his fingers like a precious seashell. From the corner of his eye, he followed the progress of the second hand on the large clock hanging above the cash register. As always, in the final moments before implementation, he felt the same frustrating awareness of his breathing and his heartbeat, which occasionally drowned out the ticktock of the seconds.

The café was half full.

He glanced around at the people and again saw in his mind the spiderwebs that traversed the air, the thin and invisible connections that linked them.

Sitting across from him at the other end of the café was a round-faced teenager, resting her head against the windowpane, allowing the music produced by marketing alchemists specializing in teenage romance to flood her thoughts via thin earphone wires. Her closed eyes, her relaxed facial features—everything radiated serenity. Guy didn't know enough about her to determine whether it was indeed genuine. The young woman wasn't part of the equation at the moment. She wasn't supposed to be part of it—just part of the background buzz.

An insecure couple on a first or second date sat at the table opposite the young woman, trying to navigate through what was perhaps a friendly conversation, or a job interview for the position of spouse, or a quiet war of witticisms camouflaged by smiles and occasional side-glances in order to avoid the prolonged eye contact that would create a false sense of intimacy. In fact, this couple was an example of all hurried relationships that anxiously revolve around themselves. The world was full of such couplings, regardless of how hard it tried to prevent them.

A bit toward the back, in the corner, sat a student busy erasing the face of an old love from his heart, at a table full of papers covered in dense handwriting. He gazed at a large mug of hot chocolate, immersed in a daydream disguised as academic concentration. Guy knew his name, medical history, emotional history, musings, dreams, small fears. Guy had everything filed away somewhere . . . everything he needed to know in order to guess the possibilities, to try to arrange them in accordance with the complex statistics of causes and effects.

Finally, two waitresses with tired eyes—who were somehow still smiling and standing—conducted a quiet, intense conversation by the closed door to the kitchen. Or rather, one of them spoke while the other listened, nodding occasionally, offering signs according to the predetermined "I'm Paying Attention" protocol, though it seemed to Guy she was thinking about something completely different.

He also knew her history. Anyway, he hoped he did.

He put down the cup of coffee and counted the seconds in his head.

It was seventeen minutes before four o'clock in the afternoon, according to the clock above the cash register.

He knew that each person in the café would have a slightly different time on his or her watch. A half a minute before or after didn't really matter.

After all, people were not only differentiated from one another by place. They also operated in different times. To a certain extent, they moved within a personal time bubble of their own making. Part of Guy's work, as the General had said, was to bring these times together without generating the sense of an artificial encounter.

Guy himself didn't have a watch. He'd discovered that he didn't ever use one. He was so conscious of time that he had no need for it.

He always loved this warm sensation, which nearly permeated the bone, during the minute preceding the execution of a mission. It was the sensation that came from knowing he was about to reach out a finger and nudge the planet, or the heavens. The knowledge that he would be diverting things from their regular and familiar path, things that until a second ago were moving in a completely different direction. He was like a man painting great and complex landscapes, but without a brush and paint—simply with the precise and gentle turn of a big kaleidoscope.

If I didn't exist, he'd thought more than once, they would need to invent me. They would have to.

Billions of such movements happened every day, corresponding with each other, offsetting each other and swinging each other in a tragic-comic dance of possible futures. None of the protagonists were aware of these movements. And he, in one simple decision, saw the change that was about to happen, and then executed it. Elegantly, quietly, secretly. Even if it were exposed, no one would believe what stood behind it. And still, he always trembled a bit beforehand.

"First of all," the General had told them when they began, "you are secret agents. All the others are first of all agents and secondly secret, but you are first of all secret and to a certain extent, also agents."

Guy inhaled deeply, and everything started to happen.

The teenage girl at the table across from him moved a bit as one song in the playlist finished and another began. She shifted the position of her head on the windowpane, opened her eyes, and stared outside.

The student shook his head.

The couple, still sizing each other up, chuckled in embarrassment, as if there were no other type of chuckle in the world.

The second hand had already completed a quarter of its circuit.

Guy exhaled.

He pulled the wallet out of his pocket.

Exactly on time, a short and irritable summons tore the two waitresses from each other, sending one of them into the kitchen.

He placed a few dollars on the table.

The student began to collect his papers, still slow and pensive.

The second hand reached its halfway mark.

Guy put down his cup, still half full, exactly three-quarters of an inch from the edge of the table, on top of the money. When the hand on the clock reached forty-two, he stood and waved to the waitress who remained outside the kitchen, in a motion that communicated both "thank you" and "good-bye."

She waved back to him and started to move toward the table.

As the second hand passed its three-quarter mark, Guy walked toward the sun-drenched street and disappeared from the view of the café patrons.

Three, two, one . . .

❧

The cute student in the corner prepared to leave.

Though it was Julie's table, Shirley would apparently have to take care of it, now that her coworker was in the kitchen. Not that she minded. She liked students. She liked cute young men. A cute student was a winning combination, as a matter of fact.

Shirley shook her head.

No! Stop these thoughts immediately! Enough with "cute" and "charming" guys and every other adjective you feel obliged to toss around.

Been there, done that. You tried, you checked, you soared, you crashed. And now you've learned. Enough. It's over. You're taking a b-r-e-a-k.

The other young man, the one with the melancholy eyes, waved to her as he began to leave.

She knew him, if one could know a man from weekly, silent visits. He usually drank every drop of coffee, leaving the half-muddy sediment at the bottom, as if waiting for a fortune-teller who would never come, and the money gently folded underneath the cup. He left the café, and it seemed to her that she detected some tension in his steps. She approached his table and made a point of not looking at the student.

After all, she was only a human being. And an entire year had passed. Clearly, she still felt the need for some type of human warmth.

She still could not get used to the thought that alone was the new together. That she needed to be strong, genuine, a lone and beautiful wolf in the snow, or a leopardess in the desert, or something like that. Years and years of chick flicks, sugary pop songs, and superficial books had managed to construct a well-built fortification of romantic illusions in her mind.

But it'll be okay.

It'll be okay.

She reached out her hand, a bit lost in her thoughts.

She heard a soft noise behind her and turned her head. It was the girl with the earphones, humming to herself.

Even before turning her head back, Shirley realized she had made a mistake.

Her brain now perceived the events as they transpired, predicting them, timing them with the precision of an atomic clock, but always a thousandth of a second late.

Now, her hand was moving the cup a bit instead of grabbing it.

Now, the cup, which for some reason was placed so close to the edge, was losing its balance.

Now, she was reaching with her other hand, trying to catch the falling cup; and she was failing and the cup shattered on the floor and she cried out, a sharp, frustrated cry.

And now, here was the student—that is, a young man, a young man who wasn't interesting at all—lifting his head toward the cry, moving his hand in the wrong direction, and inadvertently spilling hot chocolate on his papers.

And now, Bruno was coming out of the kitchen.

Shit.

"Sometimes you'll need to be a bit ruthless," the General would say. "It happens. It's necessary. I, myself, really enjoyed this. But you don't have to be little sadists in order to understand. The principle is quite simple."

Guy walked down the street, counting his steps until he could permit himself to turn around and look from afar. The cup should have already fallen. He would take a look, just one quick glance, to be sure everything was okay, to confirm. This wasn't childish, this was healthy curiosity. No one would notice. He was on the other side of the street. He was allowed to do this.

And then he would go sabotage the pipe.

Shirley saw the student curse, his arms flailing in an effort to rescue the pages covered in dense handwriting.

She bent down quickly to collect the broken pieces of the cup, and bumped her head on the table.

Shit #2.

She tried to collect the large pieces without getting cut. Her shoes were spotted with small coffee stains, like the splotches of a hesitant giraffe.

Did coffee stains come out in the laundry? Were these shoes even washable?

She quietly cursed everything and everyone. It was the third time this had happened to her at the café. Bruno had made it very clear what would happen the third time.

"Leave it," she heard a quiet voice say.

Bruno crouched next to her, crimson with anger.

"I'm sorry," she said. "Really. It . . . it was an accident. I just lost my concentration for half a second. Really."

"It's the third time," Bruno muttered angrily. He didn't like to yell in front of customers. "The first time, I said it wasn't a big deal. The second time, I warned you."

"Bruno, I'm sorry," she said.

Bruno glared at her.

Oh. Big mistake.

He really didn't like to be called by his first name. She didn't usually make mistakes like that. What was going on with her today?

"Leave it," he said quietly, accentuating each word. "Return the uniform, take your share of today's tips, and leave. You're not working here anymore." And before she could utter a word, he stood up and went back into the kitchen.

Now Guy was running.

He still had a lot to do. Everything could not be prepared in advance. There were things he had to execute at the last moment, or at least check that they were occurring as they should.

He had yet to reach the point where he could let the cups fall and then sit and watch one event follow another. He still needed to give the events a small push, in real time.

He would need to photocopy most of the material again.

One of the waitresses—not the one who was collecting the pieces from the floor and looked like she was about to burst into tears— came to him with paper towels and helped him mop up whatever the pages had not yet absorbed. In silence, they quickly cleaned the table. He left most of the papers there. "You can throw these away," he said to her. "I'll just photocopy them again."

"What a bummer," she said and pursed her lips in sympathy.

"Bring me the bill please," he said. "I think I'll get going."

She nodded and turned around, and he caught a whiff of her perfume. A small, old alarm quietly resonated in his head. Sharon's perfume.

He needed this like a hole in the head.

He blinked and continued to stuff the papers that were still dry into his bag. Then, with the table sparkling, the waitress gave him the bill.

He didn't even notice that he had stopped breathing when she came near, just to avoid smelling her by mistake.

When she moved away, he lifted his eyes from the bill and saw the second waitress, the one who knocked the cup over, leaving the café, dressed in regular clothes.

Guy sat at the bus stop and opened the little notebook.

He was in a spot where she wasn't supposed to see him, but just in case, he pretended to be reading the notebook.

He opened it to one of the first coincidences he had worked on. The mission was to cause a particular employee at a shoe factory to lose his job. The person was a brilliant composer who had never discovered his talent for music. In the first stage, Guy had to arrange for him to be fired; in the second stage, he had to expose the man to music in a way that would induce him to try to compose something.

It had been a fairly complicated task for a fledgling coincidence maker, and less exciting than other missions he dreamed of.

Guy remembered being quite pretentious at that time. He tried to do something that far exceeded his planning abilities. Reading from the notebook, he remembered that he used a particularly jumpy goat, flu shots, and a power outage that paralyzed the entire factory.

He failed, of course. They fired someone else because he didn't correctly calculate the employees' times of arrival. That was back when he only took the individual person into account, instead of looking at that person's connection to the broader picture. He hadn't paid sufficient attention to the pattern of traffic jams on Thursday mornings in his composer's neighborhood, and someone else was at the factory at the time Guy thought his mark would be present.

The entire maneuver he'd tried to execute was sketched on four pages in the notebook. Four pages! Damn, who did he think he was?

Someone else arranged for the man to be fired five months later. He also managed to return the man Guy had mistakenly fired to the newly vacated position. Guy had no idea who did this. He figured several musical compositions would never be written because of his mistake.

Not all of his mistakes were corrected in this way. There wasn't always a second chance.

Across the street, he saw the waitress who knocked over his cup arrive at the bus stop.

At that moment it seemed like the entire world revolved around the rhythmic tapping of her steps on the sidewalk. That and the small *swish* her arm made as it brushed against her clothes, and the touch of the label in the back of the blouse. When she was irritated, she paid attention to unimportant details.

She'd discovered this not long ago.

Strange, but it wasn't her abrupt firing that disturbed her now, but the feeling that it hadn't occurred as she imagined it would. Just like that, in a second, everything changed? Life was not supposed to treat you this way. Life was supposed to slowly bring you the tidings, good or bad. It shouldn't throw stones into your pond and point to the circles disturbing the water's tranquility with a malicious smile. Why did she have the feeling that what happened was like a head-on crash with a distant acquaintance just as you were turning the corner?

It had rained earlier, and despite the bright and warm sun that now bathed the street, there was the smell of something new in the air. A small brown stream flowed at the edges of the street, to the sewers, allowing a rude bus to splash her as it passed by, wetting her shoes again. She had missed her bus. Of course, it was one of those days.

She just had to get through it without serious bodily injury, or something like that, and tomorrow would be more reasonable. Tomorrow there would be time for damage assessment, for a meticulous inspection of her basic fortifications, and for a rational decision about how to move forward, and where.

She scolded herself for her histrionics. So she'd been fired from work, big deal. It wasn't a formative experience she would recount to her grandchildren or to a psychologist. It was just a lousy day. You're quite familiar with days like this. You're good friends. No drama, please.

She stuck out her hand. It could be an hour until the next bus came. It would be better to just get a taxi, take a long shower, and climb into bed until tomorrow. And tomorrow we'll see. We'll see if there's work somewhere. We'll see what to do about next month's rent. We'll see what the instructions are for washing shoes.

෨

Guy was worried. She didn't seem despondent enough. He had expected a medium-high level of despondency.

Actually, it might be good that she wasn't so despondent. She'd remain open to new ideas.

On the other hand, some light frustration peppered with a dash of sadness was likely to make her yearn for someone to lean on.

Or it could simply encourage her to stay away from people.

I should have taken this possibility into account, Guy thought. I'm such an idiot. I should have calculated her level of despondency in advance, precisely. You need to minimize the chances of error in all things pertaining to choice. It's the first lesson. Okay, not really the first. Perhaps closer to the fifth.

Perhaps it's the tenth. I don't really remember anymore.

In any case, she doesn't appear to be sufficiently despondent.

෨

"What's happening?" he asked.

One of the passersby on the sidewalk stopped. "What?"

"What's happening?" he asked again. "Why aren't the cars moving?"

"A water pipe burst," the man said. "They closed the street."

"Oh, thanks."

He'd drive around it. If he turned right here and then left, he should be traveling parallel and come to . . . no, there's no entry there. Maybe he'd turn right twice and then left via that one-way street. Or maybe it wasn't a one-way street, but a dead-end street? Sharon always laughed at him. "How did you complete officer training if you can't even navigate around the city?"

"In the city it's different," he would tell her.

"It should be even easier," she would say.

"I didn't have you in the course," he would tell her. "You completely ruin my concentration."

She would smile that smile and tilt her head a bit. An offside Mona Lisa smile.

"No, no, really," he would say. "Maps, streets, diagrams, directions. I get everything jumbled. Right now, there are only two places—by your side, and not by your side. So how am I supposed to remember how to drive to the movies, huh? You tell me."

And she would lean over a bit and whisper in his ear, "Left, then right at the end of the block, and straight at the traffic circle, commander."

So the pages were ruined—so what? He wouldn't let that spoil his day . . . or any day. Any day at all.

He would go home, toss all of the lousy papers into the darkest corner of the apartment, download a comedy, the most inane comedy he could find—something with college students, or neurotic Brits, or Spanish women who spoke really fast—and then he'd sit with beer and peanuts and enjoy them without any feelings of guilt.

Then he'd go to the beach. That was also a possibility.

In any case, beer was an important ingredient. The beer would be insulted if it were not involved. You don't mess around with beer; he had learned that the hard way.

He tipped back his head and roared with pleasure. Every time he postponed a task related to his studies, he got into a good mood.

So alive. He loved this "zone"—his happy, nice zone, the one that managed to see life beyond its obligations, as something through which you needed to flow.

Onc day I'll be a Zen teacher, he thought. I'll put people in cars and watch them roar and laugh themselves to life.

But until then, we'll make do with being nice. We'll help some old lady, we'll pick up a hitchhiker, we'll buy a flower and give it to a random young woman in the street. He was roaring with pleasure again.

☙

People respond to things in different ways.

People also had different weaknesses. Guy discovered the student's weakness somewhere in the middle of conducting his research.

None of these weaknesses worried Guy in particular, except for the student's difficulty with finding his way around the city.

So he arranged for the student to watch a military documentary the previous evening. He loved to influence people's thoughts by changing the television schedule. It was relatively easy, and it had the pleasant aroma of a wager. And he no longer dared risk a larger wager than that.

After the student had watched the film, Guy felt there was a chance that when the student asked himself where to drive after leaving the coffee shop, something similar to "left, right, left" would come to mind. In any case, the other roads would not be open.

☙

Too much time had passed. She had to catch a taxi. She lazily lifted her arm again and tried to calculate the chances of finding a new job that week.

She reached the conclusion that there was no chance, and just then a small blue car stopped next to her, and the window opened.

Distractedly, she conducted the short conversation about her destination and entered the car. A moment after closing the door, she realized that it wasn't a taxi. She had inadvertently been hitch-hiking, apparently, and now, seated next to her was the student from the café who was sure that she had waved at him. . . .

He put the car into gear, smiled at her, and began to drive.

And now, as they were moving, the ground could not swallow her up even if it wanted to.

She was cute, and quiet too. A dangerous combination from his point of view.

It seems you cannot refrain from fantasizing a relationship with any creature of the female persuasion you encounter, he scolded himself. And now get on with your life, my friend.

But, actually, if I'm going to the beach with beer . . .

He made a real effort, it should be said to his credit.

She silently counted nearly a full minute before he broke down and started to speak.

"I hope he didn't yell at you too much?" he asked with a small smile.

"No, he's not a yeller. When he's upset, he simply speaks in a very accentuated way."

"Accentuated?"

"Each and every word. Like gravel."

"How accentuated was he this time?"

"He fired me." She shrugged her shoulders.

Half a look, half worried. "Really?"

"Really." Never had the word "really" been uttered so sharply and curtly. That was the last word in the conversation, my friend, she thought. Hope that got through to you.

Part of her was like this. A part that liked to be abusive in small talk. To break the accepted continuity of question and obvious response, to say the inappropriate word or the sentence that would make everyone fall silent, feel unpleasant, squirm in discomfort and think: Okay, she apparently *r-e-a-l-l-y* doesn't want to talk.

Don't talk to me about work. Don't talk to me at all. Drive. I'm just here by chance. Simply drive.

"I, um, I'm sorry to hear that."

"I'm sorry about your papers. I saw that everything spilled onto your notes."

"It's nothing. I'll just photocopy them again." Now it was his turn to shrug.

"Okay."

"It's really nothing."

"I understand. Okay. So I'm not sorry." She smiled to herself.

"Um, yes."

"I'm Dan."

"Shirley."

"I have a cousin named Shirley."

What do I care? "Really? Wow."

"Yes."

❧

Guy counted breaths again. It was supposed to be more effective than counting seconds, he knew, but it became problematic when the pace of his breath was irregular.

He took the cell phone from the bag and waited a bit.

And a bit more.

You could call this conversation an "insurance policy," no?

He punched in the number.

❧

"I'll drop you off at the corner before your street, okay? If I go down that street, it becomes a one-way, um, I think."

"Great. No problem." She allowed herself to flash a smile.

"Your apartment is close to the beach, right?"

"Yes, quite close." A step forward.

"Do you go to the beach often?" he tried.

"Sometimes. Not so much." Two steps backward.

"I go there occasionally. It really clears your head."

"Actually, not at all. The noise of the waves breaks my concentration."

"You don't have to concentrate to clear your head."

"Whatever you say."

She smiled. It's a good smile. That is, a smile is good in general, right?

"I might go this evening. Do you feel like joining me?"

"Listen . . ."

"Really, nothing special. I'll bring beer and you can bring something if you feel like snacking. Just to sit, to talk. I'm serious."

"I don't think so."

"Usually, I would wait until a conversation developed between us, of course. Charm you with all sorts of banal insights. I'm not one of those guys who rushes things, but it's just that we'll be arriving in a moment and . . ."

"I'm not into that."

"Into what?"

"Relationships."

"At all?"

"At all."

"Sort of like a nun?"

"More like a sort of strike."

"Why?"

"It's complicated."

"How long have you been on strike?"

"I don't think it's worth . . . what's that noise?"

"I think it's from your bag."

"Ah, it's my cell phone, shit." Searching, groping, fumbling for it. "Hello?"

"Hi."

"Yes?"

"Is this Donna?"

"No." She felt her eyebrow rising up on its own, annoyed.

"Hello?"

"No, no. It's not Donna."

"Donna?"

"There's no Donna here. Wrong number."

"Hello?"

"Wrong number! Wrong number!" she shouted.

She closed her cell phone and tossed it into her bag, on the floor by her feet. "Ugh! What a crazy day."

Guy put the cell phone back into his pocket.

Okay, now all he could do was hope and go home.

And paint the wall.

Guy put the cell phone back into his pocket.

"Okay, we're here."

"Great. Thanks."

"So I won't see you there anymore?"

"No, I was fired."

"And there's no chance you'll break your strike?"

"No."

"I'm sane. Completely. I've been examined by leading experts."

"I'm sure."

A last smile, eyebrows raised. "Not even a chance of one in a thousand? You won't leave me a telephone number?"

He should've given up a long time ago.

"No, thank you."

I'm outta here.

A huge and detailed diagram of the last mission was sketched on the wall. There was one circle with "Shirley" written in it, and a second circle with "Dan" written in it, and countless lines branching out from them.

On the side were long lists of character traits, aspirations, and desires.

And there were a great many circles linked to one another with blue lines (actions to execute), red lines (risks), broken lines (things that might happen), and black lines (connections that must be taken into account). A note was written inside each circle in small and hesitant lines—"Bruno" and "Julia" and "water pipe" and "bus no. 65" and other several dozen elements that ostensibly had no connection at all, such as "basic training and dreams—documentary film" and "David, cable company technician" and "Monique, David's wife." In the left corner at the bottom was a space for calculations. The amount of coffee that would make the falling cup sufficiently spectacular, how much perfume had to remain in Julia's perfume bottle, how much water flowed per hour in the pipe, the desired depth of the puddle that the bus encountered on its route, the songs that girls liked to hum.

There was also a list of air conditioner technicians and conversation topics related to pelicans, and entry codes of at least nine banks, and ingredients of Irish beers, and television schedules of channels in three countries, and the way in which the words "good luck" were spoken in various languages, and time zones, and associative connections that could be created between Peru and goat's milk, and hundreds of other details in small letters in different colors, with lines stretching back and forth for all of the possibilities and subpossibilities, and the contexts and the thoughts and the combinations that could lead to a single point.

Yes, definitely, he was long past the stage of working with a notebook.

"Hi."

"Hi."

"Dan, right?"

"Yes."

"It seems I left my telephone with you."

"Yes, it was on the floor of my car."

"I guess I dropped it there instead of in my bag."

"Apparently. So it seems you did indeed leave me your telephone number, or at least your phone."

"So it seems."

Half a silence, a quarter of stillness, a tenth of tense expectation.

"Um. Could you come by and bring it to me?"

"Yes. Sure."

"Great."

"But I have a better idea."

"Yes?"

"I'm at the beach. You're welcome to come and get it."

"Um, okay."

"Great."

"It'll take me about fifteen minutes."

"I'm not in a hurry."

"Okay, bye."

"And . . . Shirley?"

"Yes?"

"I have drinks here, so bring something to snack on if you can."

Precisely calculated angles of tossing a telephone in anger, thin and long cracks in dams of solitude, roars of pleasure that echoed in a car for several minutes—everything would ultimately converge at this single point.

"Okay."

Night. The sea. Another young man and young woman sat to talk. Nothing out of the ordinary. Small smiles, discreetly protected by the darkness. Newspapers spread on the floor and another coat of paint added to a wall that had seen the world from all sides.

On an electronic sign somewhere in a nonexistent airport, another entry was added under "Love—Arrivals."

Under the Reason column, the words "coincidence of the second degree" was illuminated.

And another day passes.

2

When Guy woke the next day, the faint smell of paint lingered in the air, even though he had left the balcony doors open all night for ventilation.

He mentally patted himself on the shoulder. Waking up naturally is another good sign. You're starting to be a professional.

Professional enough to be able to fall asleep after a successful mission. Professional enough to know that after you did your part, you did not remain on the scene too long and did not check on the client. Professional enough not to lie all night with eyes open just to catch the moment when the envelope was slipped under the door.

Not that he really ever succeeded in capturing that moment.

Sooner or later, he always fell asleep. Sometimes only for a few moments, but that was enough. When he woke, he would discover

that someone had come and slipped a brown envelope under the door
to his apartment.

He remembered lying in bed one time, flush with adrenaline
after successfully orchestrating a coincidence that prevented a
woman from being unfaithful to her beloved. The apartment was
dark, but he left the area in front of the door illuminated and
placed his bed at an angle that would allow him to see the envelope
when it arrived.

He remembered looking at the clock and seeing it was 4:59. He
blinked one exhausted blink and dozed for a few moments. When
he opened his eyes, it was 5:03, and the large brown envelope had
been placed in a square of light, where it chuckled at him scornfully.

He jumped out of the bed, falling and twisting his leg, but still
somehow managed to run to the door and fling it wide open. He
looked quickly in all directions. The stairway was empty. He listened.
No steps could be heard. Making a quick decision, he left the door
open behind him and dashed unsteadily down the stairs on his
aching leg, two steps at a time, tightly grasping the railing and trying
not to scream in pain at every step, until he reached the street and
began to search left and right like a crazy man.

The street was empty; the first bright rays of sunlight began to
warm the cold night air.

Guy stood there, shaking a bit, his sleepy mind responding with
shock to the rapid transition from drowsy repose to frantic and painful sprinting in the cold morning. A few light shivers sent him an
unequivocal message: "Tell me, have you lost your mind?"

He turned around and went back home. By the time he got upstairs, he had decided that he actually didn't care who placed the
envelopes under the door.

He was a professional, right?

Everything else should be of no concern to him. He must carry out the job and execute it in a way that would cause his assigned events to occur in the cleanest and most natural way. That's it.

He slowly sat up in bed, savoring the few remaining moments before receiving a new mission.

Soon he would shuffle from the bedroom to the living room, and see the envelope with the next mission placed just inside the door. The first page would include a general description. Bringing lovers together was a mission he had received a lot lately. Perhaps this time would be different.

The mission could be to change a worldview; unite families; make peace between enemies; sow seeds of inspiration that generate a work of art, a new insight, a groundbreaking scientific discovery if he was lucky—who knew. The first page would contain this description, detail who was involved, provide a bit of general background and the immediate circle of people he'd have to interact with, and the usual reminders about adhering to timetables.

Then he would find a number of small booklets containing information about the relevant players. Names, places, influences, statistics of decision making in various situations, conscious and unconscious beliefs. There would also be a booklet of specifications for the coincidence to be created and the repercussions that must be avoided. He recently had been assigned to bring together two future lovers, but the briefing explained that the young woman must not meet any member of the young man's family before meeting the young man, and that no alcohol could be involved during the process of their becoming acquainted.

Several months earlier, a briefing he'd received specified that he couldn't make use of emergency medical situations in order to facilitate the coincidence, which was aimed at steering the client toward a new insight about death. This complicated the matter a bit.

The last pages of the briefing would specify which "broad" activity could be conducted in the short term. The explosion in the water pipe the previous day was an activity of this sort. In fact, the briefing nearly required the activity because it was designed to facilitate a number of more complex coincidences (level four, apparently) that transpired at the same time. Guy probably could have fulfilled the mission without the water pipe. There were a thousand ways to block a street.

Such broad activities were always a bit problematic. It was difficult to predict the scope of their repercussions if the briefing didn't explicitly define them. Perhaps it was possible, but it would require diagrams that would cover an entire ten-story building. Guy wasn't at that rank yet. A bit more time on the job, and he would get there.

And there was, of course, the usual waiver, to which no one paid serious attention. "I hereby declare that I have decided of sound mind to resign from active service. . . ." Blah, blah, blah.

He entered the living room, where the envelope was waiting.

He allowed himself to ignore it for the time being and turned to the bathroom, his eyes still bleary.

He had dreamed the dream again last night. Each time in a different place, but always the same thing. Blurry pictures of himself standing in the middle of a forest, in the center of a soccer field, inside a huge bank safe, on a soft cloud . . .

In the dream last night, he was in the desert. Miles and miles of hard, cracked ground sprawled out before him, thirsty broken lines on an endless yellow-brown surface. He moved his eyes back and forth and saw only barrenness to the horizon, and the sun scorched the top of his head.

In this dream, as always, he knew that she was standing behind him. Back to back. He felt her presence there. It could only be she.

He tried to spin around, to look away from the barren landscape and turn his body toward her, face-to-face. And as always, his body didn't obey him. He felt a gentle breeze on the back of his neck and tried to say her name and woke up.

Every few days, like a bothersome friend who can't take a hint, the dream came, each time a slightly different variation. It was starting to bore him.

When would he have normal dreams?

While brushing his teeth he let the mild smell of the paint and the tingling feeling of a new mission awaken him. He always liked to wait a bit before opening the envelope. Only an hour later, when all the morning affairs were organized and Guy felt completely alert and lucid, would he sit down on the sofa, place his cup of coffee on the table, and with the familiar light tingling in his fingers, open the envelope.

Today's was unusually light and thin. He wondered why, and then discovered that it contained only one piece of paper. An hour, place, and a single sentence: "Do you mind, perhaps, if I kick you in the head?"

FROM *TECHNICAL METHODS IN COINCIDENCE MAKING*—PART A

Among historians of coincidence making, there is a common view that "cliché-dropping" is one of the three most ancient methods of coincidence creation, and was apparently developed even before the official design of the classical coincidence-making methods by Jack Brufard.

Cliché-dropping is considered one of the least expensive and simplest techniques, and one of the safest maneuvers for beginning and apprentice coincidence makers. Consequently, you will already practice C.D. during the first month of the seminar. However, due to the complexity this entails, as demonstrated in the studies by Florence Bunshet, it is customary for the clichés to be set in advance by the trainers, while the students in the course primarily practice the technical aspects of the drop, such as strength, diction, pauses, and spacing or location vis-à-vis the object.

During the coming weeks, you will be assigned various sayings that you will have to practice thoroughly and drop at the place and time the trainer defines.

There are three customary methods of C.D., and we will practice all three of them during this course. We will first perform the exercises in a dry run and later in crowded places such as lines at health clinics, movie theaters, and banks, among large audiences during shows or in busy restaurants. The student will practice arriving at a precise location within hearing range of the desired object and at the correct time. Usually, the goal of the drop is to plant sayings that would not reach the object through his or her regular modes of thinking and thus arouse new thought processes. Of course, one should say the cliché to somebody else in such a way that the object ostensibly hears it by coincidence.

Classic C.D. In Classic C.D. (C.C.D.) common clichés are used. Good examples include: "If he believes, he will succeed," "The truth can be found within yourself," and "You can't cry over spilled milk." Today we use C.C.D. primarily in dry runs because few people are still influenced by classic clichés. Studies have shown that the public is immune to them.

Postmodern C.D. P.M.C.D. usually tries to adopt the method of contradictory clichés. "He has no chance, the little bum" was the first P.M.C.D., which was successfully tried on a jockey in a horse race by the founder of the P.M.C.D. method, Michel Clatiere. Opposite sayings usually generate a strong reaction from an object who is not totally in despair. The trainer is responsible for studying the object before the use of P.M.C.D.

Client-tailored C.D. This is the most prevalent type of C.D. today. The coincidence maker must conduct an in-depth study of the object's character in order to discover key words, events, and associations that are likely to influence him. Students will practice C.T.C.D. only in the second stage of the course, after completing the introductory lesson on personality analysis.

CAUTIONARY RULES FOR CLICHÉ-DROPPING

1. Always go in pairs; people do not tend to believe someone who is talking to himself. In this way, you will also be able to correct and offer encouragement and comments to each other. At the beginning of the conversation, speak in quiet voices until the cliché is spoken in a louder voice. C.D. performed by an isolated person (for example, in a fake conversation on a cell phone) will be performed only by certified coincidence makers.
2. Drop to the target only. If you identify another passerby that is liable to hear you, make sure the statement does not affect him. Twenty percent of the mishaps in C.D. coincidences derive from a drop absorbed by the wrong person.
3. Intelligent use of cynicism and sarcasm—For P.M.C.D. users, there is a tendency to adopt cynicism and sarcasm in order to communicate messages. Make sure that your client is capable of understanding these nuances, and use them cautiously.

4. Follow-up—Do not drop without conducting a follow-up! Always check that your statements have achieved the desired impact and make corrections as needed before proceeding.

3

The plane made a nearly perfect landing and came to a complete stop a few minutes later.

The NO SMOKING sign went off and the passengers got up from their seats and burst into a meaningless race toward the plane's exit, back to the world in which the light turned on automatically only in refrigerators and not in bathrooms.

The quietest and most efficient hit man in the Northern Hemisphere sat in his seat and waited patiently for everyone to deplane. He had always been the patient type, and there was no reason this one flight should change him. He somehow managed to ignore a certain amount of excitement that he felt. Perhaps "excitement" is a bit too strong a word. Let's say "readiness." A hit in a place he had never visited was always a refreshing change, and he wondered whether this strange sensation in his belly, the small and solid ball that developed there at takeoff and refused to disappear even after hours of flying, really was due to anxiety prior to the hit, a feeling he had not experienced for a long time, or derived from his concern for the fate of his luggage.

Or perhaps it was actually connected to something he ate.

His aunt's meatballs always made him feel strange, even when he was a child. Back then this had manifested as gaseousness, and not as a small, determined ball of iron floating in his body cavity. Nonetheless, what the hit man felt was apparently some type of anxiety. He just hoped that a good half-hour nap in front of a boxing match on television would settle his head.

That is, his stomach.

He got off the plane, smiled to the flight attendants, who smiled back at him in a Pavlovian response, and stopped for a second to look out from the top of the stairway. The sun hung in the middle of the sky, and it was hot. He might have to buy sunglasses.

As he descended the stairs he wondered how he had managed without sunglasses for so long. Indeed, sunglasses were a sort of status symbol in his profession. How could you be a self-respecting hit man and not go around with sunglasses?

Am I a self-respecting hit man? he wondered as he stood in the bus transporting him and fifty other people who ran to get there before him. He had always been treated a bit differently from the regular murderers. That was part of his thing—that he wasn't like everyone else. He operated in a different way. Perhaps he wasn't supposed to act like a self-respecting hit man but more like, let's say, a travel agent who was only fond of himself? Do travel agents who are only fond of themselves usually wear sunglasses? And what about the switchblade he usually carried in his sock? It wasn't comfortable there; it always bothered and distracted him when he walked. If he started to regard himself as a travel agent instead of thinking about himself as a hired killer, could he finally go to sleep without a gun under his pillow, like a normal person?

That's how it was when you had a profession that chose you instead of a profession that you chose. "Normal" was only a word.

Few people knew him by name. Not necessarily for reasons of secrecy. Primarily because in a profession like his, people were not interested in names.

They remembered nicknames more. The Black Plague, The Black Widow, The Singing Butcher, The Silent Hangman—those were the types of names they used. A nickname that was easy to remember was an advantage. Only a few people could talk about him based on personal acquaintance. These were usually the people who persuaded others to hire him. This persuasion most often began with a sort of executive summary for people who were not really executives, even if some of them occasionally viewed themselves as such.

The summary would begin with: "He is very, very efficient." Undoubtedly, a positive statement. Then the one who defined himself as an executive would ask, for example: "But how did he get that name?" And the one who tried to persuade would add, instead of answering him: "And he is extremely quiet."

The executive would move his head from side to side, put aside for the moment the question troubling him, and try to clarify whether "your guy" could do "the job." And only after the details he heard satisfied him would he again ask: "But how did he get that name?" And he would receive an answer like: "It's just a nickname. Perhaps it's connected to a job he did in the past." There were truths that did not need to be exposed, or at least should be provided only after "the job" was done.

He sat on the bed in his hotel room, on the fifteenth floor, with the sea glimmering in front of his eyes.

The suitcase was to his right, the cage to his left.

"That's the sea, Gregory. Isn't it beautiful?"

Gregory didn't answer.

"I hope you didn't suffer too much down below there." Gregory was busy. He wasn't in the mood to conduct a conversation.

"Okay," he said. "I'm going to bring you something to eat."

Gregory sniffed the air. He really was a bit hungry.

They could have called him "The Quietest Murderer in the Northern Hemisphere," but that would never catch on. Maybe because it was too long, perhaps because people like something special, something different. So somehow he became "The Man with the Hamster."

Not that he cared. He loved Gregory.

He took him out of the cage to pet him, and the ball in his stomach became smaller and smaller until it nearly disappeared.

4

Emily and Eric waited for Guy at their regular table.

Emily sat with her back to the window because "this way, the light illuminates everyone for me," and Eric was positioned so he could survey everyone entering the café, as well as the young women walking along the street outside. "It's purely a professional matter," he would say. "I'm practicing."

"Practicing?" Guy would smile. "Of course."

"Oh ye of little faith." Eric would lean back and raise his glass of orange juice as if it were a martini that was shaken, not stirred. "In a profession like ours, it's important to guard our instincts, to continue to discover the secret and unconscious interactions among people, and the ways in which small details influence processes. Well, you know."

"Yes." Guy would shrug his shoulders. "I know."

"And besides," Eric would say, "there is so much beauty in the world. It's a shame to miss it."

"I understand you had a successful coincidence yesterday," Eric said as Guy sat down with them.

"Apparently," Guy mumbled.

"And I understand that it again entailed matchmaking," said Emily.

"Something like that," Guy said.

"Sometimes you're too transparent," she said. "You never come on time after a successful matchmaking mission. I would expect that after so many times it would excite you a bit less."

"It's my favorite type of mission," Guy said. "I can't help it."

"You're a cheap populist," Eric declared. "Missions of love are the most reversible type, and from a statistical perspective, they are the missions in which our investment is lowest relative to the outcome. You're simply a person of ratings. A bit of work, high and fragile profit."

"And exactly how do you measure the outcome?" Emily asked.

"Since when are you categorizing missions by their rating?" Guy asked.

Eric played with his fork in a puddle of syrup that, twenty minutes ago, surrounded a large stack of pancakes. "That's exactly it—I'm not categorizing. I try to approach each coincidence we make with the same tools, even with the same respect. The way is important, not the outcome. You need elegance; you need style. It's a bit like being a magician—you make them look in one direction, and do something somewhere else."

"He's starting again," said Emily.

"Aha," said Guy, rolling his eyes.

"Say what you will, but the great coincidence makers are those who succeeded in creating elegant, fluent coincidences. Coincidences that were works of art, not a collection of causes and effects that ultimately led to . . ."

"So now art is the reason that the 'how' is more important than the 'what'?" Guy asked. He turned to Emily: "What was it the last time?"

"I think he used the thing about 'variety' last time," she responded.

"Oh, right, right. 'If you don't want to get up one day and discover that you hate what you do, you should avoid doing the same thing all the time.'"

"Something like that."

"Of course I forgot the hand gestures."

"It's okay, you succeeded in communicating the feeling."

"Thank you."

"You're welcome."

They smiled at him.

"You're pathetic," Eric said. "And I waste precious energy on you that I could spend on a splendid coincidence that would bring me together with that young woman at the bus stop with the short red hair."

"Of course. And we're the pathetic ones," said Guy.

"Come on, really," Eric said. "For example, take a look at that coincidence maker Paul what's-his-name. He worked for three years on an artistic project on the side, where he took *The Dark Side of the Moon* and synchronized it with *The Wizard of Oz*. How wonderful it is, how wonderful!"

"But, Eric, no one has ever met your Paul what's-his-name. That coincidence never really occurred," Emily said. "It's only a story they tell in the course, in order to get the students excited."

"Oh, come on, check the Internet. It happened. A great piece of work. And Paul what's-his-name planned it all himself. A genius."

"Breakfast," said the waitress who burst forth from behind Guy and placed a plate with an omelet, bread and butter, and a small salad in front of him. "I'll bring the mint lemonade in a moment," she added.

Guy looked up in surprise. He always ordered the same thing but he didn't think they'd noticed.

"You know, you really are transparent sometimes," Emily said, smiling.

He nodded and looked down at his plate. In his mind, Cassandra suddenly laughed in front of him and a memory came to mind. "You? Don't worry, you'll never block my view. I can see through you to the end of the world."

Guy, Emily, and Eric had met for the first time on the first day of the Coincidence Makers Course, three years earlier. Sixteen months of working together under the baton of the General could draw any three people closer, even those with such disparate personalities as theirs. Especially since the entire class was comprised of the three of them.

During those sixteen months, the three studied history and alternative history together, reviewed more than five hundred reports by coincidence makers from the past century, sat together in a car opposite a building for an entire night only to prove or refute Moldani's Theory of Door Opening Frequency, and quizzed each other again and again on the possible patterns of cause and effect for each of the incidents reported during the latest newscast.

There was something that happened while studying how to quantify the chances that people would take one path of action instead of another. Something that caused the people closest to you to become exceptionally human.

So they called themselves "The Musketeers" (until they stopped because they felt it was idiotic) and enjoyed betting on what tomorrow's news would be, based on an analysis of today's news. Occasionally they would pose small challenges to each other. Guy once managed to cause an entire floor to hang laundry on the same day following a wager with Eric. After two months of frustrating attempts, Emily was able to create a situation in which, for half an hour, only buses with numbers divisible by three were at the central bus station. This was after Guy claimed it would take her at least six months just to understand the pattern of bus arrivals, and the complex connections among these buses, and the rest of the transportation system in the city.

Eric succeeded in solving nearly every challenge they posed to him within less than a week. He also incessantly spoke about each such success until they no longer posed challenges to him and let him serve as "judge."

After the course was over, they continued to meet at least once a week for breakfast. They would tell each other about the latest coincidences they were working on and share small tips.

"So what do you have now?" Guy asked Emily while chewing his omelet.

"I'm still working on my poet," Emily said. "This character is pretty dense. I thought poets were supposed to be dreamers who hate banality and are thirsty for life, people for whom every moment is meaningful."

"You'd be surprised how conventionally minded they can be, just like accountants," Guy said.

"Which is what he is now, right?" Eric asked.

"Yes." Emily shrugged. "I'm trying to lead him to a situation in which he discovers his need to write, and I'm not succeeding. He is the materialistic type—well, you know. He thinks we all are machines of genes with evolutionary mechanisms, blah blah blah. No inspiration or idealism."

"Did you try to arrange some extraordinary scenery or something like that?" Guy asked. "Something that would stimulate his excitement glands?"

"The guy lives in a three-room apartment in the city." Emily sighed. "He leaves every morning at seven thirty for work, eats lunch alone, returns home, goes for an hour-long walk in the streets near his building, watches television until eleven, and reads nonfiction until going to sleep. He maintains contact with his few friends via laconic emails or telephone conversations of no longer than three minutes. He doesn't travel, has no hobbies, doesn't go to the beach or the theater or whatever. He even eats the same thing for dinner every day. How am I supposed to generate a change in consciousness in such a person? How am I supposed to make him discover his destiny when he lives life in such an automatic way?"

"Sounds like a tough character," Eric said.

"I'm not sure he's even capable of thinking in terms of 'destiny,'" Emily said sadly. "I always get the most difficult coincidences."

"How much time do you have left?" Guy asked.

"A month. I already tried to arrange chance encounters with pretty and melancholy girls. I tried to have him find a poetry book in the stairway. I even tried to arrange for a famous poet to get stuck with a flat tire right in front of his building and approach him to ask for help. The guy doesn't get the hint. It's as if he has no internal inclination for poetry."

"It's because he's so busy," Eric said.

"What do you mean?"

"He has other things on his mind. Numbers and facts when he's at work, and idiotic television content when he's at home."

"So?"

"So, fire him."

"What?"

"You know what I mean."

"You know I don't like solutions like that," Emily said.

"You're supposed to perform the job, not like it. Arrange for them to fire him, and for him to be without television for a week due to a technical malfunction. If, after a week of staring at the walls, he doesn't try to take a pen in hand and write a poem, then there really is no chance."

"This whole idea of ruining people's lives in order to advance them never sat well with me," Emily said. "The most I can do is make someone miss his dentist appointment. I don't have the heart to get him fired."

"You mean you don't have the courage," Guy said. "But Eric is right. The way it looks now, at the end of your month you'll have to report a failed attempt at coincidence making, and your guy will continue to live a life that fifty years from now he'll realize was wasted. And that, believe me, is much more painful than being fired."

"But . . ."

"At worst, you'll find him another job later, if you're really a softy," Eric said.

"And if you have time," Guy added.

Emily stared gloomily at the half-empty plate in front of her. "Ooh, I hate when things don't go smoothly."

"So you hate most of what happens in the world," said Eric, turning to look toward the street. "By the way," he added, "that reminds me of a coincidence I heard of about six months ago."

"Also a poet?"

"No, a car mechanic," Eric said.

"Did you know my first one was a composer?" Guy asked.

"Yeah, yeah, yeah," Eric said. "I'm talking. Quiet. Focus here, please. We're not discussing artistic inclinations at the moment. The man was sixty-five years old and worked as a car mechanic. A widower with one daughter. In his great wisdom, he had decided to cut off contact with her because she married the wrong guy, in his opinion. He lived in a studio apartment above the garage, which he didn't even own. Now, go and plan a coincidence that will make this type of person—who has been working for thirty-eight years at the same place, who is accustomed to spending his time grumbling about the unfair world and pitying himself for how they stole his life or his daughter or whatever, who spends his evenings drinking and his mornings dozing—renew a connection with his daughter. And make this happen—and I'm quoting the mission description—'by means of an active move he initiates and not as a result of a chance meeting with the daughter.'"

"What did they do?"

"If what they told me was correct, they tried nearly everything, going exactly by the book. Strangers said sentences within his earshot that were supposed to arouse longings in him; the radio at the mechanic's shop broke down and only played melancholy programs with sobbing mothers telling heart-wrenching stories about lost children; someone brought a car with a trunk full of children's books. Nothing."

"And in the end they got him fired?" Emily asked.

"Nooo," Eric said. "The coincidence maker was an old-fashioned type. He reached the conclusion that there was no chance that any normal change in this person's life would lead him to reassess his life. Not even getting fired. He would simply find another garage to distract himself from his loneliness or sit at home and do nothing."

"So what did he do?" Guy asked.

Eric took a sip of his juice and said: "Cancer."

"Cancer!" Emily asked in astonishment. "Didn't he go a bit too far?"

"Perhaps," Eric said, "but these are the facts: the man got cancer and underwent nearly a year and a half of treatments. After a stage of depression and a stage of anger and a stage of crazy pain, he started to talk to the people around him and ask them about their dreams. He developed an obsession about the fulfillment of people's dreams, and what drove people to live. He started to write a journal and began to realize how foolish he had been. And one day, before being informed that he was healthy, the man saw a seventeen-year-old girl arrive at the hospital as a volunteer; her face reminded him of his daughter. It was the granddaughter, of course. And then, one day after they informed him that he was healthy, he did two things: he got into the car and drove to his daughter's house, and he proposed marriage to the nurse who had treated him."

"Wow," Guy said.

"Definitely," Eric said. "Not that it changed anything. The coincidence maker was reprimanded for excessive use of force, and because the time assigned for the mission was two months, they even defined the mission as a failure at first."

"And after he drove to her home?"

"The status of the mission was changed, but the reprimand wasn't erased from the record. As punishment, he had to arrange another coincidence that would cause this jerk with cancer to publish his life story. The belief was that similar methods would be unnecessary in the future, since similar clients could read the book instead of living through such a harrowing experience. An idiotic assumption, if you ask me."

Emily and Guy sat up in their chairs. "Quite a story," Guy said.

"Yes," Emily said, "if we ignore the fact that it's fiction."

"Hey, don't be insulting," Eric said.

"It is forbidden for CMs to cause long-term illnesses, permanent injuries, or clinical death in missions that are not part of an historic process at rank five and have received approval on Form fifty-seven," Emily cited.

"How do you remember all these things, huh?" Eric asked.

"What you told us is impossible," Emily said.

"It's possible that he received a reprimand." Eric shrugged his shoulders.

"Like I said, it's impossible," Emily said. "It would be one thing if you said that he had an accident or something, but to cause someone to get cancer? How? How does one even do such a thing? Technically, we can't do that at our rank. We don't work at the cellular level."

"Perhaps I erred a bit, or exaggerated a little. Perhaps he just arranged an error in the test results that made him think he had cancer for a certain period of time, and actually he didn't have anything," Eric said.

"Exaggerated?" Guy asked.

"Perhaps," Eric said.

Guy and Emily looked at him. They had a standard look for these moments.

"What?" he asked and added, "In any case, it seems to me that what you need to do is get him fired."

"I'll think about it," Emily said.

Guy leaned back in his chair. "And what coincidence are you working on now?" he asked Eric.

"I have two," Eric said. "One of them I received two days ago. I'm supposed to somehow cause some loser to get a job within three weeks. It's quite annoying. I'm forbidden to use government agencies,

I can't cause layoffs, and it has to be work that makes him get out of the house every day. It's the type of mission that makes you feel that the guys upstairs are just trying to annoy you. Perhaps they're making a wager at our expense."

"And what's the second mission?" Emily asked.

"Didn't we speak two minutes ago about that young woman with the short red hair?" Eric smiled.

Emily and Guy shook their heads in disbelief.

"You are a nutcase," Guy said.

"Perhaps," said Eric, "but it's quite fun."

The waitress returned to their table and served Guy the mint lemonade. "I'm sorry about the wait," she said and placed another small plate in front of them. She turned to Emily: "These brownies are for you." Emily's eyebrows rose in surprise.

"I didn't order brownies."

"I know," the waitress said, jerking her chin to the side. "It's from the guy in the corner there."

They turned around. A slightly embarrassed young man, who had expected only one pair of eyes, nodded his head shyly.

"And this too," the waitress said, placing a small, folded piece of paper next to the plate.

Emily stared at the note.

"He's quite cute," the waitress said.

"Yes, Emily," Eric said and nodded with a thin smile, "really cute."

"Thank you," Emily said to the waitress before turning a furious gaze on her companions.

"Okay," she muttered angrily, "which of you two is responsible for this?"

They instinctively raised their hands in innocence.

"Why do you think it was us?" Guy asked.

"False accusations are not good for the complexion," Eric said.

"Listen," Emily said, "I know that one of you arranged a coincidence to have that guy send me brownies. I just know it."

"Is it so hard for you to believe that someone is trying to flirt with you?" Eric asked.

"With brownies?"

"Why not? They're delicious, aren't they?" Guy asked.

Emily got up and took the plate in her hand. "Okay, I'll settle this."

"Come on, give him a chance," Eric said.

Emily didn't reply and rapidly walked away from them.

"Did you arrange this?" Guy asked.

"No. You?"

"No."

They were silent for a few seconds and Eric sighed. "Oh well, it's a shame. The guy looks nice."

"Yes."

"My score is correct, right? This is the tenth guy she's rejected since we completed the course?"

"At least of those we know about," said Guy.

"Well, maybe it's because she's in love with someone else?"

Guy stared at his plate. "Shut up."

"I'm just saying that—"

"I know what you're saying. Just shut up."

Eric was still smiling his little smile when Emily returned and sat down. "So," she said to Guy, "what's your next mission?"

"It's one of the strangest things I've ever seen," she said a few minutes later.

They passed the page Guy had received in the morning envelope from hand to hand.

" 'Do you mind, perhaps, if I kick you in the head,' " Eric said. "That's definitely a refreshing mission description."

"I don't understand what it's supposed to mean," Guy said.

"You're sure it was an envelope? That is, a standard one? One of ours?" Emily asked.

"Yes," Guy answered.

"Do you mind, perhaps, if I kick *you* in the head?" Eric said, emphasizing the question with his hands.

"That is, where's the mission description? Where are the restrictions?" Guy asked. "Since when do I receive a riddle as a mission?"

"Do you mind, perhaps, if I *kick* you in the head?" Eric said. "No, that still doesn't sound right."

"It seems to me that there was a mistake here," said Guy.

"I seriously doubt they make mistakes of this type," said Emily.

"*DYM PIIKYITH*," said Eric.

"What?" Guy asked.

"These are the first letters of the words in the sentence," Eric said. "It doesn't mean anything to you, right?"

"Right."

Eric returned the piece of paper to him and shrugged. "You have a small mystery here. Enjoy."

"And what am I supposed to do now?"

"It seems to me that you should go to the place specified at the designated time," Eric said.

"And . . . ?"

"And decide whether you mind or not."

"Mind what or not?"

"If someone kicks you in the head."

5

Eric looked around, waiting for a taxi to appear.

"It's ironic," he said. "Throughout the years, I've organized at least fifteen taxis to arrive precisely when needed, but when I need a ride, half an hour passes before something comes by. And even then, the cab is taken."

Guy laughed. "The shoemaker's son always goes barefoot."

"I'm not a shoemaker's son," Eric said. "And I recently decided that I can't stand irony."

Three seconds passed and a taxi stopped next to them.

"And exactly how did you do that?" Emily asked, wide-eyed.

"Who said I did something?" Eric smiled. "Sometimes things just happen, don't they?"

"You planned for a taxi to arrive now only so you could use the punch line 'I can't stand irony'?" Guy asked. "Don't you have anything better to do with your time?"

Eric got into the taxi and waved to them. "Parting is such sweet sorrow."

"If you say so," Guy said with a smile, and the taxi drove off.

"You remember our bet, right?" Emily asked.

"Um, there's a small chance that I don't," said Guy.

"How many times do I have to repeat this?" Emily sighed.

"We're already busy coincidence makers," Guy said with affected seriousness. "We have no time for nonsense."

"Don't try to get out of it. We agreed—whenever you want, and for at least fifteen minutes, you need to arrange for ten young girls named Emily to be within the park. I need to try to arrange for there to be ten children with the name Guy."

"Okay, okay."

"Hey, belittle this all you want, no problem. There's a dinner at stake, you know."

"Can I also bring boys?"

"Named Emily?"

"Or Emil."

"On the condition that I can bring a Gaia."

He nodded his head, smiling. "We've got a deal."

She smiled back, an old sparkle in her eyes.

"The park" was, of course, the park where everything began, from their perspective.

The first day of their Coincidence Makers Course began on a reddish bench in the park. Guy arrived second; Emily was already there. He approached slowly, a bit hesitant, and stood before the young woman with the short black hair.

"Uh, is this . . . ?"

"Yeah, I think so."

She had large, dark blue eyes and a small face the color of pale marble. She smiled a bashful smile. "Emily."

"Guy," he said, and sat down next to her. Only a second later did he realize it would have been more polite if he had asked permission. But she didn't seem to notice.

Children played soccer on the grass in front of them. Farther off, several mothers and babysitters sat with little children, trying almost desperately to stop the toddlers from eating pieces of grass or examining particularly intriguing dog poop, though they were unwilling to stop talking on their phones while engaging in these efforts.

Emily held a small bag of bread crumbs in her hand and scattered them on the ground in front of her. A few lucky birds gathered and pecked the sidewalk with urban expertise.

"At least now we both know this is the right bench," said Guy in an attempt to break the ice.

"Yup," said Emily, scattering another handful of crumbs.

"So where are you coming from?"

Emily sat up straight and looked at him. "What do you mean?"

"What was your previous position?" he asked.

She looked at him for a long moment. "You first," she said. "What were you?"

"I was an I.F."

"Hmm. Initials. Great. And they mean?"

"Imaginary friend. I was an imaginary friend. Of young children, primarily. Very interesting work."

"I'm sure."

"Yes."

"So, from your point of view, this is a promotion?" Emily asked. "It's considered a better position?"

"Yes. I'm used to existing only in the eyes of one child at a time. Regular and continuous existence will be an interesting challenge for me. I'm quite satisfied."

"Did you submit a request for a transfer or did you simply receive it?"

"I simply received it, to be honest. I didn't know you could submit a request for a transfer."

"It seems logical for there to be something like that, no?"

"Perhaps. I'm not really familiar with all the . . ."

"Okay."

Emily absentmindedly scattered another handful of crumbs.

"Is this the bench for the Coincidence Makers Course?" they heard a voice behind them ask.

Both of them turned around.

"You're not supposed to just say it," Guy said. "What if any two people were sitting here?"

The thin redhead behind them looked at him with an amused expression. "Then they would think I'm a bit cuckoo and tell me no," he said. "You don't seriously think someone would assume such a course really exists, right?"

"There are rules . . . ," Guy tried to say.

"Sorry, I didn't hear about a rule against asking. And even so, you know what rules are designed for. This is the course, right?"

"Right . . . but . . ."

"Great." He walked quickly and sat on the bench between them, crossing his arms to extend his hands in both directions.

"Pleased to meet you," he said. "Eric, man of many talents."

"Nice to meet you." Emily raised an eyebrow and smiled.

"I like your hair. The smile is great too," Eric said before turning to Guy. "No smile?"

"Not only can I smile, I can offer you a handshake too." Guy extended his hand. "Where are you from?"

Eric shook his hand. "Maybe if you explain the question, I can answer it."

"He meant, what did you do before the course?" Emily said.

"I was an igniter," Eric said. "It's a wonderful thing. But you get tired of it after a few decades. Or centuries, it depends."

"What's an igniter?" Emily asked. But before Eric could answer, his face was covered by the shadow of the person standing in front of them, whose arrival had sent the birds into flight.

"Good morning, Class Seventy-five," said the figure.

"Good morning," said Guy.

"Good morning," said Emily.

"Ditto what they said," said Eric.

Standing tall in front of them was a middle-aged man with short grayish hair and light green eyes, like bundles of grass that grow in a hypnotist's yard. Through the tight white cotton shirt he wore, the three of them could tell he was someone who took care of his body. And his body, in quiet appreciation, took care of him in return.

"This," the man said, "is the stage when you begin to follow me and listen."

The three quickly obeyed. They got up and began to walk behind him.

He walked slowly, his head held high and his hands crossed behind his back.

"Okay, listen up. The name is really not important, but you can call me the General. In fact, you must call me the General, if only because it's the only name you're supposed to know and to which I'll respond. Please erase from your heads—as long as you still can—

whatever guesses are now coming to mind regarding my real name, because soon I'll be stuffing your minds with so much information that it'll be difficult for you to even budge within your own thoughts. Like a praying mantis that needs to swim in a pool of honey. Clear so far?"

"Clear," Eric said.

"And you?" The General glanced back toward Guy and Emily.

"Clear, clear," they quickly responded.

"When I say 'clear,'" said the General, "my three imbecilic trainees will make the effort of their lives, will leap over the mental hurdle related to the complicated thing called 'timing,' and will answer me together, at the same time."

He stopped and looked with extraordinary interest at the top of one of the trees. "Clear?"

"Clear," the three of them answered.

"Better. I'm very impressed. You're extremely talented. I'm even a bit moved. Oh, here comes a tear," he said and continued to walk.

"During the next sixteen months, I'll teach you how to make coincidences. You think that you understand what this actually means, or why we do this, but you're probably completely wrong.

"First of all, you are secret agents. Except all the others are first of all agents and then secondly secret, but you are first of all secret and to a certain extent, also agents. Your existence is regular and continuous, like any human being. You eat, drink, fart sometimes, and occasionally will catch a virus, but with the help of the tools you receive in this course, you'll understand the way in which cause and effect operate in this world and how to exploit this understanding in order to create small and nearly imperceptible events that help people come to life-changing decisions. Clear?"

"Clear."

"Many people think that to make coincidences is to determine fate—to lead people to new places by the power of the events. This is a childish view, lacking in vision and full of arrogance.

"Our role is to be exactly on the border, to stand in the gray area between fate and free will, and to play Ping-Pong there. We create situations that create situations that create more situations that ultimately can create thoughts and decisions. Our objective is to light a spark on the fate side of the boundary so that someone on the free will side of the boundary will see this spark and decide to do something. We do not light fires, we do not breach borders, and we definitely do not think our role is to tell people what to do. We are creators of possibilities, givers of hints, winkers of tempting winks, discoverers of options. You're welcome to think of other descriptions in your free time, later, but make no mistake—whatever you did before, you were just promoted. Because there are many reality-backstage-workers out there—imaginary friends, dream weavers, luck distributers, and the list goes on—but after finishing this course, your new role touches the core itself.

"The world is full of coincidences. The overwhelming majority of them are indeed what they are—things that simply happen by chance at a time when something else happens too, wonderfully regular things given context by good timing. And the context imbues them with meaning, and the meaning makes them important. It doesn't have to be a room in which all of the people have the same shirt, though that is nice. It can simply be that someone says something while someone sees something, and the combination engenders a new thought. That's all. No great drama. No one notices these regular instances. The idea is simple. Sometimes things happen that cause people to think someone is trying to send them a message. Sometimes things happen that simply cause people to think, without trying to attribute the occurrence to an entity seeking to spur them into action. And sometimes things happen that compel people to look at reality from a new angle, to turn this Rorschach inkblot called 'life,' to see it a bit differently. We are responsible for these three types of instances. We do not determine fates; we are hired hands of the general public—even slaves to it, if you wish. You will all have private, almost regular, lives but will be able to observe another layer of life, unlike others.

"Making coincidences is a delicate and complex art, full of details demanding the ability to juggle events, assess situations and responses, and apply a basic lack of stupidity that is sometimes hard to find. You'll need to use mathematics, physics, psychology. . . . I'll be talking to you about statistics, about associations and the unconscious, about the additional layer behind the regular existence of people, a layer they are completely unaware of. I intend to cram into your brains personality analyses and behavior theories; to demand a level of precision from you that will far outshine any quantum physicist, neurotic chemist, or apprentice pastry cook with an obsession for weighing egg yolks; to make you stay awake until you understand what causes certain birds to stand on a particular tree and other birds to stand on electric wires; to force you to memorize tables of cause and effect until you forget the name of the love of your life, if you ever had love, or a life. I'm going to explain things to you that will at first make you look over your shoulder to check whether someone is arranging your life for you while you're not looking, and in the end will allow you to sleep better than you've ever slept. I'm going to change you, reorganize everything you have in life except for your face and the order of your internal organs, and I'll teach you how to make people change, without them imagining for even a moment that someone might be responsible for it."

He stopped and turned toward them, his green eyes smiling a bit—but only a bit.

"Are there questions?"

"Um, something small," Guy said, "regarding the schedule. . . ."

"I didn't really intend for you to ask questions now," the General said. "It was a pause out of basic courtesy. You're supposed to say no. Questions will come later. A bit of tact, really."

"So . . . then no," Guy said. "There are no questions."

"Great," the General said. "And now turn around."

They turned around. From the place they had reached at the highest point of the path, almost the whole park was visible. Below, in the middle of the grass lawn, someone had hung a giant sign between the trees. GOOD LUCK UNIT 75 was written on it. "Well, look at that," the General said. "Today there happens to be a party for a group of soldiers who completed basic training. What a coincidence, huh?"

The sun advanced behind them, casting their shadows down the hill, and the four of them suppressed a smile, each one for a slightly different reason.

6

Guy looked at Emily as she walked away. She still seemed small and fragile to him, as she had on the first day of the course. But if there was one thing the course had made clear to him, it was that one must not, simply must not, try to define people in a single word. People are too complex. Falling into the trap of adjectives is the first stage of distorting your perception of the person for whom you are making a coincidence. Words are always small traps of definition, but adjectives are especially dangerous, like swamps. He used to look at Emily and think only of the word "fragile." He had since grown up a little.

He realized there had always been something a bit strange in her. A bit mysterious, if he allowed himself to commit to a description.

Guy always spoke about his previous job, and Eric didn't conceal anything from them about his earlier life, even if he sometimes invented things that had never occurred. But Emily . . . each time he tried to understand what she did before coming to the course, Emily somehow evaded the question.

"It's secret," she told him when he finally cornered her.

"A dream weaver?" he tried. "I heard that in their Psychological Department, they sign a crazy confidentiality form."

"Guy . . ." She squirmed.

"I won't tell anyone, come on."

"I can't," she said.

Or that time she came out of the General's room, her eyes red, a small white envelope in her hands.

"What happened?" Eric asked her. "What did you get? Is it a mission or something like that?"

"It's nothing," she said.

"Is everything okay?" Guy asked.

"Everything is excellent," she said and walked away quickly.

"In my opinion, she was in the special unit for distributing luck," Eric said to him once. "They're more secretive than us. They deal with hazardous materials and such, and they go around in special protection suits in the event that good or bad luck spills on them. They're even forbidden to mention that the unit exists."

"I've never heard about it, and I don't think there really is such a thing," Guy said to him.

"That just proves how good they are," said Eric.

"Eric, you're delusional."

"Oh, come on."

So he played the game. He and Emily were good friends, with one small subject they didn't broach. What pair of friends didn't have that, in fact? But he always knew there was a lot more to Emily than her apparent gentleness. "Fragile"—right.

He turned around and started to walk. Maybe he should return home, put on a good CD, sit on the balcony, and try to understand what the morning's envelope was trying to tell him.

And maybe . . . maybe it was even better not to think of it at all, but just to devote this day to clearing his head. To reading a good book, to a soothing jazz performance (if there was one) in the afternoon, to a croissant with coffee in a little shop with a beautiful view. The advantages of continuous existence, he thought to himself. You have the opportunity to do things unconnected to work.

He loved this so much.

Before he became a coincidence maker—before he received this continuous life, this body, the ability to experience the present as something that was the future until a moment ago when it became ever so slightly past—when he was an I.F., he could not have even imagined this.

Back then he had existed as a character in people's minds. He was an entirely real character for them, with a personality and fine nuances of behavior, and narrow or broad humor, as requested.

This was a completely different experience.

He once made a list and realized that over the years he had been an imaginary friend to 256 human beings, and 250 of them were children under the age of 12. Another 5 were people in various stages of mental decline or senility who were so lonely they had no alternative but to invent someone to sit with them and simply note that he existed. And one of them was a man with lifeless eyes who was held in solitary confinement for years and was compelled to surrender a bit of his remaining sanity and invent the character that Guy played for him, only in order to regain his sanity. He forgot Guy the moment he was freed.

Yes, that's what he'd done. He'd played the role of characters. Or at least he had expressed various sides of himself. When you were the imaginary friend of a lonely or sad child, you couldn't allow yourself to be in a bad mood or to show despondency, even if you were personally having a not-so-great day. You had to take the little spoon of your personality and dig deep in the cold ground until you reached water that you could serve to someone else despite your own thirst.

When you were someone's imaginary friend, a number of very clear rules applied to you.

The first rule was that you existed for that someone completely. The annoying speeches, the attempts at re-education, the moral preaching—all this had to be saved for the future, if and when you became a person. When you were an imaginary friend, you were there for your boy or girl, and you needed to lead them to a better place *they* wanted, not the place *you* wanted. And that wasn't easy. Many times, Guy wanted to grab the child imagining him and shout, "No! Not that way!" or "Just say it!" or "You must stop doing this!"—but he had to take a deep breath and remind himself that the child was the captain, while he was only the ship.

The second rule was that you could not be seen in the same outward appearance by more than one client. Guy switched countless characters and faces during these years, not to speak of names. Sometimes he only changed one nuance in order to adhere to the rules. He was tall and stern-looking, or tiny and unruly; he played sweet teddy bears and exuberant toy soldiers; he assumed the appearance of celebrities and cartoon characters and famous dolls. He was a farmer, a magician, a pilot, the skipper of a ship, a singer, a football player. He used small sweet voices, thunderous authoritative voices, smiling voices, and hushed voices before bedtime.

The third rule was that if one day you quit your work as an I.F., you could never reveal yourself to the children who imagined you. The concept was clear: if a child met someone in the real world who until now had existed only in his imagination, someone who could come up to him and tell him secrets about himself that no one else knew, someone familiar with places inside him no one else had entered—this was liable to generate doubt in the wall of the imagination of children throughout the world. From the moment you quit, you quit. Period.

Guy didn't completely agree with this. Sometimes he wondered what could really happen. After all, people grow up, change, understand. But there were no exceptions. They made the third rule very clear.

Guy still remembered most of those who had imagined him.

He remembered the ten-year-old girl who wanted someone to look at her and tell her how beautiful she was. The right side of her face was reddish and wrinkled from a large burn scar, and each time she looked in the mirror, she needed him—cast in the role of a popular Hollywood actor—to look over her shoulder and whisper, "You're really beautiful. I see this better than everyone. Someday others will see it too." For four years, he snuck up behind her shoulder when she looked in the mirror and consoled her with words as simple as dust, until one time she imagined him while she sat with one of the children in the class and did schoolwork with him. They sat at the table and argued about the question they were answering. Guy stood in the back, near the wall, watching. At some point, he heard the girl's heartbeat quicken, and she stole a glance at him. He smiled a calming smile at her, and the girl played with the pencil in her hand and casually asked the boy sitting next to her whether it didn't bother him to do schoolwork with her. "No," he answered in surprise, "of course not." And she continued: "The way I look doesn't bother you? I'm sure you think I'm horrible, that I'm horribly ugly." He looked at her, thought a bit, and said quietly, "You? You're not ugly! You're actually quite cute. I like being with you." She whispered, "Really?" And he said, bashfully avoiding her gaze,

"Ah . . . really." The girl stole another look at Guy, and he felt himself fading and disappearing, never to return to her life.

He remembered the blond child who sat crumpled in a wheelchair, who imagined Guy wearing a Superman suit. "I want to fly," the child told him. "Teach me." He remembered those who took him to their tree houses and imagined him as a pirate holding a princess they had to save, and those who turned him into their favorite cartoon characters and placed in his mouth scripted, half-clever sentences they had heard hundreds of times. If he had a dime for every time he played a talking rabbit or a sarcastic flower . . .

And there were those who always made him wonder what was going on in their little minds. The children who would grow up and become geniuses, or were just very strange. Those who used him as a paintbrush to add a colorful layer to the reality around them, a level of possibility beyond their lives, and then another and another. Those who imagined him as sounds, spinning him, straightening him, reorganizing him in the air, and ordering him to sing to himself. Those who would lie in bed at night, imagining him hovering above them as abstract numbers and complex geometric forms that intricately converged into each other, giving him the worst headache ever, and he suffered in silence for the sake of their sense of mathematical harmony.

But mainly there were all of the children who were simply looking for a playmate. Loners or those who were compelled to be alone who engaged his services with a brief thought.

He remembered the small, fragile girl who dressed him as a prince and placed a white horse beside him that was no less imaginary, that smelled more like shampoo than like a horse. Speak words of love to me, like the grown-ups, she thought in her heart, so strongly that he heard. There were quite a few girls who wanted to hear "words of love" or to experience some fairy tale of their own. What he did was a complete improvisation at first, as he was still groping in the dark when it came to matters of the heart. He quoted sentences prepared in advance without truly understanding the gears within the complex clock that is romance. But after he met Cassandra, it all became much simpler. . . .

And yes, he also remembered Cassandra. She wasn't a child, not in any way.

Being an I.F. had been a great time in his life. Heartbreaking sometimes, occasionally boring, and some clients could drive you crazy. But it was wonderful. Being a coincidence maker was also wonderful. How beautiful it was to sit opposite a tree swaying in the wind, with a cup of coffee and croissant in hand, with a past, and with a future, and with a present.

CLASSICAL THEORIES IN COINCIDENCE MAKING AND RESEARCH METHODS FOR ENHANCING CAUSES AND EFFECTS

FINAL EXAM

Duration of the exam: two hours in class+one week practicum.

Instructions: Answer the following questions. You should write the method in the exam notebook, even in the case of a multiple-choice question, if the question requires the use of a formula or includes a proof of level B or higher.

PART A: MULTIPLE-CHOICE QUESTIONS

Answer all of the questions.

According to Kinsky's Theorem, how many coincidence makers do you need to change a light bulb?

A. One.
B. One to screw it in and three to arrange for the establishment of the electric company.
C. One, and two to arrange for the one to arrive.
D. Kinsky's Theorem does not provide an answer to this question.

Starting from which factor in the chain of causes and effects is the "cloud of uncertainty" created according to the methods of Fabrik and Cohen? Add a diagram of explanation and development of the proof in your notebook.

A. The uncertainty is created from the first moment.
B. The uncertainty is created when the object decides to use his or her head.
C. The uncertainty is created when the object decides to use his or her heart.
D. According to Cohen's deterministic model, there is no uncertainty as long as there is desire or hope.

According to the method of classical calculation, what are the chances that two men from the same group of 10,000 will love the same woman?

A. Less than 10 percent.
B. Between 10 to 25 percent.
C. Between 25 to 50 percent.
D. Above 50 percent, but they'll get over it quickly.

PART B: OPEN QUESTIONS

Answer at least two of the three questions.

1. Two trains leave two cities simultaneously, heading toward each other on parallel tracks. We know that at least 25 percent of the men and women in each city are unmarried, with a character distribution according to the method of Fabrik and Cohen. Calculate the chances that two people will see each other when the trains pass and their hearts will flutter.

2. Show how it is possible to prove, according to the expansion formula of Wolfzeig and Ibn Tareq, that starting from a certain level of social proximity, happiness acts as a communicable disease. Calculate the level of social proximity required.

3. Demonstrate how the order of presenting possibilities affects the choice in one of the following cases:

   A. A salesman who suggests suits to a customer at a men's clothing store.

   B. A saleswoman who suggests dresses to a customer at a women's clothing store.

   C. A waiter who offers various types of beverages at a restaurant.

   D. The order of arranging the ballots in the voting booth.

PART C: PRACTICAL EXERCISE

Perform one of the two following coincidences:

1. Cause three childhood friends to board an airplane, taxi, or train at the same time. Provide proof that the childhood

friends studied at the same educational institution for at least three years. The trip on the airplane/taxi/train will be set in advance and will not be a one-time event organized especially for this coincidence. An initiative that includes adding an unplanned trip will result in disqualification. A bonus will be awarded if two or more of the childhood friends engage in a conversation.

2. Create a traffic jam in which over 80 percent of the vehicles are the same color; the particular color is not important. The traffic jam must last for no more than twenty minutes. You may not use traffic accidents or traffic light malfunctions. A traffic jam that also includes over 80 percent of vehicles from the same automaker will merit a bonus.

Good luck, if you deserve it!

7

The Man with the Hamster stood on the street corner and surveyed the location designated for the assassination of his next target.

He was split—or perhaps it's more accurate to say he was divided into three parts.

One part of him was aware of the fact that it was impossible to execute a good hit without checking, preparing, and planning. Everything could not just be treated as "something that happens." He had to check the victim's schedule. (No, no, not the victim. The target, he reminded himself.) He needed to calculate firing angles, identify escape routes, check the wind conditions. That's the way the job got done.

A second part of him tried to persuade himself that all this was superfluous. That in his case, it really was a matter of "something that happens." That the whole business of calculating the amount of time he needed to disassemble his weapon and return to his car was foolish, meaningless. Whoever needed to live lived, and whoever needed to die, died. That's the way it worked with him. That's why he was considered so good.

And a third part of him simply wanted to return to the room, collapse onto the bed with a bottle of good whiskey, pet Gregory until the nervous sniffing of his little nose stopped, replaced by a snuggle of complete trust, and watch a television program in a language he didn't understand.

This three-way ritual had repeated itself during nearly all of his recent assignments. He was starting to get tired of it.

The second two parts forged an alliance and launched an offensive against the first part—the logical, responsible adult among the three. It wasn't easy. He had quite a few convincing counterarguments, particularly against the argumentation of the third part, which sounded like nothing more than, "Come on, what do you care? It'll be fun." But ultimately the hired killer shrugged his shoulders and started to walk away. He would position himself on the roof and use a long-barreled sniper's rifle. Here, planning.

The only problem was that he had two such rifles, both of them appropriate for the mission. A careful calculation of the data was necessary in order to decide which of the guns would be preferable. The analysis included factors pertaining to the weather, conditions of visibility from the roof, sensitivity of the trigger, and air humidity.

He stopped walking and looked again at the street corner, then put a hand in his pocket and pulled out a coin. He tossed it into the air, caught it, and peeked at the result.

The problem of the rifle was resolved.

8

You're not good enough.

You're not good enough.

You're not good enough.

Quiet!

Emily stood opposite the scribble-covered wall in her home and tried to quiet the thoughts running through her mind.

Why did she always approach her missions with a sense of impending failure? After all, there was no basis in reality for this.

She was good. She was really good. Even Eric allowed himself to compliment her for the quiet coincidences she successfully created. So every time a new envelope arrived, why was she certain that this time—yes, this time—she would fail?

And in fact, what difference did it make? The average success rate of coincidence makers was 65 percent. Her success rate was

80 percent. To whom did she owe anything? So what if this accountant continued to be an accountant? He wanted to pursue this path, so be it! She wasn't in the course anymore. She didn't have to impress the General. Or Eric, or Guy . . .

She sat on the floor.

Again, she was doing everything just to impress others. That was precisely the reason why she felt pressure from all sides, felt trapped in this unstoppable chase, constantly looking at herself through the eyes of everyone around her. She felt a need to be amazing, to be extraordinary, to be so charming and terrific and successful and full of humor that he would finally be swept to her shores, leaving behind all the ruined ships and the open sea and the seductive Sirens.

There were a few words she really couldn't bear.

"Ticking," for example. A word that always made her feel anxious and gave her the sense of something approaching its end, of suffocation from lack of oxygen, of a bomb about to obliterate everything. "Alone" could keep her awake all night, tossing and turning in an unsuccessful effort to flee from imaginings in which she continued to lie in an empty bed while the world around her forged ahead. She could spend days on end trying to evade "failure" or ignore "reasonable." For some unknown reason, she also couldn't bear "biscuits."

But lately, there were few words she hated as much as "friend." She was so sick and tired of being a "friend," of the repartee that stood exactly on the edge of the cliff of flirtation, of the heart-to-heart talks in which she could only discuss things that didn't directly pertain to him, of the frustrating attempts to interpret whether there was something in his smile that hinted about something beyond, of the nauseating dance of trying to draw closer for a moment and then slowly stepping away without turning her back, just out of fear that this would ruin even the little that still remained.

She hated being Guy's friend.

And there was always that something else as well. A different feeling. Something so right. And that need. Ohhh, that need to see him happy about little things. The uncontrollable need to give yourself to someone just to know that you were capable of illuminating something within him. How could this be? Why did this shy lost boy make her head so dizzy?

Every time she thought about him, images came to her that seemed like fragments of a dream.

Moments of light and darkness, days of excitement and disappointment. She fondly recalled the moment when the butterflies disappeared, when she was able to smile to herself and know that this wasn't a case of falling in love; it was love. She wasn't a high school student swept up in romance; she was a puzzle piece that had found the match to interlock beside it. And she shuddered each time she recalled the moment she realized that he, on the other hand, wasn't there with her at all.

To hell with her poet.

Today was the day. She had waited for a day exactly like this—free, with no work, when Guy had nothing to do.

She had to make this happen. And she could.

She got up and moved to the other room. On the wall next to the door was another sketch, no less important to her. Guy was the one who suggested that she use the walls to plan coincidences, so why not use this "against him"?

Dozens of small circles were drawn there, events that she stretched like a spring, preparing to release them on a day when she could combine all of them in a small and revolutionary journey. "Us" was written at the top, with a chaotic sprawl of lines and forms and words and numbers below. And two circles, with the words "Guy" and "Emily," rested in the middle of this mess.

This diagram was large. It extended beyond the boundaries of the wall, past the window on the adjacent wall, and crawled to the ceiling, spreading like an oil spill and filling the room. The number of details in it sometimes amazed her. But she had to give it her best shot, take no prisoners, take no risks. She had one opportunity in which to take all of the weapons from her arsenal and toss them into the arena of her most important coincidence ever.

She would often wake up and find herself on the floor of this room, after lying there and trying again to follow with her eyes all of the planning that surrounded her on four walls and one ceiling. She would fall asleep and dream that the diagram continued to crawl and grow while she slept, moving across the floor in an effort to climb on top of her and bury her underneath it, wrapping her in data, possibilities, and old hopes.

She would do it. This evening.

She was good enough.

This diagram had been sketched years ago.

During classes in the course, instead of drawing hearts with arrows or mixing the letters in their names like a normal young woman, she would sketch complex diagrams of matchmaking on scraps of paper she tore from her notebooks and draw circles with arrows on restaurant napkins. The sketches always started with two circles with two names inside them, then grew into a more and more complex system of lines and connections that ultimately drove her crazy. Then she would toss the paper into the trash after devoutly tearing it into pieces.

And, of course, the one and only time she didn't bother to tear it into tiny pieces, Eric had found it.

It was during one of the evenings when the three of them were supposed to study together at her place before an exam.

Guy fell asleep on the sofa, a thick volume of *Introduction to Serendipity* open on his chest, his mouth ajar like an old and tired sea lion. Eric and Emily decided to let him sleep and continue to quiz each other on history.

By this time, she knew that Eric was a narcissist, though good-hearted in his way, but she wasn't fully ready for his curiosity. She left for just two minutes to get coffee and cookies, and when she returned Eric was holding her diagram in his hands, studying it with great interest.

"Eric!" she shouted, and Guy almost woke up. "Why are you rummaging through my trash?"

She went up to him and snatched the paper from his hands, tears in her eyes. "You son of a—"

"Hey, it stuck out of the pile," Eric raised his hands in defense. "And I saw my name. What did you expect?"

"What did I expect? I expected you to respect other people's privacy and not poke around in things when someone leaves the room for a moment. Apparently, these are unrealistic expectations."

Eric was silent and went back to studying his notes. Emily started to rip the paper.

"I hope you're not thinking seriously about this," he said.

"It's none of your business."

"The man is taken," he said, nodding toward Guy. "It'll just break your heart."

"Taken?" This was news to her.

"Perhaps not physically," he said. "But definitely emotionally."

"Who?"

"An I.F. from his past. Cassandra something."

"Guy is in love with an imaginary friend?"

"Yes. So adolescent of him, huh?"

"It's not funny." Emily flared. "It's not funny."

"In any case, that's the situation. And even if he were available, I wouldn't try to use coincidence making to arrange this between the two of you."

"Why not?"

"It's not your thing. You're better suited for inspiration coincidences, not matchmaking coincidences."

"Actually, why am I talking about this with you?"

"Okay, forget it. I've said what I have to say."

"And I have no problem making any coincidence I want."

"I'm sure. Do you remember, perhaps, who was responsible for the coincidence of discovering penicillin? Baum or Young?"

"Don't change the subject. I can do matchmaking just like anyone else."

"True, but not for yourself. You're too involved. I think it was Young. Her coincidences are simply gorgeous."

"Why not for myself? And the only reason you like Young is because she arranged for McCartney to meet Lennon. Baum contributed a lot more than she did."

"Baum is a bit technical for me. Discovering LSD, electromagnetism—terribly serious. Young organized the discovery of corn flakes. That's what I call a historic piece of coincidence making."

"Eric."

"And Teflon too, I think. Just a moment, let me look. . . ."

"Eric!"

He looked up from the pages. "What?"

"Why do you think I'm incapable of doing matchmaking coincidences for myself?"

Eric put down the pages. "Listen, Em, darling. You can make any coincidence you want. Really. I'm sure you'll do lots of matchmaking, and you'll facilitate a ton of inventions and you'll change the world, sweetheart. It's just that each of us is better at certain things. And you . . . emotional involvement is not your thing. It upsets your equilibrium, you get anxious, you try too much and too intensely. Not that I'm such an expert on the subject, but that's how it looks from the sidelines."

"You arrange dates for yourself all the time," Emily said.

"Yes, true," Eric said. He was a bit embarrassed, to the extent this was possible for someone like him. "But we're not the same. My emotional approach to this whole matter is different. I'm a bit, um, how should I put it . . . I go with the flow. You're a bit more, let's say . . . dramatic."

"I'm not dramatic!" She stamped her foot.

He pointed at Guy, who was still sleeping next to them. "Do you see him?"

"Yes."

"He's a classic coincidence matchmaker. He doesn't believe in the perfect woman, but is unwilling to accept anyone but her. He's a real romantic who doesn't expect love to exist in the world. This is precisely the right combination for someone who wants to connect people without getting overly anxious about it. You are not. Don't try to arrange a coincidence for yourself. It could be very problematic."

"Okay, okay," Emily said. "I heard you. Now shut up." A part of her was beginning to plan something. A real romantic who didn't expect love to exist? Perhaps she could use this. . . .

"Where did you put my notes on synchronicity?" Eric asked.

"Don't you ever dare look in my trash again, understand?"

9

Somehow, he always ended up at the boardwalk.

Guy didn't have many vacation days. It was one envelope after another, and only on the rare occasions when he had finished a case of coincidence making early in the morning did he have the chance to just stroll around and enjoy the possibilities of idleness—until the next morning's envelope. These vacation days could be counted on one hand.

For starters, he went back to bed for about two hours. Then he found a good steak restaurant and later rediscovered the ancient pleasure of sitting in front of trees that swayed in the wind and swept the thoughts from one's mind. The small club he had discovered two months ago was the next stop, with a quiet and dreamy-eyed pianist and a glass of red wine that did all it could to make him feel like a sophisticated young man. And finally, of course, as always, somehow he ended up on the boardwalk, to watch the sun nestle into its horizon bed and let the salty breeze tousle his hair.

He sat on one of the benches and looked at the sea, allowing the wine to wear off a bit and the scent of the cool evening to penetrate his clothing. There was almost no one on the beach. Only a teenager and his dog jumped and frolicked at the waterline, right in front of him, displaying how *Friendship: The Director's Cut*, might look.

Perhaps the time had come for him to get a pet too. It didn't have to be a dog. It could be a cat, or a ferret, or even a goldfish. For crying out loud, he'd be willing to compromise with a bonsai tree, if there was no alternative. The boy and the dog on the beach teased each other in a way that you only do with someone you really love. He felt a light twinge of envy that quickly passed through him and then disappeared. He took a deep breath of the sea air and released it with a small, bitter smile. Maybe it was good that he didn't have many vacation days. They reminded him that he was alone.

Guy got up slowly and started to walk home.

Someone at city hall had convinced someone else, after a lively discussion in the corridor, that summer nights were the time to get people out into the street, and the trees along the boulevard were checkered with small, colorful lights that turned nightfall into a sparkling carnival.

He let his eyes wander along the road, his body soaking up the atmosphere while he wandered. A few minutes passed before he noticed, but from that moment he could no longer ignore it. A couple, embracing and smiling, walked ahead of him; on a bench beside him, an elderly couple sat, holding hands; a boy and a girl, no older than ten, ran and cut in front of his path.

It was apparently his imagination. Like pregnant women who see baby carriages everywhere, like ex-smokers who see only cigarettes: people who feel lonely apparently see couples everywhere.

Guy looked in all directions, trying to find someone else walking along the street without a partner. Nothing. Only couples, of all types, walking quickly and focused on their destination, walking slowly and embracing, skipping, dragging their feet in unison, standing and whispering in a corner.

Yes, he needed a dog.

Among all of these couples, he suddenly saw, finally, someone walking alone, in quick steps, hurrying somewhere. Guy almost thanked him in his heart that he wasn't the only one here walking around independently, when the man bumped into a woman coming out of a small toy store, sending all of the boxes she was carefully balancing in her arms flying into the air. Guy couldn't help hearing the voice of the General echoing in his head.

"I know most of you have been anxiously anticipating this lesson," he said to them. "Students always think that Matchmaking 101 is a very romantic course. They also think it will be very simple. All you need is a young man, a young woman, and a street corner, right? Have the man walk from one direction and the woman walk from the other, let them bump into each other exactly at the turn, and voilà—books fall, eye contact, love at first sight, blah blah blah. The quantity of bullshit in this scenario could solve the problems of third world hunger."

Guy chuckled to himself as his new friend apologized to the shocked woman and hurried to run off on his way. This type of encounter succeeded once in a thousand times; in all of the other 999 times, you had to work a little harder. He hoped what he saw wasn't a coincidence someone had created. This low level of professionalism would be quite embarrassing.

But Emily was right in what she had said to him this morning. He really did love matchmaking coincidences. Not because of the romance. He didn't buy into romance. People treated love like something you "believed" in, as if it were a religion. And in this religion, you accepted the belief that somewhere there was a sort of cosmic connection between people that was different in essence from any other type of connection, and that in the framework of this connection you devoted yourself to worshipping someone else. People had to believe in something larger than themselves, he pondered. Religion didn't always provide them with this, so the concept called love gave them what they were always looking for—profound meaning that wasn't rational and transcended regular life. Without realizing it, love became just another thing you needed in a world that had replaced giving with possessing. A big house, a beautiful car, a great love. You didn't love? Your life was wasted.

He also thought this way once. But things had changed since then. He had tasted this fruit and was familiar with it. And love wasn't like that—it was much more. But he had already received his portion of love, and now it was gone. That chapter was closed and sealed. To his dismay, he'd accepted this long ago. Now it was his turn to take care of others. Thus, matchmaking was important to him. Perhaps when you helped someone to achieve happiness that you yourself would no longer experience, you also gained a small piece of that happiness. It was recorded under your name.

He approached the woman at the entrance to the store and, with a smile, helped her collect the packages.

"Thank you," she said to him.

"No problem," he said.

The pavement was strewn with small boxes of various sizes, classic children's games in new eye-catching packaging.

"It's for my nephews," she said, tucking strings of red hair behind her ear. "Twins. They have a birthday next week, and I decided to get them something that might tear them away from the computer."

Guy lifted a box of green plastic soldiers. "Yes," he said, without really listening to her. The small soldiers in the transparent box looked back at him with an innocent gaze.

"May I?" she said.

Guy snapped out of his reverie. "Ah?"

She stood there, smiling, the games again balanced somehow against her chest, and pointed to what he had in his hand. "The soldiers, may I?"

"Ah, yes, of course." He handed the box to her. "Sorry."

"Did you play with these when you were a child?" she asked. "Brings back memories, huh?"

"No, no." He tried to smile. "I guess I just got lost in my thoughts."

She thanked him again and walked away. Guy remained there for another few moments and then continued walking home along the street full of couples. He needed to buy bread and chocolate spread and sugar and coffee and a few other things that were surely lacking at home. He'd stop at the supermarket on the way.

Emily sat in her living room.

So this was how generals felt while waiting for news from the front, she thought.

Months of planning, walls full of diagrams, weeks of anticipation, until she had a day when she could organize everything, and in the end she was sitting here and waiting for a telephone call.

If she were at least doing something else in the meantime, it would be less pathetic. But she was simply sitting and waiting for the telephone to ring. And it had better ring.

Guy roamed up and down the shelves, looking for where they hid his coffee.

Yes, he knew exactly why those plastic soldiers had made the world stop for a few moments. It was embarrassingly clear. In fact, it was even documented somewhere, in some old dog-eared notebook.

It had been just the second week of the course. The homework in Associations 101 was to map each other's trains of thought. The General strongly asserted that only a few tools in their profession were as important as understanding the way in which "things remind one of things"—whatever this vague statement meant. Guy had to map Eric's associations, who mapped Emily's, and Emily mapped Guy.

Mapping Eric was quite simple. Somehow, everything was associated with women, achievements, and Marx Brothers' comedies. Sometimes Guy had to dig deeper to understand why a papaya drink reminded Eric of Vietnam, or why he thought "saxophone" when you said "chocolate." But ultimately the explanations were reasonable and the map of his train of thought was at a level that satisfied the General.

The idea of being mapped by someone else was particularly troubling.

Emily was thorough. She didn't allow him to get away with partial explanations. It was completely logical for you to associate the word "books" with "shelves," she argued, but why in the world would "shelves" remind you of *Die Hard 2*? He had to explain the strange connection his mind found between slippers and hedgehogs, between a smile and bats, between floor tiles and pastel-colored robots. But, somehow, she was most intrigued to discover that toy soldiers reminded him of love.

"You need to explain this to me," she said with sparkling eyes. They sat on the floor in his apartment. An open box of fortune cookies Emily had found somewhere was at their side. Every time

Guy felt he needed a break, they took a cookie, opened it, and tried to think about the coincidences in which they could use the note it contained. The box was half empty at this point.

"It's connected to a first date I had," he said, trying to evade the question. "That's all."

"Details," she said, rubbing her hands, "details."

"Eric drove you crazy in his investigation earlier and now you're taking it out on me, right?"

She smiled mischievously. "I'm just trying to work hard on my homework," she said with a raised eyebrow, betraying the falsehood.

So he told her. About Cassandra, about how they met, about how they were separated, about everything that happened between these two points. Emily listened and occasionally asked a question in a hesitant voice, curious, as if she knew they would never talk about it again.

This was the beginning of a tradition. During the course, they would meet, often over a cup of coffee and a box of fortune cookies. Eric joined them sometimes but usually canceled with excuses like "a once-in-a-lifetime opportunity" to get stuck in the elevator with someone, and so ultimately it became just the two of them. Complete discussions arose from a piece of paper enclosed in sweet dough. They didn't speak again about Cassandra. They didn't speak about Emily's previous work. They really didn't speak about the course. But they spoke about music, without touching upon its ability to stir associations in the client. They spoke about movies, without discussing scenes that aroused repressed emotions and without trying to discover which screenplays were written following the intervention of a coincidence maker. They spoke about their favorite television programs without mentioning the lesson in their course on "Building a Rating by Initiating Power Outages." And they even spoke about politics, while ignoring what they both knew about the true way in which popularity is built.

The truth was, he missed this. Since the end of the course, they no longer had much opportunity to speak, just the two of them. Their schedules were quite crazy, and somehow one of them was always busy preparing some new coincidence. They were new in this business and still didn't know how to manage their time without being drawn into their coincidences. Two, three cancellations, and their tradition died off. After several months, when Eric insisted on establishing a new tradition of morning meetings for the three of them, and after they found a way to coordinate their busy schedules, those cookie evenings seemed superfluous. He thought again about the boy and the dog on the beach. He could actually use a friendship like that now. A glass of wine wasn't always a satisfying friend.

His coffee sat in the third aisle, behind a different type of coffee that was a bit more expensive. He placed the jar in his empty cart and after taking three more steps he saw fortune cookies on the shelf, on sale.

Two for the price of one.

Emily let the phone ring three and a half times, then answered.

"Just a moment," she said.

She held the phone away from her ear and counted in her heart to ten. Her heart counted too quickly, so she counted a few more seconds, this time in her head.

"Ah, yes." She brought the phone back to her ear. "Excuse me, I was in the middle of something."

"Hi," Guy said. "How are you?"

"Fine," she said.

"Remember those cookies we used to eat?"

"Yes, sure," she said. "I think they even had accurate predictions a few times."

"Do you remember which brand they were?"

"No . . . it was in a sort of tin box, no?"

"Brown with a red stripe, right?"

"Right."

"I'm at the supermarket now and came across them. It seems like years since I've seen a box like this."

"Wow, what nostalgia," she said. "Buy one for me too."

"Um, you know what?" he said.

Of course I know what. It's clear that I know what. I hope you know what! "What?"

"How about stopping by? We'll munch on some cookies, like old times."

"I guess I could postpone a few things till tomorrow. . . ." she said, slowly enough to sound like she was trying to make up her mind.

"Come, come, it'll be fun," he said.

"You know what? Let's do it," Emily said. "And let's watch a movie. Your turn to pick!"

"Done."

"Terrific. I'll get dressed and leave in a few minutes."

They ended the conversation, and Emily felt as if she had finished hanging on the wall of her den the head of the bear she had hunted. She began to bounce around the apartment, trying not to scream too much. The neighbors, you know. So she just skipped like a little girl to the other room, stood close to the wall, rose on tiptoes, and kissed the wall where Guy's name was written.

It could be nice, Guy thought, to end the day in conversation with another breathing creature. He looked at the recommended titles on his Netflix app.

The Blind Side

Life Is Beautiful

Never Say Never Again

It's a Wonderful Life

Pretty Woman

It Happened One Night

He shook his head. He felt a bit strange.

He wasn't used to finding romantic comedies on his recommendations list, but it wasn't just that. There was something else. He ignored the feeling and randomly selected a movie, his eyes closed as he pressed the button.

Catch Me If You Can

Emily would be pleased. She loved Tom Hanks.

Only when he got back home did he realize the significance of his proposal.

It had been ages since he'd hosted anyone. Actually, how much time did he have now, ten minutes?

Clothes were strewn all over the living room, an old stain looked at him reprovingly from the tablecloth, and a large pile of books, pamphlets, and notebooks from the course was still in the corner, a monument to procrastination. Not to speak of newspapers that were spread by the wall he'd repainted yesterday.

He quickly collected the clothes and pushed the books behind one of the sofas. A quick glance through the blinds revealed that Emily was already on the street. He hurried along the wall, scooped up newspapers, tossed them into one of the other rooms without thinking, threw himself onto the sofa, and turned on the television so it would look like he had been doing exactly that when Emily arrived.

On the screen appeared a smiling, bearded man against the back-drop of a snowy, majestic mountain. The man's face was red and sunburned, and a thick down jacket covered him to the neck, but his eyes sparkled a deep blue.

"First of all, congratulations," said the interviewer, who was out of camera range except for his hand holding the microphone. "I understand this is your second attempt to conquer the summit."

"Yes," the bearded man said. "It didn't really work out last time. It was even quite horrendous, to tell you the truth. I broke my leg . . . quite a mess."

"Nonetheless, you decided to try again."

"You know how it is," the bearded man said, expanding his smile. "That's why they invented second chances. You can't give up on something that you know you must do. It was clear to me that I needed to try again. And besides, this time I also had especially good support." He reached out his hand, and a tanned woman with short hair entered the picture, wrapped in a jacket just as thick as the man's. She waved her hand and giggled when the man pressed his whiskers to her forehead.

Emily knocked on the door.

They sat together on the sofa and tried to remember how it went. After all of the meetings in which Eric also participated, with him always saying the right idiotic sentence, some adjustments were apparently required. They were a bit rusty at being together one-on-one.

"You can still smell the paint," Emily said, the automatic pilot flying the friend inside her still trying to control things.

"Yes, it . . . it lingers," Guy said. On the screen in front of them, the bearded mountain climber continued to talk silently.

Emily got up and opened the blinds a bit. On the way back, she picked up the box of fortune cookies and offered it to Guy. "One for you . . . ," she said as Guy took one with a smile, "and one for me," she said, extracting another random cookie.

She sat opposite him on the sofa, her legs folded underneath her.

"I'm really happy you invited me," she said. "We haven't done this in a long time. I missed it."

Guy smiled at her, broke his fortune cookie, and took out the small piece of paper. In the short moments before the power outage snuffed out all of the lights, he managed to read the sentence and raise his eyes toward Emily.

"'Don't look far. The answer to the most important question is likely to be in front of your eyes.'"

The darkness covered them in a silence rife with expectations. Emily sat upright, holding her breath.

She knew that the pale glimmer of the streetlights entering through the blinds would fall exactly on her eyes in a white diagonal line, making them sparkle. She heard heartbeats and wondered whether they were hers or his. When the flow of electricity resumed, he was still looking into her eyes. They remained silent.

Finally, he put down the broken cookie and said, "I think I realize something now, something I should have realized a long time ago."

She trembled slightly. "Yes?" she said quietly.

"I don't want us to meet again like we once did," he said, and she saw a flush of red spreading across his cheeks. "I want us to meet in a new way, completely new. I want us to try something else."

"That sounds excellent to me." She was still unable to speak in a full voice.

"I've lived in the past for too long."

"Yes . . ."

"And I didn't notice certain feelings until today."

"Guy . . ."

"And to hell with Cassandra. It's you I want."

"Oh, Guy."

When the lights went back on, Emily shook herself and returned to reality, awakening to the real world in which Guy sat in front of her and stared at the broken cookie and the piece of paper in his hand. He raised his eyes toward her and asked, "Emily, what's going on here?"

"What do you mean?"

Something inside of him seemed to have toughened. He got up and went behind the sofa, rummaged around, and pulled out a faded notebook that was falling apart. OBJECT SELECTION TECHNIQUES, PART B was written on it. He thumbed through it until he found the page he was looking for, then placed the notebook on the table. The title of the page was "No. 73: Choosing from a Box Prepared in Advance, a Variation on the Viton Exercise." The illustrations explained how to turn the box so that the subject would think he was randomly taking an object from it, but would actually take an object determined in advance.

Emily looked silently at the open notebook.

"You arranged for me to take this cookie, right?"

She remained silent and crushed her cookie between her fingers.

"Right?"

She still didn't answer. He threw the notebook to the other side of the room and sat down opposite her. "What's going on here?"

"Someone, a good friend of mine in a course I once took, told me about his first love," Emily said quietly. "He said he once thought love was a type of admiration, only with a pleasant smell. That it's a situation in which you become enslaved to thinking about someone else, that you become a groupie of someone for all sorts of reasons, and that this someone becomes your groupie too. After all, this is how everyone talks about it, no? Blinding lightning that hits you one clear day, or a cake of admiration that quietly rises in your belly, the realization—like a bright white light—of a connection to a twin spirit and all that bullshit."

"You also arranged for the cookies to be in the supermarket? You arranged for the woman at the toy store?" He couldn't really be angry with her, not with her, but he had to pretend to be. She must understand that this can't be. Can't. Be.

"And then, when a someone arrived in his life, my friend understood that they had lied to him, that he had lied to himself. It wasn't admiration, not even something close to that. The beginning was similar, but very quickly this superficial admiration grew and became something else, something truer. He felt like he was back home again. That he had come to a place where he was wanted and felt worthy and fitting. And, in particular, a place where he belonged. He felt, so he said, as if they had already met or had done something together a long time ago, and had been forced to take a break and then were able to do it again, though he had no idea what 'it' was. He never felt like it was a beginning, he told me. He always felt like it was a continuation."

"Emily, listen . . ."

She tried her best not to sound like she was begging. Just not begging. "Guy . . . you look around at the world," she said, "and you never see love that suits you because you are just not looking for it. You're looking for Cassandra and giving up in advance. You're looking for someone who was once there and no longer exists. You're a captive of something that is over, gone. And it's sad for me to see you like this, trying to fill in the colors in a picture whose lines were erased long ago, imagining something in which there is no—"

"I'm not imagining anything. I'm remembering. Only memories remain for me," he interrupted. "There's a difference between—"

"Still, you're a captive," she interrupted in return.

"It's good for me this way."

"But not for me."

They sat in silence.

Slowly, all of the circles of understanding came together. Tick, tick, tick. He knew what she wanted, what she was trying to arrange, and she knew that he knew. And he knew that she knew that he knew . . . and so on. . . .

What the hell was she thinking?

"Where was the beginning of all the . . ."

"For a very long time, I've been thinking about how to tell you this, how to give this to you, how . . ." She shivered. I need a hug, said her body. No, said his.

"I meant today. When did you start to make coincidences for me today?" he asked cautiously.

"At the beach," Emily said.

"The boy and the dog?"

"Yes."

"The street full of couples."

"Yes, and a few other things. . . ." And I need a hug, can't you see that?

Oh, what the hell, let it out already.

"I think that we started something together once and we had a break, and now we can continue," Emily said. "You don't feel like this sometimes? Not even a little? Because I do. Every time you're around, every time you're near me, I come home. I want to continue from the point we left off. I . . ."

"Emily," he said.

"Believe me," she said, "there is such a place."

She should have arranged a longer power outage, much longer. Now it was possible to see that she was crying.

"I'm sorry," he said. "You're great, you're really great. You know how much fun I have with you. But . . ."

There had to be a "but," right? A mental U-turn.

He took a deep breath. "It doesn't work this way. Not with me. You can't arrange a coincidence for us when 'us' cannot happen."

She didn't stay much longer.

There was no point.

She had asked the question and presented her complex gift of courtship, this possibility she had worked on for so long. And he had answered. A quiet but resounding "No."

Walking slowly down the hallway, trying not to fall, she realized the cookie was still in her hand. She had arranged a lot of things in advance today, but her cookie was really completely random. She broke it and took out the little piece of paper that was inside.

"Sometimes," it whispered to her, "disappointments are new and wonderful beginnings."

"Yeah, sure," she said. The light in the stairway went off, and she felt her way down.

10

Dammit, get in already!

Eddie Levy, an accountant, stood in the stairway, bent over, struggling to get the key into the lock.

His hands were steady, his teeth clenched in irritation, but somehow the simple act of inserting the key and turning it had become complicated. He cursed quietly.

He shot a glance at his watch. His internal turmoil had lasted for nearly eight minutes. It was hard for him to define this vague feeling, but he knew it was the last thing he needed at the moment.

The key finally slid into the cylinder, and he shoved the door open. When he entered and turned on the lights, he thought about the small scratches he had surely made around the keyhole, like some lowlife drunkard.

He tried to breathe deeply, calm down, clear his thoughts.

Deep breaths would bring more air into his lungs, more oxygen into his bloodstream, so the brain would receive the portion it needed to go into a lower gear and return to normalcy. He felt as if someone had shot one of those little rubber balls into his head and now the ball was bouncing in all directions.

But there was no need to exaggerate. It was okay. He wasn't an emotional person. He was very proud of that.

While people around him became servants to elusive urges, he had already mapped that territory long ago. He no longer tried to explain it. There was no point. People wanted to convince themselves that they *feel*. Recognition of the fact that this was nothing but a chemical reaction, a small electric surge among neurons, made them feel too mechanical somehow.

Eddie had no problem being a machine. It was the truth, and one should acknowledge it. A chunk of meat, a capsule of DNA, a system of organs with self-consciousness. Well, so what? That's how it was.

But now he found himself pacing back and forth in the small apartment, slicing the dense air between the walls covered with crowded shelves, trying to understand the source of this disquiet and stuff it back into the irrational hole from which it had crawled.

He stopped and shook his head.

Music. He'd listen to a little music. Somewhere, on the bottom of one of the shelves, was a dusty collection of CDs. It had been a long time since he'd listened to them. He had one CD of concertos for piano and orchestra and had listened to only four tracks—decisive tracks, with a structured musical theme, with development that could almost be presented as a formula with two unknowns.

His music, that's what he needed.

He pulled out the old battered Discman, with the earphone wires wound around it like a snake coiled around prey, and sat down in the armchair. The first sounds started to restore familiar order to the universe.

He closed his eyes, and the clear, almost militaristic tempo swept over him. He was no longer a grumpy man sitting in an old armchair. He looked at himself, at the whole world, from a distance and with a single thought; the armchair became a cloud of synthetic molecules, and sitting on the chair was a system of pumps and pipes, bellows and air openings, levers and tissues. He went still further in his thoughts, into cold outer space, and saw the small, blue, pathetic ball circling around the big burning ball. And still further, until everything became motionless specks in empty space. If one looked from high enough, everything appeared the same—atoms arranged in complex forms. Whether it was a random block of granite passing through a galaxy, or a blood pump made of muscle that someone at some point in history decided was the seat of human emotion.

The track ended.

There was no point in listening to the next track, which was slow and annoying. On any other day, he would turn it off and quickly move on to the rest of the evening. But perhaps because of his fatigue from walking or perhaps because he was sitting comfortably in the armchair and the Discman had slid far, far below to the floor, he found himself swept onward to the next part of the concerto. The soft, seductive, sentimental part that he hadn't listened to in ages.

When he woke up, the Discman next to him was dead.

The battery had run out in the middle of the movement but he had continued to hear it in his dream. His body was heavy, and when he raised his hand and touched his face, he felt wetness.

He was sweating.

Just a moment—no, he wasn't sweating.

Aghast, he realized that it was the trail of a tear. He had shed a tear while sleeping. This was the last thing he needed.

But now his fingers had touched this horrible salinity, and like the fading flash of a camera, all of the precious distance he had achieved disappeared. And the complex and random system in the armchair was replaced by a lonely, melancholy man, sitting in an apartment with the blinds closed.

It was because of her.

All he had done was go out on his usual nightly walk. After an entire day of sitting in the office, his joints needed some movement. Accounting was not a profession with loads of physical activity. He liked to take care of himself—five kilometers of rapid walking had become his routine.

At first, he saw her from afar, coming out of a building, her shoulders a bit slouched. Nothing that should attract special attention. He walked faster, and the distance between him and her lean, seemingly fragile back grew smaller. Behind the corner of the building, she turned to the right. And as he passed by her, he glanced to the side and saw her collapse in tears and sit on the ground, devastated.

It wasn't the first time Eddie Levy had seen a young woman cry. After all, during the course of evolution, women had developed into creatures that cried quite often. But something at that moment, something in the way her entire body tried to escape through her eyes, resonated with some forgotten truth inside him and made him slow down.

For a moment, he thought, really thought seriously, about approaching her and asking whether she was okay.

But he immediately came to his senses and continued walking, quickly distancing himself, still hearing her sobs, shocked by the way this melodramatic scene made him feel as if someone had ripped his heart from its place and then put it back, but upside down.

———

For several weeks now he hadn't felt "right." He couldn't put his finger on anything specific, but occasionally the type of thought he'd once believed he had managed to eradicate would infiltrate his defenses. And now this.

Eddie tried to explain away the palpitations and the internal burning behind his eyes in terms of his knowledge regarding causes and effects in the human body. You're not tense, he said to himself. You're simply flooded with too much cortisol. Just like there is no such thing as "fun"—only dopamine. Every emotion has a chemical name and component.

He looked at the long bookcase in front of him.

Rows and rows of books on every possible scientific subject in the world. Cosmology, physics, biology, neurology. You're supposed to be my anchor. You're supposed to spare me this nonsense.

Just several days ago, his bookcase had to be defended against someone who got stuck with a flat tire across the street and asked to call a tow truck. The person didn't have a cell phone, claiming he hated such devices. Could he please? It would just take a minute.

Eddie cursed silently for the thousandth time the fact that he lived on the first floor. Yes, sure, why not. The telephone is over there.

At one point, just before this character left—he was a skinny man, almost transparent, with the eyes of a child who had been bullied at school—he surveyed these shelves and asked why there was no prose or poetry. Eddie told him he had no need for them. What interested him was the truth about the world.

This man, who claimed he was a "poet," started to say all sorts of ridiculous things about love and culture and the way in which we "discover truths about ourselves" not only through science. Eddie didn't even let him finish. He threw the plain facts at him like a pail of cold water.

After sufficient study, the world was exposed in its full technical complexity and emotional sterility, he said. It was impossible to ignore this. For the sake of the truth, the precious and unequivocal truth, one needed to relinquish a few saccharine points of view. People loved their children, for example, because in the course of evolution, over years of fine-tuning, it was found that the trait of love for progeny was beneficial for the existence of the species. Big eyes, small faces—this was all part of the blind planning that was designed to arouse in us a feeling of protection. Brilliant? Perhaps. Exciting? Not really. Love was sexual attraction in disguise; religion was an invention designed to console humanity, which felt threatened by nature; fear was a survival mechanism; greed was a social convention without which the human race would succumb to existential passivity; the search for meaning was the price of self-consciousness and was doomed to fail. Systems upon systems. Those which caused us to digest food and turn it into waste, and those that caused us (he pointed to his visitor) to define ourselves as a "poet" and think that it made a difference.

Once you got used to it, it was more practical. You couldn't be hurt by the amygdala gland problems of another person, or be devastated when you were ignored by someone who was simply not attracted to your pheromones. And the main thing was that you couldn't fail in a life that had no meaning. Essentially, we're trying to survive because we're trying to survive. All the rest was mental decoration and self-persuasion. The poet—as a matter of fact, Eddie didn't even catch his name—gave him a strange look and went out to the car to wait for the tow truck.

———

But all these books didn't protect him now. For a moment, he wanted to assault the shelves in a fit of anger and fling the books to the floor, in a way that would cause them maximum pain. He wanted to take out all of the frustration generated by brokenhearted young women who spewed a radioactive cloud of compassion, put breaches in the walls of worldviews, and exacerbated a loneliness no one understood. He wanted to throw them onto the floor and stand among all the dead pages like the captain of a sinking ship.

But he wouldn't do that, of course. He wasn't like that.

He went to the kitchen, closed the door behind him, and sat by the small table.

An old red towel, a jar with a bit of coffee, a white page, and a blue pen waited for him. At the top of the white page was a shopping list in his neat handwriting, a catalogue of the things he needed to purchase on his weekly walk to the supermarket.

People were clouds of numbers, nothing more. Height, age, blood pressure, reaction speed, pulse, number of cells. Everything could be measured, everything. Behind every poignant melody was mathematics; behind every breathtaking leap by an acrobat was physics; behind every heartbreak was chemistry. The notion that her sadness was somehow reverberating through him now, in some strange, immeasurable cosmic way—indeed, this was completely wacky.

He took the pen in hand and started to draw small squares in the corner, like a small child trying to keep himself from being disruptive in class. But this didn't help when a half hour later he found himself sitting by the kitchen table, staring in shock at the white sheet.

Ten lines were written on the page before him.

Three clean, official-looking lines in the top-right corner listed sugar, paper towels, and laundry detergent. And another seven lines in the opposite corner—crooked and brisk, full of erasures and corrections—attempted to sculpt something with words that had no parallel beyond raw emotion.

Oh my gosh, he thought.

I've written a poem.

Eddie grabbed the sheet of paper, quickly crumpled it into a small, tight ball, and tossed it into the trash bin.

He had no recollection of the previous moments. It was as if someone else had taken control of his body, thought things that were no longer his, felt things that he no longer felt, and wrote this damn poem, which he didn't even understand or want to understand.

He had no need for this artistic weakness. He had only scorn for it, and always had. He was unwilling to bring this thing into his life just because a fragile woman on a street corner had unsettled him.

He decided to go to sleep and wake up like new tomorrow. This nonsense would sink back into his subconscious, and he would awaken to the world as the person he chose to be.

He lay in bed, angry at himself, and one stray thought suddenly made it clear what had bothered him so much. And he couldn't avoid facing it.

This feeling. Inside. Like something he had created, out of nothing. Not like the rest of his life, which he felt was a combination of the same basic materials over and over, the same things repeating themselves, just in a different order. It was as if this simply emerged from within himself. A new, fresh, unfamiliar answer.

Enough with this nonsense, he told himself. There's no soul. There's nothing beyond the sophistication of the organism.

Nothing? Then what was *this*?

Thousands of fragments of his old self were horrified and rushed to close the crack before something happened.

This must not happen.

Because if it happened, he would look at his life and consider it a mistake. He would look back, panic-stricken, at every choice he had ever made. His worldview was so clear—a crack or question mark in it would make it all an atrocious waste of time. Years of missed opportunities. It would be better to simply continue on. Don't change now, buddy! Don't change!

People only changed because of a crisis, not from growth. If you changed, it meant you were in a crisis. You must not fall into a crisis.

But inside, under all of the anxious fragments of science running around, his soul was screaming hysterically in the streets. He already knew that he did not *know*. That he was caught in that chicken-and-egg question that no one could solve: Did the worldview shape the personality, or vice versa? He knew that he could dismiss it all as a complex self-illusion if he wanted to, but that he could also surrender and accept that he had within himself, perhaps, just maybe, something more than a system of causes and effects. And, even worse, he realized that he could never take the razor of truth and cut reality in order to reveal the answer. For the first time in his life, in real fear that somehow was able to transform into great joy, he came to terms with the thought that however much he tried, he didn't really look at reality with elegance and objectivity, from the outside, but always from the inside. Deep, deep inside.

From between the slits of the blinds, Eddie Levy saw the moon. He could now jump back and forth between two ways of looking at it. One way saw a big rock orbiting in space, wrapped in the crushed glass of unfortunate asteroids, and the other saw it as the backdrop for your sweetheart to place her head on your shoulder and close her eyes.

He got out of bed and went to the kitchen.

There are some surrenders that fill you with sweetness. Or perhaps he'd simply lost his mind. Well, so what? That's the way it was.

He pulled the crumpled page from the trash bin, unraveled it, and made an effort to make it into a sheet of paper again. He didn't even glance at the poem he wrote earlier but turned the paper over and started to write his second poem. And the page embraced the ink, and another path opened before him in the forest.

11

Guy arrived at the street corner five minutes before the hour specified in yesterday's envelope. It was relatively early in the morning
and the traffic was only starting to awaken and show signs that it
intended, again, to block the city from one end to the other, if only
to demonstrate that it could. On the other side of the street, a bleary-
eyed saleswoman arranged a display window. She tried desperately
to hang a sign reading LOW! LOW! PRICES! with a giant red arrow in
the background. Not far from her, at the intersection, there was a
policeman who had to direct traffic due to a malfunctioning stop-
light. Slowly but surely, the street filled with people, cars, noise, and
one concerned coincidence maker.

   He tried to understand what exactly was supposed to happen, but
that strange sentence about the kick in the head didn't seem related
to any sort of possible instruction. The street around him continued

to go about its daily routine while he stood waiting for some sign or hint to arrive in—let's see, how much time remained? Two more minutes.

The get-together yesterday with Emily had ended in sharp silence. He didn't say the sentences that passed through his mind; she didn't answer them with sentences of her own. After she left he just went into the shower for an hour, his mind empty but pounding. I wish I could love you, but I can't. This seat is taken.

He'd known it would come at some point. During the course, they had started to dance this complex dance in which she sent hints, as if unintentionally, and he dodged them like small bullets of caring, in order to be able to maintain what they had. She just has to meet other men, he would say to himself. She only knows me and Eric. As soon as new people come into her life, she'll move on. Just keep it up.

Because that's the way it was: There were women who could only be good friends, right? You'll never fall in love with them, because they lacked the presence that resonated in your heart and they didn't linger with you after they left. It was true that Emily was the closest thing to someone who was able to read his thoughts. She made him laugh, supported him when he had to learn hundreds of lists of possible incidents and responses during the course, and she listened to him when he needed to spill his heart out after an attempt at coincidence making went terribly awry because he had failed to correctly calculate the who-knows-what. Okay, so what? It wasn't she that he dreamed of at night. She didn't overwhelm him or make him tremble. She didn't interrupt his thoughts every moment. He didn't soar with her.

And deep inside, another small voice added another small point to the list: she wasn't Cassandra.

This status quo was preferable; he was used to it. He realized he was acting like a neurotic tragic hero, but certain things were impossible to explain. And one of them was that he simply knew it wouldn't happen again. That wasn't so terrible. So why was it so hard for someone else to accept?

Leave me alone, he thought.

And what now?

What would happen the next time they met?

How would they be able to preserve the thin shroud of what was once friendship?

Eric would notice, of course. He noticed everything. And he'll make a feast out of this. Everything was so simple till now. Why did she have to complicate this so much?

Okay, enough. Concentrate. A half a minute before the meeting. What was he supposed to do?

Okay, okay. Let's get back to the basics.

Sometimes he had to remind himself that ultimately there were several very simple things that one needed to know about reality in order to be a coincidence maker. All the rest were details. Look at the broad picture and search for the contexts that no one else sees. Try to move one step ahead of reality and guess what it planned to do a moment before it happened.

The General associated a particular picture with every rule he taught them, an image that was etched in their minds when he explained the rule to them. Somehow, this worked. Guy's mind was full of gorillas rolling barrels from the tops of cliffs, dwarfs in nightgowns tying bundles of ferns, headless acrobats stretching across a trapeze made of chocolate, and, of course, billiard balls. The General really liked to illustrate things with balls.

There weren't many courses whose first lesson took place in a dimly lit snooker club. But with the General, he later realized, the lesson couldn't have taken place anywhere else.

The small club the General chose was relatively empty that night. Two young men played at a table in the corner, alternating from a position of intense concentration, their bodies taut over the table, to an indifferent and carefree position, a cold bottle of beer dangling at an angle between their fingers, their eyes watching the arrangement of balls on the green felt table.

A couple sat at the bar in a quiet meeting that included more silence and stares than words of real weight. They were counting on a place teeming with people where they could blend in and do little more than be together, to remember anew, after all this time, how it felt "to go out." Now, they were forced to try to really interact— conversation, content, nuances of facial expressions, the whole deal. And in the corner, the next-to-last cigarette in the pack in his hand, with a blank expression and four days and three hours of whiskers on his face, sat the guy who always sat in the corner and smoked, since he had nowhere else to go. His small eyes didn't gaze anywhere in particular, and the hand that wasn't holding the cigarette rested on his thigh, just as apathetic as his eyes, though his fingernails were a bit gnawed.

The General arranged nine balls in a diamond shape and set them up in their place on the table. He reached out his hand without bothering to look up. "Stick," he said.

Eric hurried to hand him the cue and the General took it, his half-focused, half-amused eyes directed at the balls. He walked around the table and placed the cue ball in the appropriate spot. In a smooth and natural movement, he bent over and aimed the stick for a few seconds. "So let's begin. The four ball in the far-right pocket," he said and hit the white ball strongly, scattering the colored billiard balls in all directions, like a flock of frightened birds. Some caromed off the side of the table. The purple ball, the four, rolled slowly until it dropped softly into the pocket to the far right of them.

The General stood upright and looked at the three of them standing around the table.

"Okay," he said, "you think you know what I'm going to talk about. You're sure that I intend to explain action and reaction, to mention Newton's laws and the Lorenz attractor and Littlewood's Law and ways to calculate the result, and to use this billiard table as a metaphor. But metaphors are crap. You can never really find two things that serve as a true metaphor for each other. If two things can serve as a perfect metaphor for each other, they're apparently exactly the same thing. The universe doesn't suffer waste."

He moved to his right along the table and stood next to Guy. "If you'll allow me, junior," he said, raising a brow. Guy moved quickly. The General placed his cue and took aim. "Always," he said, "there is always something in a metaphor that is inconsistent with the original idea, or vice versa. So yes, it's possible to use billiard balls that strike one another as a metaphor for events that affect each other, but there are a few basic things that are different. Guy, what's going to happen now?"

Guy shook himself a bit. "What?"

"Good morning," the General said. "Nice to see you're with us. Before you brush your teeth and drink your first coffee of the morning—what's going to happen now?"

"I . . . that is . . ." Guy took a quick look at the table, trying to understand the balance of power between the balls and the impact the General's stroke would have on them. "I think you'll hit the yellow, and the yellow will hit the orange and will almost knock it into the center pocket there."

The General struck the white ball, which hit the yellow one, which moved forward, spinning a bit, and hit the orange ball, which curved straight into the center pocket on the other side.

"I'll give you a hint for the rest of the lesson," he said. "I'm not in favor of the 'almost' method of playing."

He walked around the table to the other side.

"And stop with all the 'orange ball, yellow ball.' This is nine-ball pool. There are numbers on them for a reason. So here's the first difference between billiard balls and real life: if you want to predict what will happen in the next move, you'll discover that in billiards it gets easier as time passes. Fewer balls cause fewer events to happen. There are also very clear rules. You're permitted to hit some balls and prohibited from hitting others. You may not hit balls off the table, and so on. In this game, as you advance, you simplify the statistics that physics needs in order to explain to itself what the hell is going on here. I remind you: as coincidence makers, your goal is to discover the right ball to hit, and how and where. But in life, no element disappears and simplifies the problem. On the contrary, when you instigate an action, you make the situation more complex, if anything." He bent over the table. "Emily, what's going to happen now?"

Emily was almost ready. Almost.

"The one ball will hit the six ball, which will hit the one next to it, which will . . ."

"Too long. What's going to happen now?"

Emily took a deep breath. "The three ball in the corner pocket."

The General struck the cue ball that hit the six ball that hit the one next to it and ricocheted a bit to the left. In the end, it was the six ball that fell into the corner pocket opposite the one that Emily had intended. She clenched her face.

"A second difference," the General said. "In life, there are no 'theories.' Seven billion people strike seven billion balls at any moment throughout the planet. And these are only the human beings. You'll be surprised to discover how many other elements of reality correspond with each other and affect us. Words, thoughts, beliefs, fears.

And we have yet to begin to talk about the objects around us. Eric, what's going to happen now?"

"Okay." Eric took a deep breath and looked at the table. "The three ball in the pocket next to us."

The General shook his head in frustration. "You're making assumptions that are based on where I'm standing and aren't based on these balls." He walked around the table, bent over, and without aiming at all, sent the cue ball in the direction of the one ball, which flew straight into the opposite pocket.

"The balls don't care," the General continued, leaning on his cue stick. "They don't care about which pocket they fall into or how hard they're hit. You'll never feel uncomfortable vis-à-vis the six ball just because the seven ball reached the pocket before it. No ball will cry if it's alone in the corner. It's much easier to manage events when you don't care about them. But the people you're going to make coincidences for can break your heart. If you don't learn to be mean sometimes, if you don't realize that sometimes you need to give someone a little whack to get them going in the right direction, if you don't disengage from what's happening—you won't be able to make coincidences. On the other hand, if you don't care, if you start with the assumption that the world is your playground, you'll be even worse coincidence makers. Guy?"

"The two ball hits the seven ball, the seven into the corner."

The General bent over the table and hit the balls. The seven ball dropped into the corner pocket.

"Nice," Eric said with admiration.

"Thank you," Guy said and smiled.

"Quiet down. We're not done yet," the General said.

"Three ball in the right corner pocket," Emily said.

"You're a bit quick, no?" the General asked. "And you're also wrong."

Emily looked again at the table. "Then the two ball in the near-left pocket. But it has to be quite a shot because you also need—"

"Wrong again," the General said.

"Nine ball? To the right corner? It's not too far? And it's also behind the three ball, so . . ."

"It's not the nine ball."

Emily shook her head in disbelief. "Eight? The black ball? But you're only supposed to knock it in at the end."

The General bent over and raised the cue stick. "This is nine-ball pool, not eight-ball pool. You chose to draw your conclusions based on the wrong set of rules." He sent the eight ball racing into the center pocket and looked at Emily, who pursed her lips. "Indeed, all of these balls operate according to general rules that we're all familiar with, but it's even more complex with people. Because people define rules for themselves that are more hidden and strange. Customs, ridiculous table manners, social stipulations, and whatever. And that's not all. If you have someone who's unwilling to have the meat on his plate touch the peas, who checks whether he locked the door fifty times, or who tries to rudely turn away every young woman he meets because he feels insecure—you need to know this. Every ball in your system will have a separate world of rules of its own."

Three balls remained on the table: the blue, the two ball; the red, the three ball; and the white-yellow, the nine ball.

"Okay," the General said. "Who wants to predict now?"

Eric cautiously raised his hand.

"The clown," the General said.

"The two ball in the far-left corner," Eric said.

"Think again," the General replied.

"But you need to hit the two first," Eric said. "And if you do, you can't hit the other two because they're in the opposite direction."

"I want to put the three ball in the lower-right pocket."

Eric looked at him from the corner of his eye. "It's not possible. . . ." he said hesitantly. "The red one—that is, the three ball—is in the opposite direction of the two. And you have to hit the two ball first because it's the lowest number."

"Unless you intend to break the rules," Guy said.

The General circled the table pensively.

"That's not a suggestion I expected to hear from you," he said to Guy. "Innovative thinking is not supposed to be your strong suit."

"But that's what you're about to do, right?"

"I could," the General said, "but I don't need to."

"And if you needed to?" Guy asked.

"Break the rules?" the General asked.

"Yes," Guy said.

"It depends," the General said. "There are rules that can be broken and rules that cannot. In the case of some rules, it would be detrimental to your objective to break them, while that isn't the case for other rules. There are rules that really exist and there are those that are present only in your mind. In order to know whether you can break a rule, you first need to clarify quite a few things about it. Would you break this rule?"

Guy thought it over a bit. "Am I allowed to?" he finally asked.

The General laughed a short, choked laugh. Sort of a cough with an identity crisis. "Yes. That's what I thought. When you're going to ignore a rule, you prefer to receive permission first."

He moved closer to Guy and looked into his eyes.

"Check what you're breaking, then simply decide," he said. "Most of your rules are simply an invention you designed to protect yourself. Breaking those rules is courageous. Breaking the rest of the rules is just lazy."

He raised the stick and hit downward, strongly with both hands, knocking the thicker part of the stick against the cue ball.

The ball flew into the air and, when it fell, it hit the two ball and caromed in the opposite direction, hitting the three ball and knocking it into the lower-right pocket.

"Nice," the General said. "Emily, you should know what's next."

"Two ball in the top-left corner," Emily said in a flat voice.

"Oh, don't get too excited," the General said, placing his stick at the correct angle on the table.

"It's easy," Emily said.

"Meaning?"

"Meaning that after I failed the previous two questions, you're giving me something easy so I'll feel better about myself. So thank you, but it's quite clear."

"And because it's easy, it's less important, of course. Yes?" the General asked.

"For me," Emily said.

"And for the two ball?" the General asked.

Emily stuck her hands in her pockets. "What do you mean?"

"I mean that with all due respect, if you classify the coincidences you perform only by the level of challenge they pose to you or by how good they make you feel about yourself, you'll forget that what's important is the change you're creating in the lives of other people, and you'll reach the stage where you become confused between what is essential and nonessential. People who fall in love after you worked on a coincidence for five minutes do this with the same passion and the same sense of destiny as those who meet as the result of a coincidence you worked six months to arrange."

He moved the cue stick in a sharp movement. The two ball went into the top-left pocket.

Then he stood upright and looked around, a half smile trying to sneak onto his face.

Two balls remained on the table facing each other. One of them was white.

"What will happen now?" the General asked.

"Nine ball in the far-right corner," Emily said.

"The far-left corner," Guy said.

"It'll hit the side and fly to the near-right corner," Eric said.

The General leaned over the table and aimed the cue stick.

"What will happen now," he said, "is that the couple next to the bar will kiss."

They turned in the direction of the bar and saw the heads of the couple by the bar moving closer to each other, slowly and hesitantly. The sound of the impact of the balls was heard and the couple kissed.

The General stood behind the table now, the stick upright in his hand. Only the white ball remained on the table.

"And perhaps that's the most important thing," he said when they turned toward him again. "There's always a broader picture. There's always something beyond the system you're concentrating on. Never forget that. There are no clear boundaries. Life doesn't stop at the boundaries of the table. And there are always more than six pockets you can fall into. There is always something beyond. Always, always, always."

Emily wanted to ask something but decided not to. It could wait.

"The last question," the General said. "Where did the nine ball fall in the end?"

They were silent. None of them had noticed.

"Mark down your first and last failure," the General said, placing his stick on the table. "With all due respect to the broader picture, you don't keep track of an entire game only to miss the last play. Start getting used to it. You need to notice many more things than you're aware of."

FROM *METHODS IN DEFINING GOALS FOR COINCIDENCE MAKING*—INTRODUCTION

Even if we limit ourselves to only the past five hundred years, we cannot summarize the development of the field of happiness sciences in this short introduction. Nonetheless, we will try to highlight a few key points. You will find more details in the sources appearing in the appendix. We particularly recommend "Development of the Happiness Model—The First Thousand Years," "Development of the Happiness Model—The Last Thousand Years," and "Theories of Happiness for Beginners"— all by the theoretician John Coochy.

The classic period of mapping happiness was characterized primarily by attempts to develop a single general formula that would encompass its main features.

According to Vaultan, for example, happiness will always be the ratio between personal happiness potential and the difference between what an individual wants and what he has in reality.

$$H = p \, / \, (w\text{-}h)$$

Where H is general happiness, p is personal happiness potential (or php in some professional literature), w represents want, and h represents have.

Vaultan argued that the maximal level of personal happiness depends on each individual's personal happiness potential, and that the smaller the differential between want and have, the greater the level of general happiness will be. Thus, there are two main ways to maximize happiness: lowering w (defined as "lowering expectations" or "low expectations") or increasing h (defined as "ambitiousness" or "luck" depending on the school of thought).

CENTRAL PROBLEMS IN VAULTAN'S FORMULA

- *The Problem of Range: a utopian situation in which a person who has everything he wants is not defined in the formula, or alternatively leads to infinite happiness.*
- *The Problem of Negativity: a situation in which a person who has more than he wants is defined as negative happiness, which is considered particularly problematic.*
- *The Problem of Self Influence: the strongest argument against Vaultan's Formula was raised by Muriel Fabrik, who demonstrated in her book* Embedding the Also *that p in itself, if it indeed exists, must also be influenced by w and h, which makes Vaultan's Formula nonlinear and unsolvable with existing tools.*

FABRIK'S FORMULA

Fabrik also succeeded in proving that it is impossible to define standard units for measuring w *and* h, *and that sometimes even the same person uses different units of measurement. Nonetheless, most of her critics argued that the formula Fabrik proposed was a variation of Vaultan's Formula. At first, Fabrik proposed a formula that treats happiness as a relative object, measured only relative to other factors—usually, the happiness of someone else. However, toward the end of her life, she presented a new formula, which describes happiness as a product of pleasure or personal satisfaction multiplied by sense of meaning (or illusion of relative meaning) squared.*

$$H = pm^2$$

This formula paved the way for thinking about happiness in terms other than profit and loss and emphasized its subjective nature.

THE UNCERTAINTY PRINCIPLE OF GEORGE GEORGE

The Icelandic theoretician George George argued that it is impossible to measure either the quality or size of any of Vaultan's classic characteristics without influencing their value by the very fact of looking at them. In fact, it is impossible to examine happiness without changing it, whether it be the one-dimensional happiness Vaultan defined or the multidimensional happiness of Fabrik.

The problem that George George noted is still defined as

"George's Uncertainty Principle" by leading scholars, and the literature also refers to it sometimes as "The Problem of Self-Analysis."

THE POSTMODERN METHOD OF HAPPINESS

The crisis in happiness sciences became more severe and the field had nearly reached a dead end when Jonathan Fix raised the argument that all of the formulas proposed by scholars over the generations had actually examined the concept of "satisfaction" rather than "happiness." As a result of this far-reaching argument, researchers were required to redefine the essence of the happiness they were trying to quantify.

On this basis, the Postmodern Method flourished. This method seeks to disassociate itself from the solutions that the classic theories had proposed for the problem of definition. Paul MacArthur was the one who laid the foundation for this method by defining happiness as "something that people simply decide they have, and that's all."

As in other fields, the transition from the classic definition of happiness to the modern definition and then to the postmodern definition made a decisive impact on the operational methods of coincidence makers throughout the world.

12

A bicycle rider quickly rode past Guy, the wheels of his bicycle making a soft *whish* sound, and he suddenly understood.

You're a coincidence maker. So what exactly did you think you were supposed to wait for?

Did you expect that exactly at the appointed hour someone would ring a bell? A fancy car would stop next to you and the window would open? A helicopter would fly by and drop proclamations?

No, that would be too obvious.

You're supposed to be the one who notices nuances, the one who sees the thin connections. If this envelope was assigned to you, it means that at the designated hour there should be something here that only someone with your training is supposed to see.

"I hope I'm good enough at what I do," he said to Cassandra once, in another life, before all this.

"And if not?"

He was silent for a bit and said, "It would be very disappointing."

"I think you'll be satisfied if you become disappointed in yourself," she said quietly. "It would further support the conclusion that you've already drawn anyway. It would reinforce your negative opinions about yourself. You don't do enough and then become angry at yourself for not doing enough."

He didn't answer, wondering whether it was okay to be annoyed at the fact that someone else knew you better than yourself.

"Lazybones," she said with fondness that flooded him with warmth.

He looked up and started to survey the street with the eyes of a coincidence maker. There was the girl with the braces on her teeth who was walking, focused on her iPhone and about to bump into the young man with dreadlocks in just a few seconds; the elderly woman at the bus stop who was dozing and about to miss her bus; the barber standing at the door of his barbershop, watching the passersby and failing to notice that he left the faucet running in his barbershop. . . .

Five windows opened in the building across the street. In just one of them, someone stood and looked down at the street.

A half-extinguished cigarette was tossed to the edge of the sidewalk.

A valve stuttered in a passing car.

And then it happened.

Exactly at the designated hour, at the right second, he saw it. As if a camera inside his head had clicked and snapped a detailed picture of the street.

The sign the young woman was hanging in the display window was still not hung. But it was placed at her side and the arrow on it pointed to the right.

The arms of the policeman in the intersection were also raised in precisely the same direction at that moment. And the young man with the dreadlocks, who had lost his balance, raised his arm eastward during his small dance to regain his balance.

The barber was also looking toward the right, in the same direction the half-lit cigarette pointed after it fell to the sidewalk.

And above, high above, a flock of birds was moving in an arrow formation, exactly in the same direction.

He turned around and started to run.

What now?

What now?

Guy ran along the street, searching for the next clue.

Where was he supposed to go now?

And since when, in fact, had missions been assigned in this way?

He continued to run and saw a taxi stopping at the end of the street. The door opened and a tall well-dressed woman emerged, wearing the finest earrings that money could be wasted on. Yes, he decided, the timing was right.

Three steps, two, one.

And he was inside the car just in time for the woman to close the door behind him.

"Drive!" he shouted to the driver.

The driver turned toward him slowly. "Ha. Where?"

Guy's eyes raced around. He saw a blue car exiting from a parking spot on the right and pointed: "Follow that car!"

The driver looked at him for a moment and turned back to the steering wheel.

"That's a sentence you don't hear every day," he said.

"Go!"

They followed the blue car for nearly a quarter of an hour until Guy noticed three buses in the lane next to them. The three buses all had the same advertisement on them: "The time has come for a change. Cherry-flavored diet iced tea."

"The time has come for a change," he mumbled. "Now," he said to the driver, pointing to a red Mitsubishi in the left lane, "now follow that car."

"It's your money." The driver shrugged.

After a few minutes, the red car stopped at a small lookout point with a view of the sea. The driver got out of the car, walked slowly up the stairs, stood by the guardrail, and lit a cigarette.

Guy quickly paid the taxi driver, who looked at him, still curious. "Can I see what you're going to do now?"

"No, just drive away."

The driver sighed, disappointed. "Fine. Have a good one, bro."

"You too."

There was a pleasant morning breeze at the lookout point.

Two people stood by the guardrail. The driver of the red Mitsubishi, who smoked a cigarette and looked at the scenery, and a tall, thin man who listened to music through small earphones and quietly hummed under his narrow mustache.

Guy approached and stood by the smoker and cleared his throat.

The smoker took another small puff and glanced at him.

Guy looked back.

The smoker flinched a bit and returned the stare.

Guy continued to look at him and waited patiently.

A lot of looking took place.

The smoker cocked his head in question.

Guy smiled in response.

"Can I help you?" the smoker finally asked.

"I'm Guy," said Guy.

The smoker was silent for a few seconds and then dropped his cigarette and crushed it with the heel of his shoe.

"Really?" he said.

"Really," said Guy.

The former smoker took one last look at him, turned around, and walked toward his car, mumbling, "There are crazy people in this world, plenty of them." He got into the car, started it, and drove away.

Behind him, Guy heard the tall one with the narrow mustache ask: "What's the matter with you? People come here for a few minutes to clear their heads. Do you mind not disturbing them?"

Guy started to apologize but stopped.

He looked directly into the eyes of the mustachioed one and said: "And do *you* mind, perhaps, if I kick you in the head?"

The narrow mustache turned toward him.

And then lifted as the lips underneath it curved into a smile.

13

Pierre introduced himself as a rank five coincidence maker.

Guy immediately understood what this meant. Pierre was a "Black Hat"—responsible for particularly complex coincidences with extensive repercussions. The coincidences arranged by Black Hats often seemed terrible at first glance, but they contained the seeds of other coincidences and essential consequences. They dealt with illnesses, tragedies, horrible accidents, and things that only decades later could be understood as events that had changed the world for the better—and even then, they were not always understood.

Black Hats were admired, but they were loners. Their work had to be flawless, at a level of precision comparable only to the work of rank six coincidence makers, who were responsible for changes that shifted the histories of entire peoples. On the other hand, who wanted to become friends with someone who could make positive changes to reality that only became apparent in the distant future? Black Hats were called such not only because they were so invisible and successful in maneuvering the thin strings of reality without attracting attention, but also because their work was so black. No one wanted to be the one who generated tragedies, even if they had a justified reason.

They sat in a small café not far from the lookout point where they met.

Pierre was tall and skinny, his jaws and nose angular as if sketched by an engineer, and his narrow mustache, which danced a bit every time he smiled or spoke, adorned his thin upper lip. He wore a black suit, cuff links in the shape of a foreign letter Guy didn't recognize, black socks, and five-hundred-dollar shoes.

Pierre was a gentleman, or it was important to him to look like a gentleman, which was actually the same thing, Guy reminded himself.

"Do you know what the most beautiful thing is?" Cassandra had once asked him.

"What?" he asked.

"That I don't know how you really look and you don't know how I look." She straightened her dress a bit.

"What do you mean?"

"We look, sound, and smell exactly as my girl and your boy decided to imagine us. If I ever saw you on the street, imagined by someone else, I wouldn't know it was you."

"Because they'll imagine me in a different way?"

"Yes," she said. "I'm a bit thirsty," she added. He took a short breath and she sipped from a cold glass of juice that appeared in her hand.

He thought a little. "I think I could always identify you anywhere, regardless of your appearance. I could identify the look in your eyes, your laughter. There are things that don't change."

"I doubt it," she said pensively. "But in any case, I think it's beautiful."

"That we don't appear as ourselves?"

"Not exactly. That we're not confined by our appearance."

"I never thought of it that way."

"There hasn't been a single moment when I didn't feel that I was imprisoned by the way they imagined me. After enough time in this profession, you're no longer sure whether you are you, or someone they wanted you to be. I nearly lost myself. If no one wants to see me in reality, perhaps I'm not really worthy of being seen?"

"Of course you're worthy of being seen," he said.

"We absorb our appearances inward more than we outwardly project who we are inside. No?" she asked. "That almost happened to me too."

"And what happened then?"

"I met you," she said. "I was saved."

He was silent, embarrassed.

"We need you," Pierre said.

"Me?" Guy asked.

"What other 'you' do you see here?" Pierre asked. "Yes, you."

"I think I'm not at the right rank for the things you need," Guy said.

"That's right"—Pierre nodded—"but I need you just for a very specific piece of a coincidence I'm trying to create, and I received special approval to use a rank two coincidence maker for my mission."

This was very usual. Coincidence makers like Guy were not supposed to deal with materials CMs like Pierre handled. That is, he wasn't even supposed to be able to understand the scope of this mission.

A mission Guy worked on for several weeks was liable to be only one detail in a rank five mission. Coincidences Guy planned on an entire wall could fit into a single page in Pierre's notebook. That's the way it was after you got used to seeing reality from far enough away, apparently. Everything was connected to everything; big became small.

Guy understood that this wouldn't be the first time a coincidence he performed was part of a larger mission. Each time the objective of a coincidence didn't appear sufficiently defined or justified, the chances were good that this coincidence was just outsourced from another job. Guy never knew whether his coincidence was part of a broader picture, but he occasionally guessed that it was. After all, why would he receive an envelope directing him to arrange for a particular person to cross a particular street at a particular hour while wearing a blue shirt?

But a direct approach by a coincidence maker of rank five seemed very strange to Guy. He didn't think he was suited for such a collaboration. He wondered whether he even wanted to do something at rank five.

"Listen," he told Pierre, "are you sure you want someone like me? I only recently completed my two hundred fiftieth coincidence. . . ."

"I know."

"Even if what you need is a rank-two mission, I'm sure there are better and more experienced coincidence makers than me. . . ."

"That's true."

"Not that I'm so bad. . . ."

"You're not."

"But perhaps when it comes to things like this . . ."

"Listen." Pierre leaned toward him. "Before you start getting all confused trying to find the best way to tell me that you're not suitable without calling yourself a failure, maybe you should listen to what I have to say."

"And what is that?" Guy asked.

Pierre leaned back with a smile. "Let's call it 'The Story of Alberto Brown.'"

14

Alberto Brown was born on a particularly rainy Tuesday, after a difficult labor that lasted for thirty-five hours. He didn't cry, and the doctor had to hit him on the backside four times before he deigned to adopt this infantile method of communication. It was only after the baby cried that the doctor allowed himself to inform the mother that she had given birth to a wonderful boy.

Alberto was a big baby. Ten pounds of scowling sweetness and an extraordinary ability to raise one eyebrow in a worried gesture, which became evident just hours after he was born. His father didn't choose the name Alberto to honor a grandfather or uncle; he simply liked the name. Perhaps it reminded him of a movie he once saw. Alberto's mother objected halfheartedly, but she accepted it in the end. After fewer than two months, her husband disappeared, leaving behind a modest amount of debt, a used pipe, and a child with a name whose origin she didn't understand.

She considered changing the baby's name but felt it had become part of the small face she loved. She also believed in fate and didn't want to change her son's name because she feared this change would send him down a strange and unworthy path in life. Perhaps if she had known what the future held in store for him, she would have decided to change his name nonetheless.

The years passed and Alberto grew.

That is, really grew.

When he was two years old, everyone thought he was four.

When he was five years old, he looked like an eight-year-old.

He was a big boy. And extraordinarily strong.

He was a quiet and introverted boy. Even apathetic, you could say. Sometimes it wasn't clear whether his tranquil demeanor derived from his strength and that he wasn't bothered by other children who occasionally tried to challenge him, or from his being so lost in thought that he simply didn't notice they existed.

Alberto encountered violence for the first time in kindergarten.

He didn't really chance upon it, of course. The violence was there, saw him, and raced toward him. It appeared in the form of Ben, a big child himself, who feared the new boy would steal the element of dominance he had so enjoyed till then. The fact that Alberto got along fine with the rest of the children and was gentle and compassionate to everyone made no impression on Ben. In his eyes, Alberto was an enemy. Ben would push children, bite them sometimes, and run them down with his tricycle in particularly extreme cases. He wasn't one of those children who was willing to take "no" for an answer, even if reality itself, in all its glory, was the one issuing this negative response.

Since he viewed the situation with Alberto as an "extreme

case" and a real threat to the fragile hierarchy on which the kindergarten was based, he got onto his tricycle and raced toward Alberto with a mighty battle cry. Alberto turned his head and saw the boy moving rapidly toward him, and he realized that even though his body would apparently absorb the blow and not even budge, it would hurt. He felt a sort of fear, a pinch of anxiety, and a clear understanding that he really didn't want the tricycle to hit him.

As this thought occurred to him, at that very second, the front wheel of Ben's tricycle fell off, and the vehicle veered off its path, bypassed Alberto, and crashed into the wall behind him.

Ben suffered a fractured arm and a sprained knee. He didn't return to kindergarten for two months. When he did, he was very nice to Alberto.

In high school too, Alberto was well liked by everyone who met him. The girls liked his impressive physique and simple smile, and the boys treated him like they always treated someone they knew they were supposed to fear, but who had yet to give them a sufficiently good reason to do so: they idolized him. The teenagers who hung around Alberto in high school had only one wish—that someone would be stupid enough to try to hit him.

Wow, what would happen then? It would be great, wouldn't it?

In private meetings, they would discuss the way Alberto could break someone's neck with one hand or tear out someone's throat by smartly squeezing it between his pinky and thumb and turning his wrist slightly. They wanted so much to see that happen.

No one had ever seen him hurt a fly, but it was clear that he could if he only wanted to. They quietly tried to instigate disputes between Alberto and new pupils who arrived at school, hoping that an altercation, even a small and quick one, would expose the abilities of the friendly giant. But it soon became apparent that Alberto had become one of the new pupil's good friends or, alternatively, that the pupil himself was sharp enough to realize that it wasn't advisable to mess around with Alberto.

Therefore, one can understand the great excitement at school when Miguel entered the library one day, just when Alberto was sitting there. Alberto loved the library and spent quite a bit of time there. As a result, a considerable number of enamored girls and hopeful boys hung around, waiting for someone, perhaps, to come and smack him.

Miguel was a problematic pupil in every school he passed through, and he passed through quite a few—enough to write a short travel guide reviewing the schools in three different districts. If only his writing abilities were suitably developed and he were willing to use some of his rolling papers for creative writing instead of for cigarettes. Only when he became an adult and was arrested for committing three armed robberies would the authorities realize, in retrospect, how disturbed Miguel really was.

Miguel's problem—that is, his first problem—was his great fondness for fast cars and cheap alcohol. Each of these things was problematic, but the combination of wild driving under the influence of low-quality vodka was even more problematic, primarily because it led Miguel to forget the most basic rule: don't get caught. The policeman who arrested him was humorless and dedicated to his job. When Miguel sobered up and realized what had happened, he cursed his bad luck.

And thus, without a car and without a license, and after discovering that his favorite place to hang out had become a construction site, he had no alternative but to go to school that day, and to be angry.

The young fellow who would later become a gang leader in prison had no intention of going to class, of course. He had to find a place to sit where he could quietly be angry at the world. The library was ideal. There were a lot of things he could destroy and lots of quiet, innocent pupils who could be harassed with verbal or physical bullying. Miguel didn't come to school often enough to know that Alberto existed. For Miguel, sitting idly in the library for a quarter of an hour was all he could stand. He wasn't a person of existential thoughts. In order to attract a bit of attention, he had no choice other than to decide, let's say, to rearrange the books in the library according to an index system called "on the floor."

"Knowledge for all!" he shouted, "Knowledge for all!" He started knocking down books and dancing around them like an Indian.

About thirty pupils stared at him in shock, first in disgust and finally in great hope. He was crazy enough and perhaps even intoxicated enough for there to be real potential here for a confrontation.

Even the librarian saw this, and hope awakened in his heart too.

They sat and waited patiently for Alberto to notice.

At the point when Miguel was dancing on a large pile of volumes in an aisle between two rows of books, Alberto looked up. Miguel pulled a cigarette lighter from his pocket, and Alberto glanced around to see everyone staring at the scene without budging. He mistakenly interpreted this tense watching as a type of shock and called toward Miguel: "Hey!"

An invisible wave of excitement swept through the crowd.

Alberto got up from the table and approached Miguel. "What do you think you're doing?"

Miguel turned toward him. "Oh!" he cried. "Teddy bear is here! How are you, teddy bear?"

"I think," Alberto said, "you should get out of here and go sit somewhere else, to calm down."

Miguel looked at him with a sneer. "That's what you think?"

"Yes," Alberto said. "You're damaging the library's property. Get out."

"Me? The library's property?" Miguel feigned innocence. "You mean this?" He jumped on the pile, trampling the books.

"Yes," Alberto said, still quietly. "Get out of here now."

"And who exactly is going to make me leave? You, teddy bear?"

Thirty pupils and one librarian were filled with hidden joy when Alberto said, "Yes. If necessary, I will." A pimpled boy sitting to the side raised his eyes toward the ceiling and silently murmured, "Thank you."

Miguel got off the pile and leaned his arms against the shelves next to him.

"You," he said with the serenity of drunkards, "might look big and strong, but you're a bullshitter and an idiot, with balls the size of peas. Maybe you should run outside before someone gets hurt."

"I don't want to resort to violence. . . ." Alberto started to say.

"Of course not," Miguel said with a crooked smile. "That's what I'm here for." He reached his hand into his pocket and pulled out a switchblade. The knife made a clicking sound when Miguel opened it and flashed it at Alberto, as if he were an expert fencer. "Come on, teddy bear," he said.

"I'm telling you for the last time," Alberto said. "Don't make trouble. Get out."

The spring that held Miguel popped open. "Come on, you freaking mutant!" he screamed. "Come defend your precious books!" He banged his fist on the bookshelf next to him.

That was enough.

At first, a soft screeching sound was heard. And then another. The bookshelf collapsed with a thunderous noise.

After a second of silence, the bookshelf opposite Miguel also collapsed, burying the future gang leader under a pile of books six feet high.

Alberto went back to his place at the table. The pimply boy sitting to the side felt a certain urge to cry, but overcame it.

It was only when Alberto was older that he surfaced on the radar of really dangerous people. He had just received his first paycheck as a waiter in a neighborhood restaurant and decided to go to the bank to deposit it. When he approached the teller and placed the check in front of her, a masked man burst into the bank, brandishing a pistol.

"Everyone on the floor!" he shouted. "Everyone on the floor, now!" The other customers—two older women, one teenage girl with pink hair, and a gaunt young man with a haunted look—threw themselves onto the floor in panic, screaming the familiar screams they saw in the movies.

The robber continued to act according to protocol, yelling, "Shut up, I said shut up, dammit." He waved his pistol at the two tellers who sat behind the counter and intended to shout at them to raise their hands immediately, but then he saw that someone was still standing.

Alberto looked at him gravely.

"Why are you getting yourself into this?" he asked quietly.

"Get down on the floor!" the robber screamed. "I'll blow your brains out so that even your mother won't recognize you!"

"You can still stop all this," Alberto said to him, gesturing with his hand around him. "Bank robbery carries a very long prison term. You can still get out of here before you cause damage. You can return to normal life. No one here knows who you are."

"Down! On the floor! Now!" the robber screamed, his eyes bulging under the itchy stocking on his head. "Don't try to be a hero and don't try to be a psychologist!"

"You won't shoot me," Alberto said. "You're not a murderer, right?"

"I am! I am!" He lifted his pistol and aimed it straight at Alberto's head.

"Give me the gun," Alberto said. "Let's put an end to this."

"You stupid idiotic son of a thousand bitches!" the robber yelled. He had already shot five people in the head without batting an eyelash. One more head didn't pose a big problem for him. "We'll indeed put an end to this now! We'll finish this!" he said, and he pulled the trigger.

The policeman who later collected testimony from Alberto and the rest of the people at the bank said that it was a very rare type of technical malfunction.

"The back end of the pistol simply exploded," the policeman explained. "The bullet got stuck somehow and wasn't propelled forward. Consequently, the back end absorbed all of the energy of the bullet's explosion, and the thrust inside the pistol was trapped within such a small area that everything flew backward."

"Very interesting," Alberto said.

"Yes," the policeman said. "I've never seen such a thing happen. I'm familiar with this only in theory. But apparently this guy didn't have much luck." And he looked at the robber, who no longer needed a stocking to cover his face. No one could identify him now.

Two months later, two serious men in cheap suits knocked on the door of Alberto and his mother's home.

"Alberto Brown?" one of them asked.

"Yes," said Alberto Brown, dressed in pajamas.

"Come with us, please," the second one said.

"Where?" Alberto asked.

"Don Ricardo wants to speak with you," the first one said.

Alberto though for a moment and asked, "And who is Don Ricardo?"

The two seemed a bit perplexed. They weren't accustomed to speaking with people who were unfamiliar with Don Ricardo.

"Um," one of them said.

"Don Ricardo is someone you don't want to refuse to visit when you're summoned," the second one said, quite pleased with himself.

"I'm a bit busy," Alberto said.

"Nevertheless," the second one said.

"Wait a moment," Alberto said and closed the door.

The two stunned men waited behind the door and heard Alberto call to his mother, "Mother, do you know who Don Ricardo is?" They couldn't see the mother's eyes widening in fear, but they could hear hushed talk on the other side of the door. And just when the more impatient of the two men decided he had waited long enough and that the time had come to kick in the door and take this idiot Alberto by force, the door opened and Alberto stood at the entrance, dressed this time.

"Couldn't you have just said, 'from the Mafia?'" he asked.

The two henchmen looked at each other. You're not supposed to speak in such explicit terms, they thought to themselves. "Mafia" was a word used by the police, screenwriters, and bartenders who tell tall tales. We "do business."

"Okay. Let's go," Alberto said. "But only because my mother says I have to."

Don Ricardo sat at the end of the table. Alberto sat facing him at the opposite end of the table, some twelve feet away.

"Thank you for joining us," Don Ricardo said.

"It was made clear to me that saying 'no' wasn't an option," Alberto said, shrugging his shoulders.

"Saying 'no' is always an option," Don Ricardo said. "But the re-percussions are such that people usually don't."

"I think some sort of mistake was made here," Alberto said.

"Mistake is a very general term," Don Ricardo said. "Can you elaborate?"

"I'm not supposed to be here," Alberto said.

"Really?"

"I have no connection to your affairs."

"So why did you come?"

"My mother told me to."

"Ah, respect for parents. That's very important."

"Definitely."

"My son, Johnny, was very conscientious about respecting parents."

"Aha."

"He would always kiss my hand, he wouldn't use foul language around me, he wouldn't bring home young ladies whom he knew I couldn't tolerate. There was a lot of respect there."

"You must be very proud of him."

Don Ricardo flicked his hand, as if shooing away a defiant fly or trying to clean the air from a cloud of meaningless words. "He was an idiot who only knew how to use force to obtain things. No elegance, no creativity. He always got into trouble. I bailed him out of so many predicaments that at some stage, I stopped counting. Drugs, solicitation of prostitution, robbery attempts. One time, he robbed a liquor store and then went to eat at a McDonald's and left a pistol with fingerprints, just like that, on the table next to some leftover fries. A complete idiot. 'Why don't you just put bars on your window and be done with it?' I asked him. And still, he was my son."

"Yes."

"Though this also might not be completely accurate. I assumed he was my son, despite the stupidity in his genes."

"But you still loved him, of course."

"Of course, certainly. A certain type of love, at least. It broke my heart when he was killed."

"I'm sorry to hear that. How did it happen?"

"The jerk tried to rob a bank. He actually chose the bank well this time, but there was some smart aleck who tried to stop him and in the end he somehow shot himself."

It took some time, but Don Ricardo's cold gaze ultimately traveled across the long table until it reached Alberto and made the situation clear to him.

"According to what I understood," Alberto said, "it was a very rare malfunction."

"Yes, perhaps," Don Ricardo said. "But still, you know, I can't help thinking that if that smart-ass idiot who tried to be a hero wasn't there . . ."

"I'm truly sorry about the death of your son," Alberto said.

"I'm sure."

"But I have no connection to what happened."

"Not from my point of view."

Alberto squirmed uncomfortably in his chair.

Don Ricardo remained motionless.

"From this point of view—mine," Don Ricardo said, "you are responsible for the death of my son."

"I . . ."

"This makes me quite sad. I really don't like to involve people from outside of my business."

"Excuse me?"

"But you'll surely understand me when I say that I cannot ignore what happened," Don Ricardo said. He scratched his gray temple.

"What do you intend to do?"

"To you? Nothing, my friend. Nothing. But in my worldview, you took a son from me, so I take your mother."

Alberto felt his heart starting to pound.

"I . . ."

"My two colleagues are now at your mother's home. If I don't call them during the next ten minutes, then we'll be even. It's as simple as that."

"That's not fair."

"Like life," Don Ricardo said, pursing his lips, as if pondering something profound. And then he added: "But maybe we can find another type of deal to resolve the matter."

"What type of deal?"

"I have a friend. A good friend. Such a good friend that he became a good enemy. You know, when a person reaches my position, when he accumulates power, he cannot avoid a situation in which there are some people in the world, with no less power than he himself has, who counteract him. It's like yin and yang, black and white, Hansel and Gretel. You could call them colleagues and you could call them enemies. In any case, they are strong people. Strong enough so that we can dine together, on the one hand, and fight each other, on the other. It's not personal; that's the way this business works. Have you ever heard of Don Gustavo?"

"Never."

"Okay, that happens. In any case, Don Gustavo has always been one of the only people to block the expansion of my business. Not that I lack anything in life. Life is good, I admit. Business is also good. But it could always be better. You know, it's human nature. We always want more—no, we always *need* more. This is part of what drives us. We want to touch the stars, tickle the sky. We aim for infinity, though we'll never reach it. Perfectionism, perhaps. The human spirit aims for it. For infinity, my friend. I, for example, want very much to see Don Gustavo dead. It would be very beneficial for me."

"Beneficial?"

"Beneficial, yes. It would enable me to do all sorts of things that are currently difficult for me to do—things related to boundaries and commitments. If I want to expand my business, I need Don Gustavo to move to 'dead' status. But, you understand, I cannot allow myself to kill him. It's too dangerous. A matter of honor and handshakes. If somehow his death is linked to me, a world war will erupt. It will also be very unpleasant. Dishonorable. You don't do such things."

"I understand."

"I'm happy to hear that. Because this is exactly where you enter the picture. Someone who isn't connected to the family in any way. We can arrange poetic justice here. Johnny was a robber and you killed him, and now you'll be a robber and will kill Don Gustavo. You'll break into his home and kill him. You'll make it look like a regular robbery that got botched. You can also take whatever you want from there. I'll provide you with a diagram of the house, of course. I even have one or two entry codes, and the location of the guard posts. It'll really be a piece of cake. And if by chance you're caught—and, of course, we all hope very much that doesn't happen— no one will be able to connect you to me. And, in exchange, I'll go out of the room and will instruct my people not to cause any tragic accident to befall your mother. Don Gustavo in exchange for my Johnny."

Alberto raised his right eyebrow in a movement he knew how to do since he was a baby. "You want me to murder for you," he said quietly.

"That's a very barbaric way to describe it, but it's quite precise," Don Ricardo concurred.

"And if I don't agree—you'll kill my mother."

"You catch on well."

"Do I have an alternative?"

"Certainly. As I said, 'no' is always an option. The consequences are what we don't want. Right?"

Alberto thought a bit and said: "Right."

Don Ricardo insisted that the job take place that very night.

Don Gustavo's house would be nearly empty tonight, he said, and this presented a unique opportunity. Don Ricardo wanted to be done with this entire affair immediately. Alberto would later discover that impatience is a trait shared by many people who want someone else to die. He was given an hour to review the diagrams of the building, and two hours later, he was en route to Gustavo's house. Before he left, Don Ricardo gave him a stocking. It matched the one Johnny had worn on the day of the robbery. He said. "Is that poetic justice or what?"

Alberto was silent, wondering whether refraining from responding to a rhetorical question would be held against him.

"It's been laundered, of course," Don Ricardo said.

And thus it happened that at 2:00 A.M. that night, Alberto Brown found himself standing in the bedroom of the head of one of the biggest crime families in the country, a stocking over his head and a pistol in his hand—a pistol that had once belonged to the son of the head of another crime family. In front of him, an old, pale man was lying on the bed, breathing heavily. And Alberto was supposed to kill him.

It was clear what he was supposed to do now. Noise.

Enough noise to wake the old man in front of him, to make him sit up in his bed, perhaps scream something so that someone could hear that a robbery was taking place. It was important that it be clear to everyone that this was a robbery. And then Alberto must shoot him.

He took a long look at the old man lying in the bed and felt like he was choking. He didn't want to do this.

Alberto reached out his hand and picked up a vase that stood on a dresser at the edge of the room. With his other hand, he aimed the pistol at the Don.

He was about to smash the vase on the floor, but just then he heard a sound from the direction of the bed. As he turned his head, he saw the Don moving. The man gurgled a bit, then emitted a number of strange sounds. Another gurgle and his hands contorted, his mouth gaped open, and Alberto heard the Don take one heavy breath.

Then there was silence.

Alberto listened intently but didn't hear a thing. He returned the vase to its place and approached the bed slowly. He bent over and moved his ear close to the old man's face, then moved it closer and a little closer, before realizing that the old man was really not breathing.

He stood up and thought a bit. He reached out and touched the Don's hand. There was no reaction. He placed his fingers on the man's wrist and looked for a pulse. Then he placed his fingers on the man's neck. He shook him and shook him a bit more.

And then he left.

———

Don Ricardo was very impressed. He was very happy.

"How did you do it?" He grabbed his head, shaking it in disbelief. "Everyone is certain that he died from a stroke in his sleep. It's amazing. This is the cleanest killing I've ever seen."

Alberto quietly asked whether he was allowed to go.

"You don't understand?" Don Ricardo told him. "You're a treasure! A treasure! You're such a rare natural talent. It's amazing."

"I think we're even now, Don Ricardo."

"Of course! Of course!" Don Ricardo said.

"Then I want to go."

"Yes, yes." Don Ricardo sighed. "What a waste. You could be great, do you know that? I mean really great. The greatest. Killers like you can become very rich."

"I'm not interested."

"What a waste."

"I'm going now," Alberto said and left.

Two weeks later, two men appeared at the door of Alberto's home. This time, Don Ricardo told him he had a real business proposition to discuss. Alberto said he wasn't interested.

Don Ricardo said that the job wasn't for him but for a friend.

Alberto insisted that he wasn't interested.

Don Ricardo cited a sum.

Alberto was resolute.

Don Ricardo made a long speech about fulfilling potential and exploiting opportunities, and even quoted Thomas Alva Edison.

Alberto still refused.

Don Ricardo said the pistol that Alberto took the previous time, the one he held in his hand, leaving fingerprints on it, and which he had left in Don Ricardo's possession—was the same pistol Johnny had used to kill three people.

Alberto was silent.

Don Ricardo said it would be a shame if the police found this pistol.

Alberto remained silent, and Don Ricardo again cited the sum.

Three days later, Alberto lay in the mud and aimed his new sniper's rifle at a bend in the road where an accountant for a small crime organization was supposed to pass in his car. Alberto's employer suspected that the man was close to talking to the police. It was necessary to silence him.

Alberto lay in wait for a white Toyota. The front of a white car appeared at the bend of the road, and the moment his finger started to squeeze the trigger, a small rabbit jumped into the road and froze in front of the approaching car. The Toyota's driver, a fervent vegetarian and fragile soul, yanked the steering wheel to avoid hitting the rabbit, lost control of the vehicle, and crashed into a large oak tree.

The rabbit hopped to the other side.

Alberto took his sniper's rifle and left.

And it continued this way.

Alberto planted a bomb under a businessman's car. But on the way to the car, the businessman fell down the stairs and sustained a fatal blow to his head. Alberto quickly dismantled the bomb and got out of there.

The senior police officer who was planning to conduct a raid the following day was in Alberto's crosshairs when the microwave he was using to heat up some chicken exploded. A small bone penetrated the man's right eye and went out the back of his head.

Alberto Brown became the most successful hit man in the Northern Hemisphere, and he never even hurt a fly. In time, he simply got used to it. He just had to prepare everything—set up the weapon, arrange the trap, organize the hit, and almost carry it out. His victims simply died on their own. The people who hired him were happy, and he himself slept very well at night.

It was wonderful work for him, and it didn't demand any sort of violence.

Sometimes he felt lonely. So he bought a hamster.

And now, Pierre said, he had come here.

"Here?" Guy asked.

"Yes," Pierre said. "He has to kill a certain businessman. This case is a bit strange because it doesn't involve something criminal. It's more . . . personal."

"And how is this connected to you?" Guy asked.

"Who do you think arranged for all these people to die precisely at the right time?" Pierre asked.

"You're joking."

"Definitely not," Pierre said.

"But why, in fact? What's the logic?"

"Alberto has a very important role in foiling a terror organization in another fifteen years," Pierre said. "We must develop him correctly so that he can reach the spot where he makes the decision that will defeat this organization."

"And for this, all these people are being killed?"

"That's the interesting part," Pierre said. "All of the people Alberto was sent to kill were supposed to die anyway. Don Gustavo, the accountant—all of them. The coincidence that I was supposed to create was *to commission* the murder—that is, to make the right people want someone to die exactly when that person was slated to die anyway."

"That sounds complicated."

"Yes," said Pierre. "But I prefer that kind of complication to handling the current case."

"What do you mean?"

"The businessman he's supposed to murder now isn't actually supposed to die anytime soon."

"It's not something you organized?"

"No. It's an authentic hit," Pierre said.

"So what happens now?"

Pierre shook his head sadly. "If we don't want to break the streak, we need to arrange a coincidence that will kill the man. And at the right time, so that it'll look like all the rest. I raised this issue with the higher-ups. We have all the required approvals."

"You want me to . . ."

"You have to bring the man to a particular place at a particular time to make it happen."

"For a simple timing mission, you came to me?"

"You could say that, yes."

"Why don't you do this yourself?"

"It's a bit complicated to explain," Pierre said. "But there are matters here that require me to organize other things at the same time."

"But why me?"

Pierre brushed an invisible speck of dust from his pants and refrained from looking at Guy. "You know the man," he said. "You were his imaginary friend once. I think we can make use of that connection."

Guy swallowed and tried to smile indifferently.

"Who is it?" he asked.

"You know him as Michael," Pierre said.

A slight shudder ran up Guy's back. Michael. It was thanks to him that he had met Cassandra.

15

It was a Tuesday.

Michael was playing in the park with two of his green toy soldiers, assigning them attributes that were not very militaristic—such
as the ability to glide through the air or remain with their heads
stuck in the ground for particularly long periods of time. Guy sat
on the bench next to him, his legs and arms crossed, his thoughts
wandering. Sometimes the only thing Michael wanted him to do
when he imagined him was sit there.

When two of the soldiers started to chase each other, Guy wasn't
able to understand who was doing the chasing and who was being
chased—not that this was really important. But when Michael
started to get carried away and wandered off making various heroic
sounds, Guy called him and told him not to go too far.

A child who is too far away forgets that you exist. A child forgetting you exist means you no longer exist.

Guy actually wanted to sit there a bit longer. He hadn't experienced existence for quite a few days. He longed for himself, to a certain extent.

And besides, he wanted to keep an eye on Michael, to make sure he didn't go into the street. At least that's what he told himself.

A girl and a woman entered his field of view.

The girl was small and blond, her long hair almost reaching her waist; purple eyeglasses with a thick frame were tied with a red string behind her head. The woman was tall and elegant. Long braids ran through her red hair, covering her head like a crown, and her eyes followed the girl with tender love.

They sat on the bench opposite him, not far away, but they couldn't see him, of course.

He took another look at the woman. Something in her movements pulled at his heart. A thought crept into his mind: how rare it was to meet someone who looked like she knew what she was doing, in the broad sense of the word. So many people moved their bodies only in order to take up space, in order to do something that made them feel that they were indeed changing something. They waved their hands, shook their heads, and shifted their legs anxiously. If movements made sounds, how much noise most people would create around them, just to show their presence. She, on the other hand, was so much truer—the way she sat on the bench, the way she tilted her head to the right and looked at her girl, the way she allowed her red-and-white dress to rest upon her without concealing her identity. Why weren't all people so relaxed?

"I like your dress," he said.

She didn't notice him, of course. But that had never bothered him in the past. He would speak with people, tell them things, share with them, even if they weren't the children imagining him, even if there was no chance of them seeing or hearing him.

"I know you don't know I'm here," said Guy, "but who knows, perhaps in some mysterious way my words will affect you somehow. And perhaps not. It doesn't really matter. Sometimes you need to speak to someone who isn't listening, just so you won't go crazy."

The girl sat at the foot of the bench, playing with two dolls dressed in the best doll fashions. Every once in a while, she lifted them up and said something to the woman on the bench. The woman nodded with a smile and said something in reply.

Guy could have heard what they were saying if he'd wanted to. They were close enough. But what was the point?

"I'm John," he said. "At least, at the moment I'm John. In another hour, I might be François, and then Genghis Khan, and tomorrow I'll be Motke the painter. It's a bit confusing, perhaps, but these are the demands of the job. Because what am I if not a mirror of what someone else asks me to be? My name, my personality, my desires— everything is designed only to rescue other people from their loneliness.

"You'll never understand what I mean," he said, leaning forward a bit, trimming a few inches from the distance between him and the unknowing queen as she gazed at the treetops. "You're too connected to yourself. I envy people like you. Well, the truth is that I envy nearly everyone. You're living your lives without hiding behind a role that someone else writes for you. You see that boy there? The moment he comes closer, he just needs to pay a bit more attention to me and I'll again have to be entirely John. I won't be able to talk with you—or deliver a speech to you. I'll be his again, completely.

"I've seen so many ordinary people who do what I'm doing.

Them, I don't envy. They're in a worse situation than I. At least I need to wear just one mask each time, because only the one who imagines me can see me. But they're the imaginary friends of everyone, covering themselves with masks provided by everyone who looks at them, until one day they become people seen by everyone, only they don't really exist.

"But you're different. I see this. You are who you are. People like you are so rare. I hope you know how lucky you are. How different you are." He got up from the bench, stuck his hands in his pockets and stared at the ground, and moved a bit closer. "And also beautiful, if you don't mind me saying so. . . .

"In any case, if you're ever lonely and would like to imagine someone lonely like yourself, I'd be happy to appear in front of you and get to know you a bit better. You know, it's not so awful to be the creation of someone's imagination. You can do this for example."

He pulled his hands from his pockets and stretched them out in front of him. "Ta-da!" he said.

Three small balls of fire appeared in the air, and he began to juggle them.

"This is something that is very easy to learn," he said, his eyes glued on the balls. "The first principle is not to look at your hands. You need to follow the balls in the air and try not to see how you catch them. You can also do it with four;"—a fourth ball appeared— "it doesn't matter. Of course, the fire part is a nice privilege that comes with being an imaginary friend. All the rest is simply an acquired skill. I think. I don't remember ever acquiring it, of course. But from your perspective, it'll certainly be acquired."

He continued to juggle a little longer until he felt tears welling up in his eyes without knowing whether it was because of the faint spirals of smoke rising from the fireballs or because of something else that was gnawing at him. The fire balls were extinguished and disappeared in mid-flight, and his hands dropped to his sides.

"And that's it," he said quietly, lowering his head in embarrassment. How stupid it was to speak this way to himself. He looked up. The girl still played with her dolls on the grass, orchestrating a quiet tea party, and that wonderful woman sat on the bench and looked at him. That is, right at him.

He felt like he was frozen for a moment, and his eyes gazed into her eyes.

A moment before he got up to leave, convinced that it was only a coincidence that she was staring in the direction where he stood, she said, "Why did you stop? It was actually beautiful."

A few seconds went by and he still couldn't manage to speak. Michael was a bit far away. Please don't stop imagining me now, just don't stop now, Guy thought.

"You . . . you see me?" he asked.

"Aha . . ."—she nodded her head, smiling—"and apparently you also see me."

"It's . . ."

"Quite surprising," she said. "I didn't know exactly how to respond when you started to speak to me."

"But why . . . ?"

"I'm Cassandra," she said and pointed to the girl playing alongside her, "and this is Natalie, the girl who imagines me."

"It's really, that is . . . I didn't expect . . ."

"Yes, me either," Cassandra said. "But it turns out we're able to see each other."

They were silent for several seconds and then Cassandra asked, "Do you come here a lot, you and your boy?"

"Not so much," he said. "Usually Michael prefers to play in his room."

"It would be nice if you started to come more often," she said. "They can play and we'll be able to talk a little."

"Yes," he said. "I'll try to persuade him. If I can."

"Great." She smiled. A shiver ran along the inside of his skin.

And that's how he met Cassandra.

"I'm John, by the way," he said.

"I know. You already said."

"Yes," he managed to say before Michael took his mind off him completely, and he disappeared.

16

Emily was still lying in bed and looking at the square of light cast by the window as it slowly advanced toward the ceiling.

So why was she still lying there?

At this stage, after nearly ten hours of lying in bed, was she really staying there because she was depressed, or was she doing this because lying in bed with her eyes open was something that depressed people were supposed to do, and she was declaring herself depressed?

And what would be the next stage? Drinking? Chain-smoking while standing on a balcony and staring with burned-out eyes at the rooftops of the city? Where do you draw the line between actions carried out due to an internal need, and actions that were nothing more than a version of one ceremony or another that help us define our emotions?

How many people actually cried at weddings or shouted in

frustration or tossed their heads back when laughing or grasped a partner's face when kissing because something inside them compelled them to do this, and how many did those things because it was something they needed to do?

She turned over and looked at the clock by her bed. If you've started to think such thoughts, then apparently you've really gotten over it, she thought to herself. No excuses.

Let's go, get up.

When she washed her face, she nearly smiled at herself over the dramatic gesture of the previous night. The cathartic weeping, declaring that she realized he didn't want her and never would, the weakness in her legs, the collapse into a self-pitying heap on the sidewalk, the long, long fall into bed, still in her clothes, the feeling that there was no reason for tomorrow to come.

It's strange, she thought, how we're able to turn one specific thing into everything that drives us in life, and how we convince ourselves that without this thing there is no meaning in anything. And it's even stranger how quickly we get used to the opposite thought.

She leaned against the sink and felt choked up. Tears crept up into her eyes, waiting for the right time to flow outward. She swallowed and took a deep breath. Yes, yes, the choking feeling was real, that part of her brain still thought; there was no ceremony in this.

She hadn't planned it this way. She didn't think such a situation was possible. A situation in which, within herself, she was really giving up on Guy. And here, it was happening. She was in unfamiliar territory, in which the color of the air was a bit different and light traveled at a different speed. Her heart pounded at an unfamiliar pace. And Guy wasn't hers at all anymore.

No, no, that's not the way it was supposed to be.

She planned successes. She planned that everything would work out as it should.

Not only yesterday evening, but in general. Her life was supposed to happen in a different way, wasn't it?

What, in fact, was choking her now? The thought that she really was giving up, or the change in plans that was imposed upon her, a control freak like her?

Perhaps smoking a cigarette and gazing upon the city's rooftops wasn't such a terrible idea. She looked at herself in the mirror. An urge to get a bucket of black paint and splash it all over the walls in the other room washed over her. She wanted to cover this pathetic attempt of bringing them together, to erase everything, anything, get rid of the ability to dream itself.

It wasn't enough to wash her face. She needed to wash everything.

When she came out of the shower wrapped in a towel, a bit better prepared for the rest of the day, she discovered the envelope waiting for her by the door.

Nearly involuntarily, she immediately turned to her room to get dressed and to devote a few more minutes to herself before having to return to the real world, in which there were real "things" she needed to do.

The new envelope could mean only one thing: her accountant had started to write poetry.

It was a bit strange, considering that she had done nothing special during the past twenty-four hours. Perhaps something from all of her earlier actions finally got through to him.

This was a viable coincidence-making technique, she knew. In this approach, small events in varying frequencies were not intended to lead to a particular instant where the change would occur. Instead, these events created an ongoing process under the surface, resulting in a quiet and almost imperceptible impact.

This kind of coincidence was considered of a higher quality and more elegant than most, primarily appropriate for rank three. Eric would take pride every time he managed to create this type of coincidence. "Untraceable" he called it, as if it were executed on a private and secure phone line. It's very hard for a client to understand how tens and sometimes hundreds of events had gradually changed his life.

But that was definitely not her style. Not yet.

Maybe she should sit down sometime and analyze what she had done in order to understand how to use this technique more in the future.

She tried not to think at all about the horrible coincidence of the previous evening.

Her diagrams were still on the walls around her, circles and lines and small lists about video machines, mountain climbers, fortune cookies. . . . She tried to avoid looking at them. That's the way it went: a coincidence that she worked on for many long months turned into a pathetic attempt at courtship, while a coincidence on which she had given up simply happened on its own without her noticing.

And now it was time to open a new envelope.

She sat on her bed and spread out the pages that were in the envelope, trying to construct in her head what she should do next. It was exactly what she needed now, a new and clear mission that would help her return to reality, a flood of activity that would wash away all of the moments and places where Guy's face was imprinted.

This time, it appeared to be a simple timing mission.

Someone was supposed to suffer a heart attack. She had to arrange for a doctor to be in the area. If this were all the mission entailed, it could have been an exercise in the course. But, naturally, there were the complications that were always a part of true missions.

He must have the heart attack on a flight; its destination didn't matter, the pages declared. The doctor must be on the same flight. Of course, neither of her two clients planned a flight in the near future, and certainly not exactly when the attack was slated to occur.

She'd have to organize a flight for the two of them somehow. And, as if this weren't enough, the doctor was afraid of flying. Would another doctor be possible? Emily knew the answer before she turned the page. Of course not.

It wouldn't be easy.

Why specifically on an airplane?

Eric would say that it was related to the dramatic effect. If they asked him, the goal of this entire coincidence was certainly not to save someone from a heart attack. There are consequences, and consequences of consequences, he would say—changes in consciousness. Everything was designed for another passenger, who was supposed to feel something as he witnessed the attempts at resuscitation. That's what Eric would argue without any basis.

Eric had a theory for everything. Why make an effort to have someone you haven't seen for fifteen years enter a restaurant exactly at the moment you spoke about him? And, in general, why organize coincidences that really made no difference and only aroused a strange feeling? Eric had presented his theories to them one evening during the course, after five vodkas.

"Let's assume," he said, making hand gestures that were a bit grander than necessary, "let's say that all the people in the world are lined up in a long line, sort of like standing on a scale. At the far left—that is, over there—are all of the people who really think that everything is completely coincidental. That nothing has meaning, that there's no point in searching for it or asking about it, that life is a result of a toss of cosmic dice that no one actually tossed, and that it's okay that this is how things are. And on the other end are all of the people who are sure that there's a reason for everything, and I mean everything. That there's someone or something that organizes everything, and that nothing happens randomly.

The people standing at the two extremes are the happiest people in the world. At both ends. Do you know why? Because they don't ask why. Never. Not at all. There's no point, because either they believe there's no answer, or they believe that someone is responsible for the answer and that it's none of their business. But these people aren't even one-thousandth of the population. Most people stand in the range between them. No, they don't stand. They go, they move. They constantly move in one direction and then the other. They think they're on one of the sides, but occasionally, nonetheless, they ask themselves why and don't understand that they'll be happy only if they let go of this question, for whatever reason.

"That's why there are meaningless coincidences. Every time someone encounters this sort of coincidence, he moves a bit on the scale. To one side or the other. And this movement can be difficult, like a fingernail screeching on a blackboard, or pleasant, like an infant's caress. That's why we perform them, these coincidences. In order to get people moving on the scale, because this movement on the scale, any scale, is called life. That's the way it is. The main thing is to move. And now, pass me an olive from the bowl there and watch how I hit that girl on the other side of the bar with the pit, right on her head."

———

Emily was now immersed in calculations. This was the first time she'd received a mission with two centers, two clients, that wasn't a matchmaking mission. She would need to develop two tracks of coincidences in order to cause the changes in consciousness in both of them. A business meeting or family gathering for one of them, and perhaps a prestigious conference for the other. And somehow she would have to deal with the doctor's phobia. Somehow.

She spread the thin booklets on the bed. A booklet describing the situation, a booklet containing details about the "patient," a booklet about the doctor, restrictions on possible coincidences (there was nothing special—they could even sit in the same section in the airplane, but for some reason they couldn't wear the same brand of shoes), a bit of background on the region and the upcoming period of time. . . .

Her heart skipped a beat for a moment when she found another page inside the envelope.

It's not that she hadn't seen it before, but she was surprised by the thought that came to mind the moment her eyes rested upon it. For one second, one very quick second, it seemed relevant to her.

In every envelope, at the end, after all of the booklets, was a Waiver.

The personal data of the coincidence maker, a bit of general information about the reasons for resignation, and a place for a signature. An option to quit, at any stage.

Usually she didn't even take this page out of the envelope. No one took it out. A coincidence maker—that's what she is, it was her essence now—was not a profession from which you resigned. The fact that no one knew what happened after you signed the Waiver also contributed to the general reluctance to do so. Only two coincidence makers had ever signed and quit the service of their own accord. Emily had no idea what had happened to them afterward. From her point of view, it had never been an option.

Until now, she suddenly realized. She peeked again at the page lying at the edge of her bed and discovered that the thought of quitting had been incubating in her mind for some time. And now, today, it had grown enough to trouble her.

She pushed the Waiver off the edge of her bed with her foot.

She had a heart attack to organize.

A few blocks away, an ordinary person was walking along the street.

That was only one of his many abilities—to be ordinary.

He understood the power this ability entailed long ago. In a world in which so many people chased after their tails in order to be different and extraordinary, a truly unusual ability was needed in order to blend into a crowd and be ordinary. Primarily, there was a need for mighty willpower because he was not ordinary in any way.

And on the other hand, he didn't like it very much. He liked to be in the center of things, at the top of the pyramid, the life of the party.

He was a very colorful person; at least he thought so.

For colorful people like him, it was harder to pretend to be ordinary. He had so many extraordinary things to carry out in the world.

But now he was ordinary and walked along the street without attracting anyone's attention.

If someone were to ask the people who passed him on the street, "Did you notice a tall guy walking by at such and such a time?" they likely would shrug their shoulders and say, "No, no. I have no idea what you're talking about."

If this same person were to ask them, "Was there a guy here, perhaps, who was leaning against the pole for an hour, as if he were waiting for something?" They would respond, "I don't pay attention to everyone who leans against a pole." If he persisted and said, "But he was there for nearly an hour, and was looking up at that window the whole time," they would still say something like, "Do me a favor, leave me alone, okay? I didn't notice anything special."

To appear ordinary was the closest thing to being invisible.

He was still on the street corner. With the patience of an ancient glacier, he leaned against the pole and shot another glance at Emily's window. He wouldn't have to wait much longer.

Timing—that was also one of his important abilities.

A square of sunlight had nearly reached the opposite wall.

Emily was unable to last five minutes before peeking again at the corner of the shiny paper looming beyond the edge of her bed. A small triangle of paper, much more tempting than she had thought. She should have tossed it in the trash rather than just kicking it to the floor. It continued to gaze at her.

Actually, why not, she thought. And then she shook herself again and tried to return to thoughts about the next mission. Not that this helped. Like a new pupil in a meditation course, she discovered that she was unable to gain complete control over her thoughts. Again and again, she was tempted to think about the Waiver lying at the foot of the bed. Again and again, the feeling returned that here was an opportunity to change her life completely.

Again and again, the thought crossed her mind that she no longer had any reason to remain here.

What do you really want? she asked herself. To continue to drag your life between coincidences for people you don't know while the person you love runs around in front of you searching for something he'd never agree to find in you? In fact, how long was it possible to remain torn like this? To know everything and say nothing? To dance barefoot on the tip of a knife and smile as if it didn't hurt?

Here—here is your opportunity.

She sat up in bed and looked outside. She could do much more than this. She could deal the cards again. She no longer had anything to gain here, so why shouldn't she take herself to a place where she had nothing to lose?

Suddenly, she noticed that she was crying.

Where had *this* come from? She quickly covered her face with her hands, like a little girl before a piano recital.

She didn't want this anymore. She didn't want the endless calculations, she didn't want this chase, she didn't want this burning emotion laid on her heart like an overheated towel, searing through.

Enough, enough, enough.

She was allowed to admit that she was exhausted, right? And she was allowed to admit that she no longer believed in happy endings, or the assurances that "everything will work out," right?

Right?

She wanted new, she wanted clean. She wanted smooth. She was even willing to go back to what she had been before. Perhaps that's what happened when you signed a Waiver, who knows.

Perhaps you forget.

Perhaps you start over.

Who knows?

She was supposed to be strong and optimistic, of course. But now she just wanted to be different. Completely different.

And faced with the choice of becoming "completely different" through hard work and internal persuasion, and a long and exhausting climb out of a pit with scarred walls, or the possibility of attaining this through one quick signature . . . she was allowed to admit to herself that she wanted to choose the easier path now, wasn't she?

He took a short walk to the end of the street and back.

He couldn't stand under her window for too long. It would appear suspicious.

Besides, he had a little more time, he knew.

He sniffed the air, waiting for the right moment.

He felt like having a hamburger.

But that would have to wait.

Emily sat down at the kitchen table and wrote the letter of her life.

If she was going to leave, she had to leave at least a small expla-nation.

The tears on her face had dried while she sat and filled the empty page with line after line. When she was done, she lifted it with a trembling hand and quickly read what she had written. Everything had to happen quickly now, before she changed her mind. Before she felt optimistic again. Half-depressed people always worried that hope would catch them unprepared, and all that despair would go to waste. She folded the pages of the letter and stuffed them into a long white envelope.

As soon as she sealed the envelope, she felt it warming up in her hand. Before she realized what was happening, the letter burst into flames. Emily dropped it, surprised. The page turned into hot ash even before it touched the floor.

She'd actually known this would happen, hadn't she?

There were secrets that must not be revealed, that the world did not allow being discovered because it was against the rules. She would never find closure. This was another good reason to get out.

More certain than ever, she hurried to the bedroom and grabbed the Waiver from the floor.

She returned to the living room and started to fill out the details. Now she was being spontaneous, right?

She was making a decision in the spur of the moment, a rapid and irresponsible decision; how wonderful! She was spontaneous—that meant she was authentic, right? That she was alive, right?

She quickly filled out the form. Suddenly she was able to control her thoughts. Everything was focused on doing this quickly and not looking back. She had a quarter of a second to change her mind before signing her name in the designated place at the bottom of the page, but she leaped over this quarter of a second without looking down and signed her name.

His time had come.

It was happening.

Like the soft ring of an oven when a cake's baking time was up. He must be precise now. He started to move toward her house and felt the small iron wire in his pocket.

Lock picking, another important ability. Actually, not. Perhaps it was more of an acquired skill.

The moment she lifted the pen from the page, the urgency vanished from Emily's mind.

She leaned back limply and allowed the tension that had built up within her to dissolve, together with the Waiver, which had slowly disappeared in front of her eyes, fading into the air. One deep breath, and then another, and she opened her eyes in terror.

What in heaven's name did I do?

She tried to get up from the sofa, only to discover that her legs lacked the strength to support her.

Precisely at that moment, after her urge of self-destruction had fulfilled its role and left her body, after she was officially no longer a coincidence maker, she saw the complete picture before her eyes. This was the decision of my life, she thought, and this was how I made it?

Her breathing became labored. It was as if the air had become thicker. This isn't what I really want, she said to herself; it wasn't me. A desperate commander screamed to the pilots who could no longer hear him, "Abort! Abort!"

She wanted to hurry and erase her signature, but the page was no longer there, and nothing remained of her being a coincidence maker except the ability to look at the broad picture and suddenly see all of the lines that led her to this point, that had led her over the brink. No, no, no, this couldn't be.

A faint noise at the door drew her attention, and when the door opened and she saw the figure standing at the threshold with an apologetic smile on his face, she recalled the question that gnawed at her mind during the first days of the course, and which she never dared to ask.

Before her body sunk lifelessly into the sofa, before she shut her eyes, at her very last breath, she wondered whether all this would have happened if she had dared to ask, back during the course: "Do coincidence makers have coincidence makers?"

FROM THE WORKBOOK FOR THE COURSE FREE
CHOICE, BOUNDARIES, AND RULES OF THUMB,
PART III (HUMAN BOUNDARIES)

In her book *Embedding the Also,* Muriel Fabrik described six
basic mistakes that most people make when making a choice.
Her method became established as the standard that was accepted for many years by coincidence makers who sought to
map the possible mistakes of their clients.

Abstention. The most common mistake, according to Fabrik,
is simply not to choose. In such a case, the client will not
allow himself to take a risk or take advantage of any chance,
and will prefer to have "reality" decide for him. This mistake
derives from the fact that making any choice also means
relinquishing its alternatives. "The abstaining client" sees
this relinquishing and not the choice, and chooses a passive

stance. The choice to do nothing, Fabrik explained, is also a choice, but it is simply a bad one. [For additional research on the problem of abstention, see Cohen's book *Why Get Entangled?—How to Make Coincidences for Spineless Clients*.]

Fear. Fabrik argued, among other things, that the correct choice is usually also the most frightening choice. This is not because it is necessarily the most dangerous choice, but because a bit more courage is needed in order to choose it. Most clients prefer a long and complex process of deliberation in which they ultimately choose what they would have chosen in any case from the outset—the less frightening choice, or the one they are familiar with and that does not demand a change in currently held beliefs or thought patterns.

Self-delusion. Some clients understand that the correct choice is indeed the more frightening one. In order to avoid this fear, they create a complex mechanism of self-deception that leads them to both fear the incorrect choice and choose it. (Usually this is the decision not to do anything; see the first paragraph.) In the literature, this mistake is also called "misplaced courage" or MC.

Regret. The client returns again and again to the point of choice and reexamines it until there is no choice that fulfills its objective anymore, and all of them become erroneous choices. One of the first rules of Michaelson's method of "Golden Coincidences" derives from this mistake: "Do not allow the client to go back and deliberate, particularly if he is a level B idiot or higher."

Surplus of options. Many clients try to organize as many choices as possible in order to be certain that they are indeed "choosing." Coincidence makers also sometimes err in thinking that the choices are better and more meaningful when the number of possibilities is greater. In fact, Fabrik argued, starting from a certain threshold and above, a multiplicity of possibilities harms our ability to make a good choice and does not help us, and it significantly raises the likelihood of making one of the four mistakes outlined above.

Originality. Clients who suffer from a lack of self-confidence and an anxiety of influence tend to choose a particular possibility only because it seems to them to be original or extraordinary. The data Fabrik collected indicates that over 80 percent of choices made with the aim of being extraordinary are ultimately categorized as "banal, stupid, and disastrous."

When you come to make a coincidence, remember: while a coincidence maker is forbidden to influence the client's free will, he is permitted to preempt possible mistakes or, alternatively, to use standard mistakes of choice in order to steer the coincidence in the right direction.

17

Michael sank into his executive chair and tried to read the same paragraph for the third time. He sat in his office on the thirty-fifth floor, inhaling the furniture's oak aromas, surrounded by oil paintings made by Dutch artists in the mid-seventeenth century, and was still unable to calibrate his mind for work.

There were days like this.

He'd had too many days like this since that wintry day. He tossed the document he was reading onto the desk and got up from his chair, turned to the large window behind him, and looked out at the city.

At first, he tried to fight against these days. He tried to understand exactly what was making him feel so bad about himself, what was distracting him so much. That recurrent dream at night? The fact that his wife again didn't bother to turn over in bed toward him when he got up in the morning and left the house? A baby carriage he passed on the way to work?

He thought that if he could put his finger on what had upset his equilibrium that day, he would be able to sweep away this daily malaise and again become the efficient, astute, charismatic businessman he was supposed to be.

As time went by, he had learned to accept that there would be days like this.

Days when he would get up in the morning and feel the hole that gaped in his heart. The black hole that swallowed up the ghostly figure who was once his wife, the optimism that once accompanied the mornings they woke up together.

A quiet knock on the door.

It opened a bit and his secretary appeared.

"Michael?" she asked.

He turned around, slipping into the role of the smiling boss. "Yes, Vicky?"

He always told his secretaries to call him by his first name. In fact, he instructed all of his employees to do so.

"There are a few things here I need you to sign," Vicky said.

"No problem." He crossed the large room, and she closed the door and handed him a number of papers. He skimmed them absentmindedly.

Each time the impulse was stronger. This time, he felt they were standing even closer than usual.

He signed one of the papers and moved on to the next one, and pretended that what was written there really needed his thorough attention. Her fragrance filled his nostrils. He was excruciatingly aware of the distance between them, of the angle at which they stood, with his right shoulder close to her left shoulder, of her long blond hair (today, how wonderful, she decided not to tie it back), her green eyes, her lips, the way her blouse hung. . . .

He was always a person with self-control, but how much loneliness can a person bear?

He moved on to the next page, the last one. She was breathing a little heavily. He felt it. He wasn't alone in this feeling.

He could just move a bit so that their arms touched, or reach his hand out and stroke her lower back. There would be nothing vulgar about it. It would be wonderful, he knew.

This woman.

He was so lonely.

He knew, simply knew, that if he made the slightest move, she would be his. He had felt this for a long time from the way she moved around him, in the way she looked at him. What he wouldn't give for . . .

He returned the papers to her. When she took them from his hand, their fingers almost touched.

"Is that all?" he asked.

"Yes," she said.

They stood facing each other.

Close. Too close. Too close for it to be coincidental. He looked in her eyes and saw that she was looking back at him. But he was the one who had to make the move. All he had to do was to bend forward a bit. . . .

Four seconds passed. Four seconds of a mutual gaze were never only four seconds between a man and a woman. He turned around and began to walk back to his desk.

"Excellent," he said, as if nothing had happened.

"Great, thank you." She played along. "Bye."

She left the room.

He took a deep breath and felt how the effort to do the right thing had nearly crushed him this time. He sank into the chair, turned it toward the window, and rubbed his burning eyes. Well, apparently today was one of those days.

⚲

Guy saw the secretary, a bit flushed, leaving his client's office.

The knowledge that she was unable to see him was a bit embarrassing. He felt like a Peeping Tom of the worst kind. Ever since he had stopped being an imaginary friend, the sense that someone was looking at you and not seeing you had become foreign to him. He was surprised by the power of the feeling.

Pierre had made what Guy needed to do unequivocally clear. It was almost like a commando mission. Enter, execute, exit.

Guy was merely a small cog in the complex world of coincidences that Pierre was creating in order to cause Michael to die at the appointed time, and this had to happen that very day, within a few hours.

"Will you be here when I return?" he asked Pierre.

"No," Pierre said. "I have a few urgent errands. We'll see each other in a few hours."

Thus, he was alone now, just outside the office of someone who had once been the child Michael. Of all the children in the world, it had to be him.

But sometimes you just needed to do it.

He tried to remember exactly which character he wore when he was with Michael. The color of the suit, the shade of the eyes.

He took a deep breath and, as he had done years ago, walked inside through the closed door.

❧

Michael knew why these days were coming.

They were coming because he and Mika were now living like roommates instead of like a married couple. Even worse, they were like roommates who were staying together only because their lease had yet to expire.

The love of his life would barely exchange a word with him. Ever since the accident, she was living like a ghost. Going to Pilates during the day, sitting and staring at the television in the evening, turning her back to him and quietly weeping at night.

Mourning, it turned out, could be quite repetitive.

He had met her when he was still a young entrepreneur full of ambition, when he still went to conferences for the lectures, and not only to be seen. When his ideas were the thing that motivated him and not the inertia of accomplishments.

A common friend (because then he could still be sure they were really friends for the right reasons) introduced him to the woman with the most smiling eyes he had ever seen, and he thought it would be nice to spend a little time with her.

Two weeks after their first date, he knew she was the woman he would spend his life with. He had always laughed at people who made such statements. Only later did he realize that there was no other way to explain this feeling.

They were at her home. They were trying to plan where to go out that evening and discovered that, in their heart of hearts, they both were sick and tired of the same places and people and options. They discovered that they shared a secret: both of them were fed up with what the rest of the world called "having a good time." After they had tried all of the different coffee combinations, all of the restaurants and nightclubs and theaters, it suddenly occurred to them that what they really wanted was just to be alone together.

Michael was certain their relationship would die that very evening. He wasn't accustomed to a connection that lacked a continuous and regular exchange of witty content that passed from one side to the other against the backdrop of a social pastime. If they weren't planning to go out or engage in some activity, what would their relationship be based on? That's how he operated in all things pertaining to women: he won them over with wit, exciting shared interests, and all sorts of wonderful diversions—but not with frankness. As in a fight club, the first rule in a relationship was not to talk about the relationship, he thought. The main thing was to keep them far away from the worst thing—banality, to always offer excitement or surprise, and to keep away from silences, from talk about the weather, and from routine.

He was afraid that since they had decided they had nowhere to go, and that they didn't feel like going out at all, a corrosive silence would enter into their relationship, and the drabness of everyday life would destroy the enjoyable and exciting thing that had developed between them.

And then, when they sat there together in her living room, surrounded by a huge collection of old books and vinyl records that he noticed for the first time, hearing the neighbor humming on the other side of the wall, unconsciously synchronizing their breathing, remaining silent, he suddenly discovered a different type of connection. It was no longer about fun. It was something else. Slower, less demanding, thick and embracing. You didn't really know that you loved someone until you'd been properly silent with her, apparently.

Out of this thickness, Mika got up and went to her bookshelf. Then she sat down on the sofa and signaled for him to sit next to her.

"Come, listen to something nice," she said and opened the dog-eared book.

They sat there all night, with her reading in her gentle, melodious voice and him listening to the silence between the words. And when the morning broke, he knew that she was the woman of his life.

And subsequently, once or twice a week, when the level of their love surged high enough and when the level of their fatigue was low enough, they would read to each other at night.

He read Gaiman and Safran Foer to her, she read Hugo and Camus to him; he amused her with Pratchett, she rocked him to Hemingway, he caressed her with Coben, she surprised him with Twain.

All of them were their guests. Thrillers, dramas, the familiar, and the obscure. Even Dr. Seuss. All of them were part of the dialogue of lovers they created between themselves, far from the eyes of the world, during long nights of reading to each other.

On the third of December, in the morning, everything changed.

Michael regarded that day as the center point of his life, the peak point in the Gauss curve of events from which his soul was built; until that point everything ascended and rose higher, while from that point onward everything started to come apart.

Mika had been his wife for nearly two years.

The inspiration of his life got into the car that morning, primed for another day of work as a math teacher. She started her small car and switched on the countdown clock for the end of their love with a slight turn of the wrist.

The only woman who was able to induce his high and choking laugh without him feeling embarrassed drove off, an Ella Fitzgerald CD playing in the background. The air conditioner was set to ventilation mode. The woman with whom he had already decided to try to bring children into the world hummed to herself, like always, because she was the humming kind, and she occasionally glanced in the mirror. When he received the telephone call that morning, he didn't realize how deeply the rift would gape in their lives after she, the only "she" he ever had, looked at the mirror one time too many and ran over a three-year-old boy.

He never understood exactly what happened.

How did a three-year-old child reach the street without anyone noticing? And why? And where were his lousy and pitiable parents?

Like a lit candle that someone extinguished with a fan, Mika was snuffed out that day.

When she returned home, even before the slow trial and the sleepless nights and the endless weeping and the self-hatred, he was unable to crack her new armor. He couldn't stop those screams in which she tried to explain to him that she doesn't want doesn't want doesn't want anything more from life because she doesn't deserve doesn't deserve doesn't deserve anything and the first therapist and the second therapist and the third therapist and the marriage counselor and the pills and the vomiting every time she got into a car and the diary full of small letters that she wrote, gripped in a frenzy, then set ablaze in desperate tears behind the house one frigid and thorny night, and the cold back and the short barbed arguments in which they tried to hit each other where it hurt and her loathing of everything she had ever done and of all the optimism that was once part of her—even before all these things, already that same evening when she returned home, he felt that a thick black cloth had been wrapped around her heart, choking it.

He tried all different sorts of remedies.

He would take her on a short vacation and imagine how they would open up and talk a bit about what happened, and how she would cry and he would comfort her and they would embrace and then talk a little more and then manage to change the subject, and how they would go for a short hike in the morning and how he would say something foolish that would finally make her smile, and then a slow and beautiful process of internal healing would begin when they returned home.

He would quarrel with her, intentionally, and imagine how he would later return home and theatrically fall upon his knees and ask forgiveness, and how she would then be able once again to grant him that wise look, and how she would cling to him and tell him how much she needed him, and he would strengthen her and lift her and cure her only with kisses, nothing more than kisses.

He would avoid contact for entire days and imagine how she would eventually call him on the phone and ask him to talk with her, and how he would relent and both of them would cry on the phone and he would remind her of silences they both had forgotten and show her that it was possible to go back and that she was worthy of being loved the way he loved her.

All of these imaginings were meaningless.

They would spend three silent days in a cabin, and the small quarrels would become monsters, leading him to say a quarter of a sentence that unintentionally tore another small strip of her soul. And she never called him on the phone so he could tell her she was worthy.

The sense of surrender that had recently overcome him was actually not something he imagined. He never thought he would reach the point of staying an extra hour at the office after finishing his work, only because he didn't want to return home to the trench she was digging around him.

He never believed he would put himself into such foolish workplace situations, so morally questionable, only in order to feel a bit alive, only to experience a little of the urge to self-destruct, because why should she be the only one to go crazy? And if someone, on that December third, had told him that he was going to be so lonely and so frustrated and dissatisfied and angry to the point of being one breath away from an affair with his secretary, the biggest cliché in the book, he would have fired him on the spot, for his impudence and stupidity and for drinking on the job.

Yet here he was, and he knew that the next time it would happen.

"Oh, shit," he heard himself saying, and pressed his red eyes with his fingers and looked out again at the city.

"Yes, I understand what you mean," he heard a voice say behind him and quickly turned around.

When he saw the figure sitting, amused, on his desk, it took him a few seconds to understand who it was. And when he understood, it was clear that this was a particularly bad day.

Once, before Michael was defined within the bounds of his business card, before he had enough pocket money to buy self-confidence, he was a short child who didn't really understand the dynamics of human relations among people under the age of ten.

He would roam around by himself in the schoolyard during recess and wonder how the other children communicated with each other so naturally. He would be dumbfounded and clam up every time he had to conduct a conversation, play in a group, or speak in front of a class of small people. He wasn't sure how others viewed him, and he was sure they would judge and examine him on every syllable.

He was the young embodiment of those who prefer not to take action in order to avoid failing, and he considered every interpersonal activity as falling within the range of unreasonable risk.

Only later, when standing in front of the class during a catastrophic lecture on the lives of whales, which he had prepared for homework, would he feel the huge excitement of appearing before a crowd. Something inside him broke and was rebuilt, and a week later he was participating in a soccer game in the schoolyard, scoring a goal, and revealing himself to the world. It was that simple.

But until then he had his little soldiers, he had the neighborhood park where he observed the lives of bugs and conducted small, dirty scientific experiments on the uncomplaining natural world around him, and he had Medium John.

Medium John was his imaginary friend.

He wasn't particularly tall like Michael's uncle, so he wasn't Big John. And he also wasn't short like Sasha, the smallest child in the class, so he wasn't Little John either. He was Medium John. At first, Medium John was with him mainly during the winter, when he couldn't go out to the park. They would sit in his room and spend time together. Sometimes Michael would talk to him and tell him about school and about what he didn't do that day, and John would say really wise things, or at least they sounded really wise. His words would both reinforce Michael's decisions and offer the possibility of changing. Michael would lie in bed and try to understand what he meant exactly. Sometimes he would imagine John again and ask him what he meant, and John would again provide an explanation that could be interpreted in every possible way.

But usually they would play with the soldiers, or Michael would tell John things about the world, or he would play with the soldiers by himself and John would sit there and help him feel that he wasn't alone.

Later, when the weather allowed it, they would go out to the park, and Michael would run around and engage in a meticulous examination of the wildlife hiding in the park. Occasionally he would call John and show him a new discovery. John would nod his head with a smile and sometimes come to take a look, but usually he sat on the bench, looking at Michael and guarding him from afar.

He had to because he had a beautiful suit, and he couldn't get it dirty in the park.

Every once in a while, he would say things like: "You don't always have to decide. You can simply feel, flow with what is happening, and the decision will emerge on its own. Living is something you do now, not later." The meaning of this wasn't so clear, to say the least. Michael felt a bit more comfortable with other sentences, like: "Most of the big things in the world didn't happen because someone was particularly wise, brave, or talented, but because there was someone who didn't give up."

And there was that weird time when they couldn't go outside to play because Michael's mother didn't allow it for some reason. He played with the soldiers by himself and Medium John stood and looked out the window. At a certain point, Michael raised his eyes and tried to understand what in heaven's name Medium John was doing by the window. He stood there almost motionless, and Michael felt compelled to ask: "Is everything okay?"

Medium John replied: "Someday, in the future, someone will tell you all sorts of stories about what love is. Don't believe what they tell you. Love is not a boom; it's not explosions and effects. It's not fireworks in the sky or a plane flying by with a large banner. It slowly pours under your skin, quietly, without you even noticing, like anointing oil. You just feel a type of warmth, and one day you wake up and discover that under your skin you are wrapped with someone else."

"Does that mean that everything is okay or not?" Michael asked.

So, yes. That's how he was, Medium John. But usually he said things that were clearer. And then, he was the responsible adult who disappeared after the first goal that Michael scored in his life.

And now Medium John, still in a suit that no longer looked as impressive as it had all those years ago, sat on the table with his legs crossed and smiled at him with the same tell-all-tell-nothing grin.

Michael turned back toward the window and convinced himself this wasn't happening.

"I'm here for a reason, you know," Medium John said. "Apparently you need me again."

I don't intend to answer him, Michael thought. Was this what a nervous breakdown looked like? People you imagined at age eight or nine come back to you when you're grown up? Was it time to start taking pills?

"You're not crazy," John said. "You simply need someone to talk with. That's the way it always was when you called for me."

"I don't need to talk with you," said Michael.

"Oh, you answered—that's progress," John said. He got up from the desk and stood next to Michael, looking out at the scenery with him. "So, what's happening, Michael? We've advanced in life, I see."

"Nothing's happening."

"You look very troubled."

"I'm talking with an imaginary friend from my childhood, someone with a marine haircut and a second-rate suit. That's not natural."

"It's completely natural," said John. "People do this all the time."

"No, they don't."

"Okay, maybe not specifically with me, but people conduct little conversations with themselves all the time. You'd be surprised how much. Sometimes only in their minds, sometimes out loud. This occurs among people of all ages. People who need help often turn to themselves."

"I don't need help."

"Are you sure?"

Michael didn't respond. In the street below, the traffic pattern of the small vehicles repeated itself.

"You're not angry," said John. "You're not desperate, you're not even really alone. You're longing—that's what you are."

He stopped and waited for his words to sink in.

"You long for the woman you once knew, and who's no longer there when you come home. On the one hand, you're afraid that she's gone forever, and on the other hand, you're not capable of moving on and leaving her behind because something in you still hopes she'll return."

"You're talking nonsense," said Michael.

"But"—John ignored him and continued—"each time, you try bringing her back in one fell swoop. You think that you need to re-store the old love, the old understanding, your old Mika. It doesn't work that way. It will be a new Mika. Wonderful and loved, but new, with additional layers. A new love is never created all at once. This you already know. It happens slowly, step by step, one drop after another."

"I'm no longer at the age when I can start things from scratch."

"Of course you are. You must. You'll rebuild something famil-iar. You need lots of patience and you need to calm down."

"I'm tired. It's too late for us, John."

"No, definitely not."

"Yes it is, dammit."

They stood there a few more seconds, silent, and John said: "Love, I think, is an emotion that's very difficult to quantify. Very difficult to measure. We feel it so rarely and we're so totally swept into it that we are never really capable of defining for ourselves how much we want and need and love something. And that's okay—there are things in the world that aren't supposed to be measured. Longing, on the other hand, is a much clearer emotion. According to the quantity of longing, we can know how much we miss the person who has vanished from us. You're lucky, Michael. You're experiencing longing when you still have a chance to restore the love. Most people begin longing only when it's too late. And you, you can look from the depths of the pit you're in now and understand how high you can reach if only you give yourself a chance. As long as she's not dead, Michael, you can rediscover how to love her and to be loved by her. 'Too late' is an expression pertaining to events of a different type.

"For most people, longing is only proof—proof that comes too late—that they truly loved. You can mobilize this. It's definitely not too late for you, Michael."

When Michael turned around to look at him, Medium John was gone.

18

Alberto Brown decided to kill his target after the movie.

It was a comic action film, the type Alberto liked. He had al-ready seen it twice. Just unrealistic enough to still be enjoyable. He had approximately three hours before his man would emerge from the building. He would then turn left and walk exactly twenty-five yards until he reached the entrance to the parking lot. Alberto would have twenty-five yards in which to kill him. He wondered how it would happen.

There were no renovations under way at the building, as far as he could tell. Therefore, the idea of a hammer falling from the twentieth floor didn't seem likely. Another scenario he dismissed was a car losing control and careening onto the sidewalk. Along the entire length of the twenty-five yards, there were posts to pre-vent such accidents. His target also appeared to be quite fit, so a sudden heart attack didn't seem logical. Perhaps a mugging that went awry?

He had a small yellow notepad in which he documented all of the ways in which his targets had disappeared from the world. Strange accidents, sudden attacks—he had seen it all, it seemed. He tried to find some sort of pattern. It couldn't be that all of this was happening to him just by chance. On the other hand, it could be that he was a guy with luck, or perhaps the exact opposite. Maybe both.

Okay, he'd soon find out how this was going to happen. Very soon. The movie was starting. If he went to his position above the street immediately after it ended, he'd arrive there an hour before the hit itself. This time frame appeared reasonable.

He purchased a ticket.

Medium John stood in the bathroom at the end of the floor and looked at himself in the mirror. Slowly the reflection changed from the long, tough face of someone whom only one person in the world could see, to the softer face of an ordinary coincidence maker.

The eyes of this coincidence maker were moist. A few superfluous blinks and there would be a real risk of a tear.

Had he bought it? Did anyone buy everything his imaginary friend told him, just because it was him?

Back then, Cassandra claimed it was so. Faith and love go together—that was her standard line on this subject.

She closed her eyes and asked, "Are you ready?"

"Yes," he said.

She stood with her back to him, but when she said, "Are you sure?" he could still hear that she was smiling.

"Yes," he answered again. "I don't understand how you do it. I don't think I can. Not even with you."

"Faith and love go together," she said. " 'Love me' and 'have faith in me' join forces, walking hand in hand, throughout the course of history."

He stretched his arms out in front of him, a bit nervous.

"It's an interesting sensation," she said, "the moment before. I've never been in a situation of trusting someone."

"Just fall back already," he said. "I'll catch you."

"I've never had a reason to trust someone. They were the ones who trusted me. They needed me; I didn't need them. And suddenly I now understand that there's someone I need to trust, who won't hurt me."

"Um," he said, "I think you're taking this in the wrong direction. We're talking about trust here, not about hurting. I would never hurt you. Positive thoughts, okay?"

"Yes, yes, I know. But this is actually what gives trust its power, no? That you could hurt me?"

"Yes . . . yes . . . perhaps."

She laughed. "It's simply wonderful."

"Wonderful?"

"It's no wonder that people do this exercise. You can't be connected to someone who can't hurt you. That's the beauty. Never in my life have I allowed anyone to be in this position. It makes me feel . . . really . . ."

"Really what?"

"Human," she said, spreading her arms and falling backward.

———

He rinsed his face, letting the coolness of the water bring him back to reality, like after sleeping. The mirror in front of him reflected someone who was confused, small drops dripping from his chin.

He tried to explain to himself what he was feeling. It was like trying to catch a frightened fish with slippery hands.

Perhaps one feels this way after unfaithfulness.

Unfaithfulness toward someone who relied on you to be there in his difficult moments and say something to pick him up. While, in fact, you've just wrapped your despicable intentions in pretty sentences. Someone who always thought you were standing by his side, and perhaps you had been, but now you're using all of the blind trust you received as an Archimedes fulcrum to leverage the world in the direction *you* want. And he'll never know.

For a split second, it seemed to Guy that he also detected a sense of relief.

Relief that it wasn't worse. Relief that he was able to perform this loathsome mission without saying something that he didn't believe in, like "the power of change." Because he truly believed in longing as a measure of love. He believed that it wasn't too late for using giving as therapy. Not that it made any difference. This child, that is, the one who was once a child, would no longer be alive at the end of the day and would be unable to make use of all these things. But he hadn't lied entirely. He wasn't completely unfaithful. He was able to be a friend, this last time.

And maybe, deep inside, there was also a bit of happiness in him.

Because he was able to give something of himself to someone. Really from himself.

He had been engaged in service for so long. To echo the thoughts of those imagining him, without expressing his real opinions. To make coincidences without taking a stand on what he believed was right or wrong.

And here, he'd been able to stand next to someone, and really—unbelievably—assist him, with the help of ideas that were completely his, perceptions that he had formulated on his own, thoughts that the other person had never thought.

He looked at the figure in the mirror and for the first time didn't feel like he was staring at someone else's reflection.

If only it were so easy to give advice to himself.

He didn't have to be a compliant reflection.

Not for anyone. Not for Pierre, either.

He accepted too many things as self-evident, as meaningless decrees. He would just have to go to Pierre and persuade him that Michael didn't have to die today.

Something new throbbed within him. Perhaps it was responsibility. Perhaps that was the thing that had been lacking during this long period of time.

And he felt alive—like he did with Cassandra.

19

"To fly," she said.

"That's all?" he asked her. "Just to fly?"

"For a start," Cassandra said and shrugged her shoulders apologetically. "Perhaps after a little more time, I'll figure out what else I want."

"Really? If you could imagine yourself, if you could create yourself however you wish, you'd only choose 'to fly'?"

"Create myself however I wish?" Cassandra laughed. "It was enough for me to create myself. Do you know how many characters I've played in this job? And all of them were beautiful and amazing, believe me. No one imagines me ugly or stupid. Natalie, for example, does excellent work with me. I love this hair. But it's the hair she imagines for me, not my hair. Of course, it's fun for me to be noble and self-confident, like she wants me to be. But now I have you, and I mainly want to be myself. So yes, if I could imagine myself, it's exactly what I would do. I would imagine myself, not someone else. But I'd still like to fly. To fly up high to a place where I could flee all of those who judge me, to move with the wind."

"Okay, I admit," he said, "that could be quite nice."

"And you?" she asked. "What would you imagine if you could imagine yourself?"

"Hmm," he said. "I don't think I have something specific that I really want to imagine, to tell you the truth."

"A minute ago, you made fun of me for . . ."

"I know, I know. It's just . . ."

"And you're always talking about how you're fed up with doing things that others imagine you doing, and that you want to do things by yourself and for yourself."

"Right." He scratched his head in embarrassment.

"So what do you want to do?"

"I . . . I don't know. . . ."

Suddenly, he looked around and was uneasy.

"Where's Michael?" he asked.

"What?" said Cassandra.

"Michael, where's Michael?" He got up and looked around anxiously.

"He left," Cassandra quietly told him.

"No, no," he said. "It can't be. He has to be around here. The fact is, I'm still here."

"No." Cassandra avoided looking into his eyes. "I saw him. He took his soldiers and went home."

"So he must be looking at me from the window, or something like that."

"I don't think so."

Medium John looked up toward the building. The window of Michael's room was closed.

"He's sitting at home and imagining me here?" he wondered out loud.

"I find that hard to believe."

"So how is it that I'm still here? If he isn't imagining me, how is it that I'm still here?"

Cassandra hugged herself and looked to the side.

"It could be . . . that is . . . apparently, I'm imagining you here."

He turned toward her, surprised.

"You?"

"Yes."

"I didn't know it was possible. . . ."

"Neither did I. . . ." Cassandra said. "But I saw him leaving, and I didn't want you to disappear on me. So I imagined you continuing to sit here next to me." He struggled to find words, and Cassandra interpreted his silence as anger. "I didn't make you do anything!" she pleaded with him. "Nothing. I only imagined a presence, not behavior. Everything was you. Really. Really."

He moved back toward the bench and sat next to her.

"Okay," he said. "Thank you."

They sat for a few moments without words.

"It's okay, right?" Cassandra asked anxiously.

"It's the most okay thing in the world," he said.

The sun had started its slow descent in the sky.

A lone dog passed in front of them, engaged in the calm pursuit of a wisp of unfamiliar scent.

"I didn't know we could imagine each other," he said.

"Actually, why shouldn't we be able to?" she asked.

She played a bit with the lace on her collar, and it seemed she was trying to decide whether to say something.

"What?" he asked.

Cassandra bent over toward Natalie, the girl imagining her, who was busy playing next to them the whole time. "Natalie? Sweetie?"

Natalie lifted her head.

"It's starting to get late," said Cassandra. "I think you should head home."

"Okay," said Natalie. "You'll come with me?"

"No." Cassandra smiled at her. "I'm going to stay and rest here a bit, okay? We'll meet here again tomorrow."

"Okay." The girl got up and absentmindedly brushed off her dirty knees. "Bye, Cassie."

"Bye, sweetie," said Cassandra.

The girl walked away, and Cassandra turned back to him.

"Imagine me," she said.

"I don't . . ."

"Imagine me. Keep me here."

"But how?"

"Please." She started to disappear, almost blinking. "I don't want us to be limited in time. Imagine me."

He felt his heart racing.

What did it mean actually, to imagine her?

Who is she? What is she? "But I don't want to determine what you'll be," he whispered, closing his eyes.

"Keep me here." He heard her as if from a great distance. "Don't you want me to stay?"

"I do," he said.

Not the way she looks, or her smell or touch. These are details. Something else, there must be something else. He reminded himself of the feeling that her presence induced in him. . . .

And he imagined her.

The two of them sat by themselves on the bench.

The sky above was streaked with red and purple.

His Cassandra at his side, tears in the corners of her smiling eyes.

"Not behavior," he said to her. "Just a presence. Like you said earlier. I just imagined you here. Do whatever you wish."

She nodded slowly and smiled.

Her long hair fluttered around her head. She laughed.

"What happened?" he asked.

"Are you imagining that my hair is flying?" she asked with a smile. "There's no wind at all. . . ."

"Hey," he said. "This is my first imagining. I'm not so experienced yet."

"Neither am I," she said. "But you don't see me improving your shave or changing the color of your eyes."

"What's wrong with the color of my eyes?"

She laughed. "Nothing. They're perfectly fine. They're great eyes."

He shook his head. "It's not logical. I'm imagining you imagining me imagining you imagining. . . ."

"Yes, yes, I get the point. It's a circle," she said. "Get used to the idea."

"But it's not logical," he repeated.

"Since when is logic connected to love?" she quietly asked.

"Connected to what?" He was caught off guard.

"What happened? Did I say the forbidden word?" she asked with a smile. "That's the way it is with everyone, right? A closed circle like this. . . ."

They imagined each other, being careful not to exaggerate.

We are truly a small closed circle, he thought to himself. The world could disappear, all of the people in it could stop imagining, and all of the reality, even the true reality, could rot and break and dissolve and be sucked into nothingness, and the two of them would remain, holding each other this way, while the rest no longer existed.

"Do you want to fly?" he asked.

"Yes," she said.

"Should I imagine wings for you?"

"No, just imagine me gliding in the air. That's enough."

She started to float in the air now, and he instantly started to float after her. "Hey!"

"Stay close," she said.

They rose higher, gliding next to each other, not taking their eyes off each other.

"Just don't stop imagining me now," he said quietly. "Don't let go of me."

"I won't," whispered Cassandra. "Don't worry."

They left the treetops below them and started to ascend to a place where no shadow blocked the colors of the sunset.

"You too," whispered Cassandra, her eyes wide open. "Don't stop. Don't let go."

"Never," he said.

FROM *KEY FIGURES IN THE DEVELOPMENT*
OF THE COINCIDENCE-MAKING PROFESSION,
MANDATORY READING: H. J. BAUM

Hubert Jerome Baum is considered by many to have been the greatest coincidence maker of all time.

At the beginning of his career, Baum was a certified dream weaver, and during his service he received three different awards for originality and professionalism in building dreams. During that period, he was still one of the youngest people in the field, but in the archive files of his department one can find at least fifty-five references to dreams of a particularly high level of complexity and polish, and at least one hundred seventy citations of dreams that left a positive effect on the lives of his dreamers.

About two years prior to retiring from dream weaving, Baum won the prestigious Doson Prize for "the use of dreams for healing traumas" and became the youngest dream weaver to ever win this award.

After this period, Baum moved to the Special Department for Designing Associations but left after several years. In one of the biographies written about him, *Baum—Knocking Down the First Domino,* he explained that he felt a strong need to engage in activity that was not confined to an office.

When Baum started his work as a coincidence maker, the field had grown only slightly from its infancy. Coincidence makers at that time engaged mainly in organizing coincidences of the third level, at most, and even then they were merely cliché-drops or "loud" coincidences of the type that seem coincidental due to their improbability.

Taking advantage of his extensive experience in dream weaving, and with the help of the knowledge he had accumulated in the Special Department for Designing Associations, Baum created a new, complex, and more elegant approach to coincidence making. In his view, coincidences are also a type of "weaving," and Baum initiated a number of organizational steps that changed the way in which coincidence makers have worked ever since.

Throughout his service—which still continues, according to many sources—Baum was responsible for some of the most complex and impressive coincidences in history, such as the mold in Alexander Fleming's laboratory and the discovery of penicillin, organizing the discovery of electromagnetism, the discovery of X-rays, and organizing a window of time in which a storm began to die down, allowing the invasion of Normandy. In addition, he was responsible for other major historical and particularly complex coincidences, most of which are still classified and some of which will apparently never be revealed.

Baum is considered a master in two main fields: changes related to and/or using the weather (which demand considerable research and a high degree of precision), and the use of multiple identities in the framework of coincidences. The costumes and identities that he particularly liked include a tall train conductor with an unclear accent, an old gardener, and a portly hairdresser usually named Claris.

Baum makes rare public appearances in his real character, but was recently seen at the graduation ceremony of a coincidence makers course in Spain. His present location is unknown, as is his status as an active coincidence maker.

20

Pierre ran through the fine details of that day again in his mind.

Half of the plan had already been executed. He had to get to the bus stop soon; he was scheduled for an argument in which he had to get very upset.

It was always hard for him to get upset. Before he could, he had to take that heartbeat and set it in the right place, he reminded himself.

He didn't look like Pierre now, of course. He was dwarfish and balding, with a spasmodic gait and sweaty stubble.

During the past three months, when he roamed around this radio station, he didn't talk with people very much, but after a while they simply assumed he was supposed to be there and ignored him, as if he were a little dirt on the windshield that wasn't important enough to merit washing the whole car. He was very familiar to them now, and they had no clue who he was.

The amount of attention one person attracted was always inversely related to the total number of people in the given area, it turned out. The station was big enough and its hallways were long enough that the level of attention he attracted was exactly under the red line he had defined: exactly the level at which no one would want to initiate a conversation, but everyone felt familiar with him.

He exited the radio station slowly.

No one took notice of him, as usual. On the table, outside of the place they still called the "record library" for some reason, were piles of discs, arranged according to the order of the programs that day.

The secretary at the entrance, the director of the record library, the broadcaster who went around with an unlit joint just to look cool—none of them were there when he quickly walked past and switched the discs in the two boxes.

It was very simple. The broadcaster would think he was playing a certain song, and by the time he noticed, it would be too late to search for the original disc. He would stutter something about a small technical glitch and then accept the situation and play the other song. Sometimes even without lighting a joint, you were liable to think a bit slowly.

And so he would play the song that Pierre chose.

It was the very first lesson in the coincidence makers course Song Manipulation.

This was like, so basic.

He smiled.

21

Emily sat at the white platform and waited for a train.

Apparently.

It definitely looked like a train platform, though it was completely white. But the tracks below, not far in front of her, were unmistakable. So, apparently, she was waiting for a train. The red suitcase at her feet was another significant clue. Not that she had packed it or anything.

On the other hand, she also didn't remember traveling to the train station. One moment she was in her apartment, signing the Waiver, completely alive, and now she was here, at a station, and dead too.

She didn't feel dead. She felt the cool air entering her chest through her nose, she felt her weight pressing against the seat, she even felt a little hungry. But she was dead, that was quite clear.

A stressful thought. Although you had no idea what was going to happen, you felt that the worst was already behind you, so you really had nothing to worry about. What a strange type of curiosity this was, lacking even a tiny bit of fear about things to come.

She looked around, trying to locate herself in space. The platform stretched endlessly to the right and left. White and pristine, without any seats except for hers. In front of her, the platform ended in a step. Under the step, below, were two black train tracks laid on the ground. Behind them was white grass that moved in the light breeze and continued into the distance. Small trees, also white, filled the horizon with a zigzagged strip.

To her right, a little behind her, she now noticed a tall, square column with a loudspeaker mounted on its top. Yes, apparently a train was supposed to arrive soon. She turned farther and saw a small booth behind the column. It was also white, of course, and had a small window. Above the window was a sign with pale gray letters: INFORMATION.

Information?

There's information here?

She got up from her seat, fighting for a second the urge that remained from her previous life to take the suitcase with her. No one would try to steal the suitcase. And even if they did, what difference would it make?

She slowly approached the information window, trying to prepare herself for whatever might happen. Behind the window sat a small woman, wearing a lively blue cotton shirt. Wrinkles of a smile sent calm branches around her face, and the ends of her short black hair tickled the crease in the side of her neck. She looked like an illustration that could be placed next to the word "friendly" in the dictionary.

The small woman raised her eyes and looked at Emily with a smile.

"The feeling when you see this sign?" she asked. "Eight letters, and the third letter is an *r*."

Emily looked at her, a bit confused. "Excuse me?"

The woman picked up what was in front of her, on the table under the window. It was a half-solved crossword puzzle. "Eight letters," she repeated. "It couldn't be 'terrific,' because the first letter isn't a *t*."

" 'Surprise,' " Emily said.

"Correct! Right!" the woman rejoiced and scribbled quickly. "That also solves two-across for me, thanks to the *e* at the end."

"What's two-across?" Emily asked.

"What you need to take in proportion," the woman said. "Ten letters."

Emily thought a bit. "And what's the answer?" she asked in the end.

" 'Everything,' " said the woman.

"Everything?"

"What, isn't that so?" The woman wrinkled her eyebrows. "It actually fits. I already have the *i* from before, from six-across."

"And what was that?"

The woman examined the page in front of her. "Here it is: 'The name of the young woman waiting at the station,' " she said. "Emily, right?"

"R . . . ight," said Emily.

"Then, that fits," the woman said. She folded the crossword puzzle and moved it aside. "So how can I help you?" she asked.

"Um . . ." Emily said, stuttering a bit. "That is, I didn't want something specific. I mean, I do feel a need for a little information, but I don't have enough initial information to even know what to ask."

"Do you want me to also provide the questions?" the woman asked.

"No, I just . . ."

"No, no, it's okay. No problem. Try 'Am I dead?' for example."

"I . . . I'm . . . I'm dead?"

"Yes!" the woman cheered. "But not really. A kind of dead. Very good, you ask excellent questions. What about, 'When will the train come?'"

"I didn't think to ask that, I . . ."

"Well, come on, 'When . . .'"

"When . . ."

"Will the train come?"

"When will the train come?"

"Whenever you'd like." The woman waved her hand. "Now try something of your own."

"What did you mean exactly when you said 'But not really'?"

"Oh, an excellent question."

"Thank you."

"You're making nice progress."

"Thank you."

". . ."

". . ."

". . ."

"And the answer?"

"Ah, yes, of course," said the woman. "I almost forgot to answer. You're not really dead because, let's be frank, only people die. And you, how should I say this, were not really a human being. That is, perhaps you were, but you had a status that was a bit different."

"I was a coincidence maker."

"Aha. And now you're on the way to the next role. A type of waiting room."

"A waiting room?"

"Something like that."

"So why does it look like a train station?" asked Emily.

"How should I know?" The information woman shrugged her shoulders. "That's the way you chose to experience it. Each person chooses to experience this in a different way."

"And you . . . ?"

"Just someone you're experiencing in your own mind, yes."

"I'm imagining you?"

"No. You're experiencing. I'm not imaginary; I exist. You're simply choosing to see me in this way. Thank you, by the way. I like this haircut."

"Don't mention it."

"But, by the way, why did you use so much white?" the small woman asked.

"I don't know," said Emily. "Until a few seconds ago, I wasn't aware that I was creating this."

"Not that it isn't beautiful. Very clean."

"Thank you."

"Don't mention it."

Emily examined the station again, searching for clues of things to come.

"So what's going to happen now?"

"Like any coincidence maker," the information woman said with a smile, "you're waiting here for a spell. When you're ready, the train will arrive and take you to your next station."

"Which is?"

"Life," said the woman.

"Life?"

"Life. The real thing. The best job of all. Regular, full life, everything included. Free will, conflicting emotions, memory, forgetfulness, success, disappointment, the whole mess."

"I . . . I'll simply be part of mankind?"

"Or womankind, to be exact."

"With parents?"

"Two, to be precise."

"In the real, ordinary world?"

"Definitely, my dear."

Emily breathed deeply and allowed the understanding to seep in.

"You understand," the woman said, "that perhaps you've died as a coincidence maker, but as a person, you simply have yet to be born. So, one could say that you're dead, but that's not completely accurate. And I cannot give you erroneous or imprecise information."

"Is this what happens to everyone who signs the Waiver?" Emily asked.

"It's more correct to say that this happens to every coincidence maker who retires. Willingly, by request, or unwillingly," said the woman.

"Unwillingly?"

"There are other ways to die besides signing a document, you know."

"And when I'm a person, I'll remember that I was once a coincidence maker?"

"Heaven forbid," said the woman. "That's what the suitcase is for."

Emily looked back at the red suitcase that stood next to her seat. "The suitcase?"

"Yes. The suitcase contains all of your memories. When you get onto the train, they'll take it to the luggage compartment."

"And . . ."

"And it will get lost, of course. That's what happens to suitcases. They're not supposed to arrive at the same destination as the passenger. When they arrive, it's a type of mishap. At least, that's how it is here."

Emily turned around and went back to the seat. The distance

on the way back from the information booth seemed farther, for some reason, than the distance to it. She sat down and picked up the suitcase and placed it on her knees. It was lighter than she had expected. She put her hands on both of the locks and pressed. She heard a double *click* and the case trembled under her hands. She looked for a moment at the strip of white trees on the horizon and opened the suitcase.

Here was her first coincidence.

Here was that kiss, which she could never forget, though she always thought she should've remembered it more distinctly. It was a bit worn at the edges from repeated use in her dreams. Here was that time when rain had started to fall in the middle of the class The History of Coincidence Making in the Modern Era, and she couldn't wait to go out and smell it.

And here too was that smell, placed under the taste of lemon-vanilla ice cream. And here were all of the cups of coffee she had ever drunk, in order, from the weakest and least meaningful to that one she mistakenly prepared with two spoonfuls of coffee, which kept her awake until four in the morning.

Here were the dreams she had dreamed. Folded, a bit moist, as if she hadn't really woken up, arranged one on top of another, the worst ones at the bottom, swallowed in darkness in the depths of the suitcase, the wonderful and crazy ones sparkling mischievously on top.

Amazing—how did all this fit into such a small suitcase? The feeling of grass under her feet; the bitter taste of failure; her favorite shoes; the name of the waitress who always served her, Guy, and Eric at their café; her heartaches, prickly and flashing; her "almosts;" her successes; the small insights that came to her late at night just before falling asleep (and in the morning, she was sure she had already forgotten them); the twenty rules the General had insisted they learn by heart; Guy's responsibly beautiful eyes when he was contempla-tive; the noise that neon lights make; the paralyzing fear that over-came her immediately after she signed the Waiver.

And here too was the letter. The letter she wrote to Guy a mo-ment before she quit. The letter she had wanted to leave behind before she discovered that it was impossible. Here it was, in its en-tirety, not burned at all and still in the long, white envelope.

She took a few short breaths and then took the envelope in her hand and closed the suitcase with a click.

She hurried to the information booth. The small woman lifted the pen in the air, her gaze focused on the crossword puzzle in front of her. "You feel now?" she asked. "Five letters."

" 'Ready,' " said Emily.

"Hmm . . . possibly," said the woman. "I'll check now whether this fits with fourteen-across." She raised her eyes again. "Yes, how can I help you, dear?"

"Every coincidence maker who moves on—that is, to life—all of them pass through this place?" asked Emily, her voice quivering.

"Yes, yes, I think so," said the woman. "It doesn't happen much. There aren't so many of you actually, and you aren't very anxious to die, but in the end you pass through here."

"Could you do me a favor?"

"What else am I here for?" A small smile.

"Could you give this to someone?" Emily passed her the envelope.

The woman took the envelope and examined it. Somehow, Emily knew the woman knew exactly what was inside.

"You found a way to get around the rules, huh?" the woman asked.

"Sort of," Emily said. "I need you to give this to someone when he arrives here. He's about this tall, and—"

"I know what you're talking about," said the woman. "That is, who you're talking about."

"Yes?"

"Of course. You're talking about fourteen-across. 'That young man.' That fits in exactly with your 'ready' from before," said the small, smiling woman. Emily felt the urge to skip, to run to the end of the platform and back.

From afar, the whistle of an approaching train could be heard.

"And that," said the woman, her grin broadening, "is a sign that you're really ready now."

22

The lobby of the building was teeming with people. Guy sat on one of the small couches, off to the side, and watched the suits hurrying to cross the space between the entrance and the elevator and back.

He still couldn't get himself to go outside and walk to the place where he was supposed to meet Pierre. A quick glance at the big clock hanging in front of him made it clear that he had to get up and move soon. He was so tired.

Yes, changing one's form could be tiring, it turned out, but that was only part of it. His internal self warned him against actions that were contrary in essence to everything he was accustomed to.

Should he try to persuade Pierre? What was his case? What arguments would he make exactly? Based on which data would he present an alternative theory to him?

None of the executives hurrying through the lobby paid any

attention to the melancholy young man sunk in the couch. And, in fact, why should they pay any attention to him?

If he approached the automatic doors at the entrance now, would they register him and open up, or was he so insignificant and spineless that even their sensors would realize that there was no one there to open for?

And perhaps he would simply stay on this couch until the sun went down and Pierre came to check what in the hell happened, why he had ruined the whole plan. It would apparently be the end of his career. Well, fine.

How full of energy he had been in his first mission. And even before, in the final exam of the course. Cutting his way through the jungle, walking quickly, eyes focused, his leg muscles screaming in pain, determined to find his client before moonrise. It was easy when you didn't understand the repercussions.

It had been a lousy mission, and he still didn't understand what exactly he'd accomplished, but at least he'd managed to somehow convince himself that it was important.

And now, when it really was important, he was unable to move. A failure.

He walked up to the emergency exit and pushed the door.

Guy hesitantly pushed the office door.

"Well, what part of 'come in' wasn't clear?" he heard the General say, and he hurriedly pushed it wide open.

The General sat behind his wooden desk and raised his eyebrows in anticipation. In front of him on the desk was a large brown file, a densely typed piece of paper, and a small bobblehead dog moving its head up and down. Guy wondered whether the

General always made a point of tapping its head before telling them to enter the office.

"Come in," the General instructed him with his hand. "Sit."

The office was spartan.

A square window always cast a square of light on the empty, smooth work desk, regardless of the hour of the day. In the corner was a large globe that also undoubtedly served as a storage place for liquor, and in the opposite corner was a coatrack on which nothing ever hung. To the right was a large bookcase with glass doors. It was empty except for one book with a yellowish-white cover, and a small flowerpot from which a single leaf sprouted. Guy always wondered whether it was real or plastic.

There were no family pictures. There was no computer, of course, and not even a calendar.

However, at the corner of the desk, far from the nodding dog, was one of those executive toys. Guy thought it was called Kinetic Balls. Five shiny silver balls, each hung by two strings, waiting for the bored boss to lift one of them in the air and start a regular pendulum motion from side to side.

Guy sat opposite the General and waited.

The General took a piece of paper in his hand and hummed to himself.

"So"—he turned to Guy—"how was it?"

"I . . . ," said Guy, "that is, I think it was fine. Wasn't it?"

"You tell me."

"Yes, yes. It was fine."

"What was fine?"

"The course."

"The course?"

"You asked me about the course, no?"

The General leaned back and looked at him intently. "You know what I like about you?"

"Yes. That is, no," said Guy.

"The excellent balance between your need to receive external approval and your ability to perform the minimal activity in order to attain it."

"I think I don't understand," said Guy.

"Ah, you're not supposed to understand everything I say," said the General. "At least not at the moment."

"Umm, okay," said Guy.

The General continued to observe him.

"My grades?" asked Guy.

The General didn't reply. He seemed to be thinking about something. Guy waited. "Be careful," Eric and Emily had told him before he entered. "He's in a good mood today."

"Yes, the grades." The General shook himself from his reverie and glanced at the sheet of paper in front of him. "Awful in history, not bad in everything pertaining to the theory of human manipulation, excellent in technical analysis of coincidences, and so on and so forth. Don't worry. Indeed, it's ridiculous that you don't know the key figures in the history of coincidence makers, but we didn't bring you here so that you'd fail on the theoretical exam. We know how to select our people. I'm also quite certain that you'll succeed on the practical exam. In fact, I'm quite sure that all three of you will."

"I'm happy to hear that," said Guy.

The General got up and started to walk around the room, his hands in his pockets.

"There are two types of particularly good coincidence makers," he said. "They can be compared to two types of people. Those who lead their lives and those who let life lead them—passive and active people."

"Excuse me?"

"The active coincidence maker can be brilliant but also dangerous. He understands that he has control over the world and he knows how to use it. He likes to view himself as a creator or an artist. Your friend Eric is active. Sometimes this is quite irritating. During the course, this little creep organized at least three dates for himself with the help of unauthorized coincidences, and he also would've won the lottery if I hadn't forbidden him from carrying out the final steps in his plan. If he weren't a genius, I would've kicked him out. But that's the risk when you take on active coincidence makers.

"You, on the other hand, are so passive that it's a pleasure to watch. You don't see yourself as an artist, but rather as a clerk. You're so accustomed to having life propel you from place to place that the concept of coincidences seems completely natural to you. You're the dream of every operator. You receive an envelope and make a coincidence, receive an envelope and make a coincidence. How comfortable. But, on the other hand, it's a bit sad to look at you closely."

Guy wasn't really listening. Emily had warned him that the General had a tendency to be caustic and tried to undermine your confidence in a sophisticated and exaggerated way before assigning your final mission of the course. "He gave me a lecture for a quarter of an hour about how good it is that I lack confidence and how this would enhance my tendency toward perfectionism," she said anxiously. "Another two minutes and I would've simply gotten up and left. Or I would've kicked him in the knee, really hard."

But now it was difficult to ignore the General.

He thrust his face straight in front of Guy's.

"If you want to advance in this profession," he told him, "if you want something that is a bit more than being a pizza delivery boy of events, you need to try to abstain from abstentions. Perhaps it's not as easy as you're accustomed to, but it's more rewarding. Understood?"

"Understood," said Guy, trying with all his might to stand his ground and not pull his head back.

In the end, the General handed him the file containing his final mission for the course and then approached the globe at the end of the room and intently studied the continents, as if he were discovering them for the first time.

Guy opened the file and leafed through it.

He looked up at the General. "It says here that I have to . . ."

"Yes."

"But that's actually . . ."

"Correct."

"It's only to make a butterfly flap its wings one time."

The General laughed a short laugh. "That's what happens when you don't seriously engage in the study of history. Don't belittle this mission. It's not simple to make a butterfly flap its wings one time."

"I understand that it might be a bit complex, but . . ."

"They're stubborn little bastards, these butterflies. In the past, they didn't realize their importance, but today they know exactly what they're worth, and it's very difficult to persuade them to move a wing if they don't want to. Finding one is the easy part. Persuading it will be the difficult part. And we didn't talk about the timing yet."

"This is the course's final mission? To travel to Brazil, roam around in the forest, find a butterfly, and persuade it to move its wings one time? It's so . . . so . . . eighties."

"Not wings. Wing. Read carefully."

"But Eric was assigned to organize a meeting of three people who are going to establish a new town. Emily received a mission to make some guy from Prague invent a card game. . . ."

"And this is what you received. Internalize and execute. Not everything you do has to be dramatic, like landing on the moon. Small and ordinary actions are also important."

"I think that—"

"It seems to me that we're done here," said the General.

He lifted one of the silver balls and let it fall in an arched movement. From the other side of the row, two balls jumped up.

"That's not impossible?" asked Guy and pointed at the rebellious office toy.

"That's the principle of everything we do here, you fool. Go and do a butterfly," the General told him. "And I mean this in the cleanest sense of the word."

Guy took the file and got up to leave, his eyes still bothered by the sight of the jumping balls. One on one end, and two at the other end.

"Sometimes it works this way," the General told him.

"I understand," said Guy.

"You don't understand, but you will."

23

"You look like you were run over by a bus."

Guy looked at Pierre. "I'm not in such a great mood," he said.

"I know that you're not comfortable with this assignment, but sometimes we need to do things like this; you know that."

"It's not fair, and I'm not sure I can do it."

They were at an old, isolated bus stop. Guy sat on one of the broken seats, his back hunched and his elbows resting on his knees, and Pierre stood opposite him, his arms crossed.

"Listen," he said. "It's really a cinch. I'm not going to sell you all the crap about the omelet and the eggs and the trees and the wood chips and all that."

He moved a bit away from the bus stop and looked at the bend of the road on the horizon.

"The facts are simple. Michael—your beloved, apparently—needs to die so that the string of successful hits by Alberto Brown won't be broken. This string of hits must be maintained so that Alberto Brown will win enough credit during the next four years to enable him to enter one of the largest Mafia families in the United States. This credit will make him such a legendary figure that five years later, he'll be chosen as the head of the family and initiate a merger with three other large families, creating the largest crime cartel in the past two hundred fifty years. This merger will enable him to forge ties and enter into business with a number of small terror organizations. And then, a few years later, when everything is ripe, my last step will be to make him bust the cartel into smithereens and deliver a fatal blow to the terror cells associated with it, which will usher in at least thirty years of peace, in more than one place."

He turned toward Guy. "To kill one man in order to spin a co-incidence spanning nearly sixty years. And it's not even something direct."

"Pierre . . . ," said Guy.

"Don't you 'Pierre' me," Pierre said quietly. "I have things to do. I have things to arrange. I've organized everything for you already. The driver is tired and worried and isn't focused on anything. You'll get on the bus. You'll sit up front, next to him. You'll wait like a good boy until you reach the appropriate spot, and then you'll ask something at just the right time so that he'll turn his head for a moment and hit our client."

"He's not our client."

"From our perspective, this coincidence revolves around him, so technically—"

"He's not our client!" Guy shouted.

Several seconds of silence stood between them.

"You shouted at me?" Pierre asked.

"If anything," Guy said quietly, "he's my client."

"You shouted at me?"

"I was the one who had to make sure that he wouldn't be lonely. I'm the one who played with him and convinced him that he could realize his dreams. I'm the one who protected him when he ran around. I'm the one who tried to explain to him that friends come and go, even though I myself wasn't sure that I'd ever have friends. And I'm the one who has to kill him now."

Pierre was quiet for a bit and then asked again, in a cold tone: "You, you little runt, you shouted at me?"

"There must be another way." Guy lifted his head. "And I think you're intentionally trying to avoid it."

Pierre turned toward him.

"Listen to me now," he said, his eyes red with anger, "and listen well. While you're busy arranging for two wacky students to bump into each other in a hallway, I'm organizing the births of presidents. While you're putting a stupid pop song into a radio program in order to create background music for cheap romance, I'm organizing the births of those who will assassinate the presidents whose births I previously worked to arrange.

"You're nothing, you're a nobody. You're a lowly functionary with a tendency to run off at the mouth. You think you're changing and organizing things in the world, but all you do is execute meaningless existential jokes. And while you're doing all this, you yourself are wandering around without any objective beyond your next lousy envelope. You made someone decide to fly to Australia on a journey of self-discovery, so you think you're able to see the complete picture? You're not capable of drawing even the three and a half things that constitute your own life on your wall.

"Look at yourself. You're a domino tile, waiting for someone to knock you over. That's your whole impact on the world. You're a stationary target. Besides that heroic rescue operation of yours—

has there been one thing, just one, that you've done in life that came from within you, and not because someone told you to do it?"

Guy tried to maintain his composure. He stared at the ground with pent-up anger. "I loved," he said quietly.

Pierre gagged. "You loved? *You loved?* That imaginary friend of yours? Since when is imagining the same as loving?"

He shook his head in disbelief.

"Love demands change. Love demands work. Love isn't a piece of candy you get for being a good boy so you have something that makes you feel good. It's hard work. The hardest in the world. What effort exactly did you invest in your imaginary friend? You took a character that pleased you and showered it with enough sweetness until you convinced yourself that you were 'in love.' Lazy people have no love."

Pierre was fuming now, unable to stop. "Oh my God, I knew I should've given up on you. I knew. This was a mercy mission from my point of view. You don't think I could've organized a hit in an abandoned park? An elevator accident? You really think that I need you dressed up as a damned imaginary friend in order to persuade him to leave the building and cross the street at the right time? For someone who arranges halves of accidents and calls himself a coincidence maker, you think a bit too much of yourself. You've been doing the same things for too long, deliberating for hours about organizing a little stomachache for a five-year-old girl. Yes, yes, I know all about you. I reviewed your missions. This was supposed to be a mission that would boost your advancement, that would force you to make a ballsy decision. You think the world can be changed with flowers? No, no, sweetheart. Flowers have never yet changed the world. Spears, perhaps. Rifles, definitely. Bombs have changed the world and will continue to do so, trust me. But not flowers. And if you want to start to move things in the world, big things, you should stop this emotional touchy-feeliness of yours."

"I like to change little things," Guy said quietly.

"So stay here, in your small, protected square. Organize meetings of couples who will divorce after five years, make people understand their 'dreams' only to discover ten years later that they have no way of realizing them and that they gave up everything for them—for nothing. Sketch drawings on the walls to the end of your days. Until you sign the Waiver, bitter and full of frustration. Like your friend."

Guy looked up in shock. "What?"

"Emily," said Pierre with a contented smile. "She too didn't have what it takes, apparently."

Guy's face became ashen.

Emily signed the Waiver. What the hell was she thinking?

He tried to concentrate on his thoughts but discovered that Pierre's scornful voice was still penetrating his mind.

"Do you think she actually realized that she was doing the mop-up work of other coincidence makers? Organizing in patterns the sawdust that falls on the floor when real coincidence makers are sawing? Perhaps. Maybe she was just fed up. That happens when you feel your role is insignificant."

Pierre turned back toward the street. A small dot came into view on the horizon.

"The bus is approaching, sweetheart. You still have time to develop a backbone. You can still get your first taste of how it feels to generate real change in the world. Or you can stay here, tell yourself how ethical you are, and remain as significant as a banana peel on the sidewalk. That can cause someone to slip and fall, you know."

Guy heard the bus engine roaring forward.

The hot air at the bus stop swirled around them. Pierre was still standing erect, facing the street. Guy was still sitting, slouched on the broken seat.

"How dare you?" Guy said finally.

"Excuse me?" Pierre raised an eyebrow.

"When exactly did this happen to you, huh?" Guy asked, raising his voice over the sound of the approaching bus. "When exactly did you reach the level of hubris that made you lose your sanity and think that you're so special that you can decide on the death of someone, simply because it serves your purposes?"

"Listen now—"

"No, you listen to me!" shouted Guy. "You're a creator of presidents and organizer of revolutions, but you can't arrange a way out of this situation without an unnecessary death? No, no. I don't believe it. You can! You could organize much more than this. But it wouldn't be dramatic enough, right? That wouldn't give you the tingle that makes you feel powerful, that you're somebody! Those bits of reality that I change, sir, are people's lives. At what stage exactly did you forget that? At what stage did you start to treat everything like a big game in which you needed to accumulate points?"

"Calm down. That's not what I meant when I said 'develop a backbone,'" Pierre said coldly.

"Shut up!" Guy screamed. "I prefer to remain 'small and insignificant' forever rather than lose my soul in order to look at things like you do. *You* choose how to make your coincidences. *You* choose. They don't happen on their own. And now I'm choosing how to make my coincidences, and it's not going to include anyone's execution."

"Calm down—"

"Shut up! My whole existence, I've been carrying out orders. All this time, while I've been running around like crazy, organizing and preparing and making coincidences, I've actually been passive. As an imaginary friend, I was passive because I had to be. I was forbidden to express my opinion or to change anything that was contrary to the feelings of my imaginer. One time I rebelled and dared to stand up to my imaginer and I was punished with years of nonexistence.

"And then I got the opportunity to be active, to change things, to move them to what I feel is the right place. But instead of that, I became subservient to envelopes. I let myself become part of the system, simply because it was comfortable and pleasant and offered a sense of belonging. From my first envelope until today, I only saw a mission that had to be performed. I advanced along the safe path to become like you, someone so absorbed in self-admiration for excellent performance that he doesn't see the souls of those affected by his coincidence making. But no longer."

The bus was thirty or forty yards away. They could smell it now.

"I'm not getting on it," said Guy. "You can do it yourself."

"You will get on it," said Pierre. "There's no other option. With all due respect to your fiery speech, we need to carry out a mission."

"And with all due respect to *your* fiery speech," Guy said, "you know where you can stick it."

The bus stopped next to them.

The door opened.

"Two things," Pierre said, placing his foot on the first step, "I'll do this now, but you, my friend—you're not going to make any more coincidences involving people. I'm going to personally make sure that you'll be assigned the matchmaking of reptiles and bugs for the rest of your life.

"And secondly, with all the bullshit about how you're sick and tired of being passive, maybe you should consider the fact that your little rebellion is based on *not* doing something. Not very active, if you ask me. As always, even when you rebel, you choose the easy way."

The door closed behind him with a dense blast of air. The bus started to drive away until it was out of sight.

Guy sat there for nearly another minute, and the blazing sun illuminated the spiraling clouds of dust around him.

And then he got up and started to run.

24

Okay, that could've been handled better, he thought.

The surroundings quickly swept past him through the windows of the bus.

He didn't have to get so carried away. And he should've stuck with his original plan and refrained from improvising. But he didn't go beyond the limits he had set for himself. No big deal. We're still advancing according to plan.

He felt uncomfortable about the things he'd said. Guy didn't deserve to hear those things. He was really okay, all in all.

Yes, he had gotten carried away.

The bus entered the city. Here, it was about to happen.

What was that stuff about "organizing the births of presidents"? That was really a critical mistake. There was no such thing as "organizing the births of presidents." People choose to become presidents after they were born, not before. The fourth rule of free will. It was included in their exams. If he noticed that mistake, it could ruin everything. After all these years, he still made rookie mistakes sometimes. "Births of presidents"—come on, really?

In any event, he had to hope that there'd be no more disturbances and that all of the calculations were correct.

After all, this was only one small hitch; this feeling of disgust was completely unnecessary.

Here's the intersection.

In a moment, the bus will need to turn right.

And here he is, still not suspecting anything. And now, just at the right second, he needs to lean forward a bit and . . .

"Hey, weren't you supposed to stop at that bus stop there?"

The bus driver turned his head toward him. "What?"

But he wasn't looking at the driver. He was looking at the person who now appeared in front of the bus. He saw his hands waving, and for one second their eyes met before the crash.

He couldn't help thinking, Mission accomplished.

FROM THE LETTER DISSEMINATED AMONG STUDENTS IN THE COINCIDENCE MAKERS COURSE WITH THE AIM OF ENCOURAGING INITIATIVE

To all of the students in the course:

As you know, in about a month you will complete your course of studies and begin a period of apprenticeship as coincidence makers.

PLEASE NOTE!!!

Over the years, a regretful practice has taken root: Graduates of the Coincidence Makers Course have created what they call "Graduation Coincidences" (GCs).

The consequences of an "amusing," "cool," or "clever" coincidence performed without professional guidance and without prior approval are liable to be severe!!!*

There is a strict prohibition on all activities of unapproved coincidence making, as funny as they may be!!!

A student who creates a GC risks being disqualified and expelled from the course!!!
You have been warned!!!
Let's complete the course safely and quietly!!!

---

*Coincidences that are ostensibly harmless, such as two Hollywood actresses arriving at a ceremony in the same dress, organizing strange hitches in live television broadcasts, or filling a café with people who all suffer from diarrhea are also liable to have far-reaching repercussions. Any irresponsible organizing of coincidences is liable to pose difficulties for coincidence makers, who will have to work hard to mitigate the cumulative impact.

25

The room was a bit cool when Alberto entered.

He always turned on the air conditioner before he left. It was important to come back to a pleasant room. But now he wasn't paying any attention to that.

He didn't lie down on the bed and gaze outside either, or sit on the balcony with a glass of whiskey and ice. He simply started to pack, wondering whether he was pleased or terrified. A hit man wasn't supposed to be terrified. He was pleased, apparently.

He had seen his target leave the building. Tall, dressed in a dark blue suit, quick steps, precise, hands clenched inside his pockets. Another target. All in all, just another target. But then, three surprises occurred.

The first surprise was that his target suddenly turned and decisively started to cross the street.

He had expected him to go to the parking lot. But Alberto discovered, as if for the first time in his life, that targets had lives of their own and could decide to cross the street as if there were something interesting on the other side.

He tracked the man in the suit in his gun sight, trying to calculate the best time to shoot him before he reached the other side of the street and went out of his range of sight.

The second surprise was that his man stopped in the middle of the street.

For a moment it seemed like he intended to go back. Alberto had no idea what could distract someone to the point of stopping in the middle of the street and contemplating like that. A second later, he understood.

It's going to be an accident, he thought. Excellent. The whole thing lasted just a second and a half. His target hesitated for a moment, looked back, and stopped for another moment, which was just long enough for Alberto to focus the crosshairs on his chest, to get to the point between inhaling and exhaling, to switch the rifle to single-shot mode, to place his finger on the trigger, and . . .

And then came the third surprise.

A short screeching of brakes, a white taxi that stopped in front of his target, an irritable driver who put his head out the window and shouted. The man in the suit raised his hands apologetically and continued to slowly walk to the other side of the street, out of the range of his gun's sight.

Alberto's finger was still on the trigger, and he felt like he was choking.

Nothing. Nothing happened. He knew it was the moment when it was supposed to happen. He felt that tingle, that strong desire blended with a sense of confidence, the slightly heavy breathing that had marked these moments for him in the past.

This moment came and went, and nothing happened.

And if he didn't get ahold of himself now and kill his target in the two and a half seconds that remained, it wouldn't happen.

Everything moved in slow motion.

The target down below, walking contemplatively to the other side of the street.

His gun sight, which ran after the target until it closed in on him.

The clear understanding that now he had to kill a person—for real. Not wait for him to die on his own. Kill him.

The crosshairs positioned exactly in the right place.

The finger on the trigger. The decision to shoot. The command his brain sent toward the finger, which ran down the back of his neck, turned right by his shoulder blades, moved across the shoulder, slid like black oil down his arm and reached the finger, and then, and then, and then . . .

And then, the defiant finger refused to execute the command.

The target disappeared out of sight.

Alberto Brown wasn't really capable of killing a human being.

As he sat on the plane and the runway started to pass in the window alongside him, he realized that he wasn't pleased and that he wasn't terrified. He simply felt a great sense of relief. He had withstood one real test. One simple choice, after which the quietest and most efficient killer in the Northern Hemisphere became just a man with a hamster. Just a man.

A man who now would go into hiding, who would have to change his identity, and perhaps would be unable to stay in the same place for very long; a man who left a loaded rifle on the roof of a building because he was so full of frustration and fear and happiness that he purchased a plane ticket to the first place he saw on the Departures board.

But just a man.

The door closed gently behind Michael, as if he were being careful not to wake anyone, though he knew that she—the only person in the house—was probably not sleeping, even if she was lying in bed.

It was late. He hadn't come straight home from the office.

After he crossed the street to a store on the other side and made his small purchase, he felt something different, new. The air outside was cool, and the first breath he took after leaving the store was like an infant's first breath: really surprising. As if only now he remembered how to breathe, as if he had died and returned to life. And then he shook his head and looked at the small bag in his hand and wondered, almost out loud, how he had ever thought this could change something.

He quietly leaned his briefcase against the door, and gently laid the keys on the table by the entrance. One of his hands moved automatically toward his neck, ready to loosen the tie, and he remembered that he had already done that earlier, when he let his legs and thoughts carry him along the streets. He'd roamed around for hours, asking himself again and again what the hell he thought he was doing, and why this attempt would succeed unlike all the rest, which had failed.

A light was still on in the kitchen, and he entered and poured himself a glass of cold water. His legs quickly and decisively kicked off his shoes and lovingly accepted the coolness of the floor through his socks. He stood in the kitchen and drank the glass of water in small sips, stopping every second or two and breathing a bit. He was surprised to discover that he was actually excited.

Less than an hour ago, it had looked like a closed case. After returning to the office parking lot after his roaming, the bag in his hand was unbearably heavy, full to the brim with exaggerated expectations. He had opened the trunk of the car and tossed it inside, almost with loathing, and cursed himself for his naïveté, cursed Medium John for the illusion he had planted in him, and cursed the entire world.

As he drove home he felt like he was returning to himself slowly. The oppressive feeling, to which he had grown so accustomed that it had become second nature, returned. This is your life, this is who you are—now deal with it. The book lying in the trunk was just one more desperate attempt at love, but this time he nipped it in the bud. It would only be a waste of time. Of his time and hers.

He sat in the usual evening traffic jam and inhaled the air-conditioning with the familiar smell.

On the radio, the broadcaster had stuttered something about "a slight mix-up . . ." and a song started to play.

Michael finished drinking the water and placed the glass in the sink.

They must have thought he was crazy, he thought, and allowed himself to smile. And why shouldn't they?

What else were people supposed to think when they saw, in the middle of the traffic jam, a tall man in a suit open his car door, step outside, and start to dance and shed tears to the sounds of the radio? What would they know about songs that became emotional Trojan horses? What was the chance of one of them understanding or guessing the look she had in her eyes when she played this song on her stereo and told him, "You're going to dance with me now, I won't take no for an answer!"

After all, the only thing they saw was someone standing in the middle of the street, his car almost shaking from the volume of the speakers, and him gyrating like an idiot, simply because that was how he thought you were supposed to dance back then, because it made her laugh. How could they understand?

They didn't beep their horns, they didn't open their windows, and they didn't yell. Or maybe they did, for all he knew. He wasn't really there. He just danced and danced, and all of those layers that he had wrapped around himself in recent years, all of them cracked and disintegrated and fell off him like a mantle of dried, muddy despair. With eyes closed and hands flapping, he abandoned all orderly thought, and when the song ended and he finished jumping, he got back into the car and closed the door and turned off the radio. And he also closed the gate in his mind that allowed the entry of any idea that started with the words: "But it's impossible to . . ."

And by the end of the trip, even after his pulse had slowed and he had calmed down, the book in the trunk had become something throbbing and real again. He made a point of not wiping away the tears but instead let them dry on his face and leave their clear salty sediment, like a battle scar, on his cheek, proving that he had participated in a war for his soul and had been victorious in at least one battle.

He slowly went up the stairs and quietly entered the bedroom.

She was lying there, her back turned away from him.

He didn't want to arrive with expectations.

He wasn't there to fix her, or to change her, or to liberate her.

He was the one who needed change. He was going to work on himself.

He realized this the moment the song started to play.

He sat down on the bed, his back leaning against the headboard, the book in his hands.

"You've never read this?" he remembered asking her.

She shrugged her shoulders then. "Guilty as charged," she confessed. "I always promised myself I would, I knew that I must, yet somehow, in a sort of strange coincidence, I never happened to get my hands on it."

"We need to read it someday."

"We must." She nodded at the time.

Maybe she was sleeping now, maybe not.

Maybe she would hear, maybe not.

It didn't matter. He didn't expect miracles or dramatic changes. He prepared himself to take small steps. He opened the book.

"Here is Edward Bear, coming downstairs now, bump, bump, bump, on the back of his head, behind Christopher Robin," he started to read aloud.

He would continue to read, till the end, or until he fell asleep.

He saw that her breathing was changing slightly; he knew she was listening. By the time he had finished reading the book, the first rays of light had entered the room, turning the specks of dust into small, slow-moving stars. And he placed the book next to the bed and allowed himself to sleep for an hour or two. Months later he would remember that at this moment, even though she was fast asleep, and her face was still gray, it was turned toward him.

26

For the first one hundred yards, it was still anger. Then came one hundred yards of fear, and a sense of urgency. Now he was simply hurrying to do the right thing.

Guy sprinted through the streets, his chest rapidly rising and falling, his strides long and fast, his brain calculating routes.

He knew this city, he knew it well. He didn't need to draw anything on a wall now. He saw in his mind the entire city from above, the way in which the traffic flowed and stopped in complex patterns, the people hurrying in the streets, the way the city breathed. It was as if someone had turned the lens a bit and, lo and behold, everything became sharp and clear.

He had known this city well for a long time. But now he discovered that he could actually do all of the calculations in his head. He didn't need a notebook, a wall, anything. He could run in the street and know exactly when each of the pedestrians would appear in front of him and where they would go. He could see the route the bus would travel, calculate the chances that it would stop at the bus stops, know its precise cruising speed when it hit Michael's indecisive body. He was no longer at rank two. He saw this; he saw the picture of the entire city.

And he was part of it, part of the equation.

He had been an observer for too long.

An observer who intervened and navigated, who examined and checked, measured and moved things an inch to the right or half an inch to the left, but always just an observer. A small and disciplined soldier who moved mountains with the power of a pivot point he never set.

Like a mug of coffee that fell from a table, he was just an instrument, not looking to the right or left, because he was afraid to formulate his own opinion. He was afraid of being someone who occasionally slammed on the brakes, pulled over on the side of the road, and wondered: "Perhaps . . . ?"

He would stop the bus. He would make a new coincidence on his own. A better one, a more correct one. He wouldn't be a butcher, he'd be a surgeon. Because all this time, when he thought he was making coincidences, he was just another link in the chain.

The anger returned and flared in him when he thought again about the disdain in Pierre's eyes a moment before he boarded the bus. But the little bastard was right. He always chose to be passive. Even when he did the most active things, they weren't his. His actions filled his surroundings with energy, it's true, but *he* was passive.

So now, he was taking action.

And this time he had even less to lose.

This had happened to him once before, just one time.

He remembered. He was an imaginary friend of a desperate prisoner in solitary confinement, narrow and smothering. He had sat next to him in the dark cell, silent most of the time, occasionally humming a song to him. He saw him quietly eating the foul-smelling food, lying in the corner and shivering from the cold, kneeling in his vomit and trying to regain his sanity. But Guy wasn't allowed to do anything that his imaginer didn't want. Every once in a while, a mouse would come to the cell, sniff around, and disappear, and Guy felt that the prisoner was ceasing to imagine him and instead turning all of his attention and love to the mouse. Occasionally, a distant car horn could be heard and sometimes even a hoarse birdcall. Each of these things was enough to make his imaginer abandon him and desperately cling to what existed on the outside.

"I think he's losing it," he told Cassandra during their last conversation. "I think he's going to give up."

"How do you know?" she asked.

"He no longer imagines me humming songs. He imagines me only out of habit. He doesn't really want me to be there. It's as if I'm there and he only consents to it."

The next time the prisoner imagined him, Guy found him a moment before his death.

He had cut the cloth that covered the filthy mattress and prepared a strong noose. Guy appeared in front of him and saw him standing on the toilet in the corner, with the rope already tightened around his neck.

"That's it," the prisoner said. "I have no more strength. I'm going to her. At least there, with her, I won't be alone."

And Guy was supposed to say, "Go in peace, she's waiting."

He was supposed to say it.

That's what the prisoner imagined he would say.

But he said, "No," and saw the prisoner's eyes dilate in astonishment.

He only had a few seconds to act before the prisoner decided that he was insane and the fear would erase Guy from his imagination. He jumped and grabbed the noose and pulled it over his imaginer's head. And a moment before the prisoner's brain instinctively rejected him and he faded away, he still managed to whisper to him, "There's still a lot to live for." And then he vanished.

He didn't remember a hearing or a reprimand, but he was stripped of existence for years. He didn't even know exactly how many.

When he returned to his role as an imaginary friend, the boy who had imagined him sitting on the bench near Cassandra had grown up. He never met her again. He didn't even have time to worry about leaving without telling her in advance. He had almost no time to think about her sitting there with her girl time after time, discovering that he was not coming anymore. He was afraid to think about the possibility that another imaginary friend was there in his place.

It was the only time in his entire existence when he had dared. When he had been active. Was it any surprise that as a coincidence maker, he never chanced to be more than an instrument?

Guy turned quickly to the right.

Here, he was back.

Him. Not his physical representation, not his job description, not his thoughtless actions. Him. He was here again.

He would stop the bus here, just after the next turn, three blocks before the vehicle was supposed to hit Michael. He would disrupt Pierre's calculated timetable and organize a new coincidence that would restore Alberto to his desired place without unnecessarily killing anyone. He could do it.

In his mind, he saw the place where the bus was supposed to be. It had to travel a slightly longer route than the one Guy ran. Guy knew all of the city's bus routes by heart, and this bus was on quite a long route.

He burst into the street, suddenly realizing how physically unfit he was—how much this run had caught him unprepared. Here, he leaped in front of the wheels of the bus, which arrived precisely according to plan. Here, he waved his hands and tried to shout "Stop!" and discovered that his breath was so short that the shout went almost unheard.

And here, the bus didn't slow down, and one look at the driver showed that he wasn't even looking at the road. The driver had glanced back toward someone who had asked something exactly a second earlier.

And here, the small, short terror that rolled in his guts when Guy recognized this someone. Someone who didn't look back at the driver, who hadn't asked in order to receive an answer, but who was looking forward, at Guy, straight into his eyes, while the bus cruised forward and rammed into his body.

27

The flights flashed on the electronic board.

Three of them were scheduled to depart in minutes, but as hard as he tried, he couldn't understand what was written there, and what their destinations were.

Guy sat on a metal bench in the center of the airport. He was sure there were other people there. After all, he heard a commotion and saw figures passing on his right and left. Still, something inside told him that they were just part of the backdrop, and that he was actually alone.

In all the times he had imagined death, he had never seen a duty-free store, but it turned out that the reality was different.

Opposite him, at the other end of the entrance hall, he saw a line of check-in counters. None of them were manned, except for one. A chubby, balding ground attendant, his head shining a little in the neon lights, sat there, chewing on a pencil, apparently working on a crossword puzzle. Of all the people in motion around him, holding in their hands what he could only describe as the concept of a suitcase, no one approached the check-in counter. The chubby attendant sat there, totally absorbed in solving his crossword puzzle.

Guy examined his own body. No, he didn't appear to be particularly crushed. He looked quite intact. Apparently his smashed body stayed behind, on the street. Was he supposed to feel so indifferent about this?

And why an airport, for crying out loud?

It was strange; he had always thought that after everything was over, existential questions would be resolved, rather than new questions being set at your doorstep. Life was full of surprises, it turned out. And death too. A small, brown suitcase was lying by his foot. He lifted it and examined its weight, surprised to discover that it wasn't constant, that it was alternately heavy and light. He placed it on his knees and opened it.

Inside was his life.

Somehow the suitcase contained much more than he thought it could hold. At some point, he discovered that he was rummaging through it with his hand submerged up to his shoulder. There's a physics problem here, he thought, but actually what difference did it make. . . ? He searched and pulled out objects, letters, pictures, reviewing them quickly.

The face of the first child who imagined him; the taste of his favorite cheesecake; the first time he went to sleep, when he discovered that there was actually such an option; Eric's short, annoying laugh; the sound that leaves made when they crackled underfoot; the sharp pain when you pulled a muscle; Medium John's face peering at him from the mirror and changing; Cassandra laughing.

He poked deeper into the suitcase. If his entire life was arranged here, then that moment should be here too. Where was it?

Finally, he found it, in a corner, placed under his first morning run. A circular, shiny memory. He lifted it up to the light and looked through it.

Winter, snow squalling, bitter cold; he stood on the edge of a barren and terrifying cliff, somewhere in a desert of ice. You couldn't see anything two inches past your nose. His fingertips were losing their sense of feeling, the shoes on his feet were not well insulated. In back of him, he could hear and see the black outline of the wolves growling at the two of them. Cassandra stood a foot or so away from him, but he couldn't see her clearly. The cliff started to lose its stability and he heard her say, "Okay, I'm ready to go back."

He imagined her and she imagined him and they were in the park again, and she was saying this sentence.

He turned the memory a bit toward the light in order to feel it completely, clearly.

"So what they say is apparently true. When the right person is beside you, you feel a sense of belonging anywhere."

He sat there and surveyed the memories that had shaped his life, until he suddenly noticed that something strange was happening around him. When he looked up, he discovered the reason. He was alone. Unequivocal silence filled the empty airport, and the only thing that moved was the head of the ground attendant who sat on the other end. He put back everything he had taken out of the suitcase and closed it. The time had come to find out what was going on here.

"Just a moment," said the attendant when Guy stood in front of him, the suitcase balanced between his legs.

The attendant continued to chew the pencil until he looked up at Guy.

"Maybe you can help me," he said. "What am I supposed to give you? Eight letters. Starts with an *e*."

"Excuse me?" asked Guy.

"I'm supposed to give you something." The attendant scratched his head. "But I'm not good at remembering things before their time comes. The whole business of advanced planning doesn't work well when you are just an idea. It's difficult to think beyond 'now,'" he said.

"You're just a thought?" asked Guy.

"Of course," said the attendant. "You don't really think that death is an airport, do you? I'm something you're creating at the moment."

"Really," said Guy, looking at him obliquely.

"Yes, really. All of you give me this look. And each time, I have to explain it again," the attendant said.

"I'm afraid this is the first time I've died," said Guy. "You haven't explained anything to me yet."

"No, not to you," the attendant said. "To everyone who passes through here. And you're not really dead."

"No?"

"No. At least until you board the flight. Officially, you're not dead."

"Everything in the world has a procedure?" Guy wondered out loud.

"When you say it that way, it sounds like something bad," said the attendant and added, "'envelope.'"

"Excuse me?" asked Guy.

"Eight letters, starts with an *e*. 'Envelope.' I remembered," said the attendant, and he pulled out a long white envelope. "Apparently, I'm supposed to give this to you now."

Guy took the envelope from his hand.

"Is this the user's manual for death, or something like that?" he asked.

"No, no," the attendant said. "Someone who was here a while ago left this for you."

Guy tilted his head in surprise. "For me?"

"Yes," said the attendant, smiling, the pencil still lodged in his mouth. "You can sit here and read it, if you want. And then we'll take your suitcase and bring you onto the plane."

"This suitcase . . . ," said Guy.

"All of your memories," said the attendant.

"I take them with me?" asked Guy.

"Not exactly," said the attendant. "You need to leave it with me, of course."

"And then?"

"And then we'll lose it."

"Lose it?"

"Yes."

"That is, intentionally?"

"Of course not! We lose it by mistake. But this always happens. It's part of the thing."

"What thing?"

"The thing of starting to be alive."

Guy felt a bit confused.

"I thought you said I'll be dead when I board the plane."

"But later you get off the plane," said the attendant, as if stating the obvious.

"And . . . ?"

"When you board the plane, you complete your life as a coincidence maker, and when you disembark from it, you begin as a person."

"A person?" Guy asked tensely.

254 • YOAV BLUM

"A person," said the attendant.

"You mean a real person, a human being, a mortal, a client of coincidences, all these definitions?"

"Yes, yes," the attendant said, still with great patience.

"All of the coincidence makers pass through this airport and are then born as human beings?"

"You're getting into the technical details with me now," the attendant said, scratching his back. "In general, the answer is no and yes."

"And that means?"

"Not all coincidence makers pass through an airport. Only you, because that's how you chose to experience this. But yes, the next stage after being a coincidence maker is being a person."

"And after a person?" asked Guy.

"Don't push it," the attendant told him. "Or, in other words, I have no idea."

"Okay." Something filled Guy with renewed hope. "So I'll just bring my suitcase and board the plane."

"The envelope . . . ," the attendant reminded him. "Maybe you should first read what it contains."

"I can read it on the plane," said Guy.

"No, no, no," the attendant told him, "you can't take anything on the flight. You have to put it in the suitcase with the rest of your memories so that it too will get lost."

"But I just received it," Guy argued. "And it's not exactly a memory from my life."

"From the perspective of the procedure, it is," said the attendant and gestured with his hand. "You can sit there and read. The flight won't leave without you, don't worry."

"Okay," said Guy, and he turned to walk away.

"And if by chance you think of what 'the taste in the mouth' is, six letters, tell me," the attendant called after him.

Guy returned to his place and sat down next to the suitcase.

He felt something unexpected: a great sense of calm. To be a human being. He would definitely be okay with that. He could give up his collection of memories for something like that.

He would read the new procedures contained in the envelope, get himself organized, perhaps drink something (if he could create an airport in his imagination, he could also create a soda machine), and move on to his new life. Life number three. All in all, he was improving, right? This time, he would make better choices.

There was no stamp or address on the white envelope. Just his name, in small letters.

When he opened it and took out the bundle of pages, he was surprised to discover that he could identify the handwriting, and when he read the words, he felt his heart sink.

28

Dear Guy,

So where do I begin?

Apparently, there are two types of people in the world.

There's the type who simply lives his life, focusing on the moment and what to do in it. When love comes along, he smiles at it and allows it to enter, but he isn't really enthralled. He would've done fine without it, but it's nice that it came.

And there's the second type, my type, who feels like he's longing his whole life for someone he has yet to meet, who's constantly waiting for the moment when the longing will stop and someone will walk through the door. We look for meaning in every small gesture. A knock at the door, a stranger who passes by us in a crosswalk, a waiter who smiles—all are signs, all are options that must be checked out. Maybe suddenly, who knows, someone will come and fall exactly into the hole in our hearts, like a toddler who fits a triangular peg into a triangular hole, a square peg into a square hole.

So, then, in the park at the beginning of the course, even though we had just met a moment earlier, it was enough for you to say you were an imaginary friend for the alarms to start going off in my mind. It took about another two weeks, a few questions, some clarifications, and it was clear. Your stories about the past, the words you used, everything fit. And when you mentioned "Cassandra" for the first time, that was it—a round peg in a round hole.

And I—I had to keep quiet.

For a long time, I asked myself: What was the specific point in time when I realized that I was in love with you? What was the equilibrium point, before which you like someone and after which he's the center of your universe?

It's like catching the point when you fall asleep. You lie in bed and try to stay awake, but not too awake, and to be aware of the point when you cross the line into a dream, but then discover too late that you're already inside it.

I have no idea why this happened and when.

But at least now I know that it won't pass. Now I know that you're stuck outside my door and will never enter, that an invisible fence of thorns stands between us, between my current love for you and your imaginary love, that there are things that don't happen. I should have known.

Okay. I'm babbling. We'll start at the beginning.

My first memory is of sitting on a soft sofa with an eight-year-old girl with green eyes leaning on my shoulder, waiting for me to stroke her hair. I had a different name, a different appearance, but I was already completely me then. And after-ward, I stroked her hair every day for many days.

I stroked her hair when it started to thin out, and when it disappeared completely I stroked her bald head, and when she regained her health and the hair started to sprout again, I stroked her wonderful spiky bristles. And when she no longer needed my stroking, I disappeared from her life.

You know the feeling.

Yes, I too was an imaginary friend.

And at first, at the very beginning, I also loved every moment.

There's a difference between male and female imaginary friends, apparently. Much more tenderness, generosity, and understanding is demanded of us. I loved this gentle way of giving, the way in which I could heal wounds that no one else could see.

At first I mainly accompanied boys and girls, just as you did. I strengthened and supported them, I said the right words. Later, to my surprise, a slightly different phase began.

As the years went by, I found myself being imagined more and more frequently by teenagers, by adolescents. And by men. They no longer wanted me to just stroke their heads. They wanted more. Some of them were looking for human warmth, some of them wanted a feeling of power, some of them wanted tender things, some of them wanted twisted and ugly things, and all of them had failed to obtain these things in real life, and so they imagined me instead.

As time passed, I felt more and more used. I embraced the children who wanted me as a friend, and I took consolation in the teenagers who practiced first love on me, but I hoped to quickly get past the moments in which I was a fantasy.

You understand, when I started all this, I had great plans. I planned to mobilize all of the strengths within me in order to change and support, and to be at the side of someone who needed me. But as time went by, I discovered that most of them didn't even want me. They only wanted me to activate the plastic doll they put around me, the mask they forced on my face.

To change? To support? Be beautiful and let us imagine you as we wish. No one wanted to imagine me as I am, and I didn't understand why. I'm not enough?

When you're imagined in this way, you realize that the world operates differently. It operates according to the "I must have more" system and not according to the "exactly what I need" system. What I have to offer, no one wanted to take.

Even the most gentle and lonely men in the world didn't imagine me as a human being, but only as something that helped them activate themselves. Most of them didn't even call me by name. They simply dressed me in the character of a model they saw in magazines. Some of them gave me kitschy names from films they had seen. Only the children sometimes let me introduce myself and call myself by name.

And when they did, I introduced myself as Cassandra.

They never loved me, those men.

Lusted, perhaps. Desired, definitely. Needed, undoubtedly. But that was it. It's impossible to love someone who does and says everything you want, who responds to every hidden thought of yours. I was merely an extension of them; what kind of love is that? Love derives from friction between two people. Like matches, like an ice skate, like falling stars that light up when they scratch the air, we need friction in order for something to happen in our lives.

I tried to find cracks in the rules. Small loopholes that would allow me to make the things I did less empty, to be more than an imaginary friend, less of a doll with a vacant look. I studied all of the rules and regulations related to the world of imaginary friends. I discovered, for example, that it is permissible to say or do things that aren't directly imagined, as long as they aren't completely contrary to the will of my imaginer. It turned out that I could end a "meeting" as I wanted, and not as my imaginer wanted, under very particular conditions. So what? It was almost never possible for me to say no and disappear.

I discovered minor rules that appeared irrelevant, like, for example, that every imaginary friend is allowed to submit a request to become a "permanent friend" of a particular imaginer, and thus become the imaginary friend of only one imaginer. But I didn't have anyone to request.

And then I met you.

An imaginary friend who sparkled like a diamond in a pile of rags.

What are the chances? Tell me, what?

I remember that after our first meeting, after you left, I remained there for nearly a quarter of an hour, with my small, cute Natalie absentmindedly imagining me, sitting next to me, my entire body trembling.

Someone I could talk with, someone who could understand what I was experiencing, someone I could tell things to, lean on, belong with, from the same small group, share a common language with. In my rosiest dreams, I didn't think I'd find another imaginary friend, someone else who could be a friend.

And in the end, it turns out, you were not only a friend, but much more than that.

How did this happen? What captivated me? I have no idea.

The vulnerable moments in which you would raise an eyebrow before saying something you were unsure of; the fact that you were very firm, on the one hand, and would try so hard to be liked, on the other; your smell, elusive and unassuming; the way you spoke to your imagining child; your passion for finding meaning in everything you encountered.

Your rare smile, a bit too flat, yet somehow still captivating. And your laugh.

The way your whole body awakened when you started to laugh about something I said, as if just then you were starting to live, and until then everything had been a dress rehearsal. A small, involuntary jump that turned into an embarrassed cough that became a hopeless attempt to keep serious, that transformed into sweet internal thunder that burst out from you, instantly turning you into a child in front of my eyes. How I love that laugh.

With that laugh, apparently, you got under my skin, without making any effort.

And perhaps that's the way you cleared a drawer for me in your heart.

The fact that someone took a small step backward in order to give me confidence and allow me to see that he was on my side, and that he told me without words, come, I've emptied a little place here for you, for who you are, come put whatever you want here. And suddenly, I was no longer in familiar territory, no longer detached. There was no longer any plastic covering, no shiny mask.

Each time we met, I was sure it would be the last time.

My imaginer, Natalie, no longer spoke with me very much, and it seemed that the end of our period together was near. If you only knew how hard I tried to persuade her that we should go down to the park again the following day or the day after.

And each time we went to the bench and discovered that you were there, I felt like I was passionate with bashfulness. I never thought it was possible to combine such opposites, and yet I did. What a fool.

When we started to imagine each other, it was clear. I was deep into the realm of love.

I was never so sure of myself as when I submitted the request to make you my sole imaginer. Is that the point when you are in love? When you not only choose someone but also accept him ready-made? When you change something inside of you for him? Perhaps.

It was so simple: one moment we sat on that bench and talked, and the next moment, when you disappeared in the middle of a choking laugh, responding to the call of another imaginer, it was clear that I didn't want anyone but you in my life. And that was the only way to achieve this.

I submitted, and I was accepted, and from that point Natalie no longer imagined me. Only you did.

Renaissance. A short and happy period. Bursts of happiness when you chose to imagine me sitting at your side, not using me, not putting words in my mouth, not making me do anything except be myself, just waiting to see how I would make myself real to you. How many imaginary friends can say they were imagined with such freedom?

How short this period was. When you broke the rules and told your imaginer something you were forbidden to say, you disappeared from my life. Both of us waited for each other, each one in a state of nonexistence. No one imagined you, no one imagined me. Time stopped. But when you returned, you didn't believe that I had waited for you. You didn't imagine me anymore. You gave up. So quickly. My little lazybones.

I know this today, after collecting bits of stories about what happened to you. But back then I only knew that I suddenly found myself on a bench, after finishing my role as an imaginary friend, and that I was now embarking on a new role.

You can imagine this feeling. To think that you've lost everything and you need to pave a new path, and then to meet someone, just a moment later, who says that he was an imaginary friend.

The moment you said that, I tried to shout that I was too, but I couldn't. The words got stuck in my throat, as faint as dust, and I didn't understand why.

Only later did things start to make sense to me. Lightning struck twice at the same spot. You were the same one for whom I had already fallen captive. On the first day of the course, the coincidence of my life occurred, but I couldn't do anything with it.

You understand, because you were my official imaginer, that I was forbidden to reveal my identity to you. It was so frustrating, to slowly realize who you were, to hear you tell stories from the past that I already knew, to hear you talk about that "Cassandra" of yours, to evade your questions about my past.

To fall in love with you again, to be disappointed by you.

I made inquiries. I sent an official request. I asked for special permission to tell you who I was.

Three times I submitted a request. I filled out the long forms at night, trying to explain how unreasonable this was. The

General gave me the responses in small white envelopes. Those were the only times I saw him express emotion.

"I'm sorry," he said.

They didn't grant approval, of course. Officially, I was considered someone you imagined, but you weren't considered someone I imagined. And that was it.

But I also tried other methods. I truly thought it would work out. We had already connected once before. You had already loved me. You could love me again, right?

After all, we had built this relationship once, one piece of trust after another. This was supposed to happen to us again. It was so natural.

It turned out that it wasn't. That's what I understand now. When I let you imagine me, I stole from you, and from myself, any possibility of being together in reality. Because you were no longer looking for me. You were no longer even looking for love. You were just stuck remembering, building castles in the air with the part of me that no longer existed.

Indeed, if I had gotten up one day and said, "I'm Cassandra"—I wasn't able to do this, but let's assume I was— would that have changed your feeling for me in any way? And if so, didn't that mean the feeling itself would have been nothing more than self-persuasion derived from the memory of who I once was?

Where was I in all of this?

But you loved me once—me, me, me. Why was I no longer sufficient? Because I wasn't imagined? Why did you become someone who wants "more" and not "exactly," like everything I fled from? Because I was real? Because I was there all the time, not dripping into your life only at the appropriate moments?

How did this happen?

You were the door toward which I fled. An imaginary friend like me, who understood the emptiness and the temptation to be someone else all the time.

And then, when I became real, you no longer wanted me?

How was I supposed to feel?

I'll tell you how. That everything was a lie. And that today too, like then, actually, I don't deserve to have someone love me as I am.

Yesterday evening, I understood everything. Finally.

You're not here. You're not with me.

You're in love with an imaginary woman, and you'll never allow yourself to give up on her for someone who exists, even if they are one and the same.

Until today, I dreamed about you almost every night.

I would find myself in an unfamiliar place, standing frozen and feeling you standing behind me, in the middle of a desert or on a cloud, inside a long tunnel, in thousands of other places. I always felt and knew that you were standing behind me. And each time, I would turn toward you, slowly, with enormous difficulty, as if a herd of horses was trying to stop me, and finally discovered that you were still standing with your back to me.

And when I tried to call you, you would disappear.

That's the way it was in the dream, and if we're honest, that's the way it was in life too.

Last night, I didn't dream about you. I'm releasing you.

I'm moving on, to the next role, whatever it might be.

And I wish you happiness with your memories and

imagination, and hope that someone will one day succeed in breaking the spell you cast upon yourself. For your sake.

Still feeling the same thing,

Yours,

Always,

And perhaps no longer,

Emily

29

Eric sat by the bed where Guy lay.

He wouldn't have to wait much longer. He wondered which transit station Guy had chosen for himself. A train station, a bus station? He had heard of some who made the transition via a movie theater. It was very hard to predict these things.

The device next to the bed monitored Guy's heartbeats, and Eric watched it intently. He focused on the shaky line on the small monitor and silently started counting down to the final heartbeat.

A nice device, almost poetic. A single line with a simple statement: if there were no ups and downs, you were no longer alive.

It was a lot more comfortable when there were instruments around, it turned out. With Emily, it was much more difficult to determine the specific point when her heart stopped beating. But here, here the soft beeping did half the job for him. Poor Emily, how frightened she was when she saw him there at the door, a second before she fell to the ground, a second before he lunged at her and stretched his hand toward her heart.

"The doctors don't know you're going to die," he whispered to Guy. "They still haven't detected the internal injury. That's what happens when the doctor sees you after thirty-six hours without sleeping."

Guy didn't move.

"You know, I'm always surprised to discover how easy this is," said Eric. "It's all just a matter of how much time you're willing to invest, how much patience you have. People are so accustomed to looking at cause and effect as something immediate. The moment you make the mental jump to a world in which they can be spread over a very long time, it's much easier to understand them."

The instruments continued to beep, expressing agreement, or something similar.

"It was nice knowing you," Eric said. "You should know you're quite a funny guy when you want to be."

He fell silent for a moment and pondered.

"When you wanted to be," he repeated.

He bent forward a bit, sitting more comfortably. His elbows were resting on his knees, his fingertips pressed against each other.

"I hope you won't be angry. When you find out. If you find out." He tilted his head and thought. "I very much doubt that will happen, to tell you the truth. But if it makes any difference, I really like you. You were one of my favorites. I like the ones who lack confidence and are unaware of their lack of confidence. To a certain extent, it's like a beautiful woman who doesn't know she's beautiful. Your blind spot toward yourself makes you more interesting."

Very soon, he'll need to be ready to reach out his hand at the right moment.

"I told the nurse that I'm your brother," he said. "I hope you don't mind. I have no idea why she believed it; we're not similar at all. People see in you what they want to see, it turns out. With a sufficiently worried face, they're certain that you're a family member, even if you aren't so similar.

"On the other hand, I had to change my appearance quite a bit for you. After all, you know how much I detest mustaches. They itch and make the face ugly. I always thought the mustache was invented by someone who forgot to shave because he didn't have a mirror. But when you choose a name like Pierre for yourself, a thin mustache is almost a moral obligation, right?"

Guy didn't respond.

"Have a good trip, buddy," Eric said tenderly. "However you choose to travel."

Guy's last heartbeats appeared on the monitor, and Eric reached out his hand.

At exactly the same place, and at an infinite distance from there, Guy folded the letter and sat limply, his arms drooping in front of him.

He looked up and again discovered that the airport was completely empty. Just the bald attendant sat at the other end of the hall and looked at him curiously.

He looked down and saw the small suitcase waiting for him, practically staring at him with eyes full of hope.

If he had any energy when he started to read, none of it remained now. To hell with everything.

He got up slowly, the envelope and the folded letter in one hand, the suitcase in the other. He walked toward the check-in counter. The eyes of the attendant were still fixed on him.

The distance he had traversed before so quickly now seemed end-less. He moved slowly. He didn't care. Finally, he arrived and put down the suitcase.

"I would like one ticket, please," he said in a flat voice.

It was as if the attendant awoke from a deep sleep. "Terrific. No problem," he said. He looked down at the screen in front of him and typed quickly. "Did you happen to think about my question?" he asked hopefully.

"Excuse me?" said Guy.

"The taste in the mouth," the attendant said, still typing. "Six letters."

"I have no idea, sorry," said Guy.

"It's okay," said the attendant.

He continued to type at a rapid pace.

Guy thought for a moment. " 'Bitter.' "

The attendant looked at him quizzically before raising his eye-brows in joy. "Right! Right! That fits with the *b* in twelve-down," he said. "Good job!"

"Happy to help," Guy said sourly.

The attendant didn't take notice. "Place the suitcase here please, on the conveyor belt," he said.

Guy did as he was told.

"And also the envelope with the letter," the attendant added.

"I . . . I want to keep this, if possible," said Guy.

The attendant shook his head sadly. "That's impossible, unfortu-nately."

"That's all that I have left from . . ."

"You can't carry memories from a previous life," the attendant said. "Rule number two. Number one is not to urinate in public places, number two is not to take memories from a previous life."

Guy looked at him, frustrated.

"Umm, I'm not good at jokes, apparently," the attendant said. "Sorry." He pointed at the suitcase. "Put it there, inside."

Guy opened the suitcase and looked for the last time.

Some of the memories came closer now. Memories of Cassandra and memories of Emily crowded side by side, like distant relatives rediscovering each other. . . .

"There's something I need to check," said Guy.

He rummaged through the merging memories until he found what he was searching for. Slowly he stood up over the suitcase with two memories, one in each hand. Cassandra's laugh and Emily's.

He held them up to the light and examined them, one in each hand, and the two laughs rolled, sparkled, and twirled in his hands, the light passing through them and falling on his face. They were exactly the same. How, how had he failed to notice, how?

He put them back into the suitcase, and they hurried to move closer to each other and embrace, giggling.

For several moments, he looked at the envelope in his hand without saying a word. He looked at the attendant, who again signaled that he should put the letter inside.

He bent over and put the envelope into the suitcase, covering a few memories of Emily and of Cassandra with it, then closed and locked it again.

"That wasn't so hard, right?" The attendant smiled and handed him the ticket.

The conveyor belt began to move and the suitcase started to fade into the distance until finally it disappeared in the small opening at the back of the terminal.

"And thus," Guy said quietly, "my life as a coincidence maker ends and life as a person begins."

The attendant typed absentmindedly on his keyboard. "Well, okay, but that's not exactly true," he said.

272 · YOAV BLUM

"Excuse me?" said Guy.

"Maybe not every coincidence maker is a person, but every person is also a coincidence maker," the attendant said. "You didn't go over this in the course?"

"Apparently we didn't go over a lot of things." Guy smiled.

"Oh, a smile!" The attendant rejoiced. "I thought it would never come." He smiled at him in return. "You're at Gate One," he said and pointed. "Have a good trip."

"Thank you."

He turned and walked away, still smiling to himself, but not for the reason the attendant thought.

Somewhere on its way to getting lost was his suitcase, and it contained everything that had happened till now, including a long white envelope with his name written on it.

But the letter itself—the letter itself was stuffed under his shirt, next to his heart.

"It's a bit like being a magician—you make them look in one direction, and do something somewhere else."

While he'd bent over to place the envelope inside—making sure to flash it in front of the attendant—he was also stuffing the folded bundle of papers cautiously under his clothes. It was probably the sharpest, smoothest, and most decisive movement he had ever made in his blurry life, and he felt as if all the rest had only been preparation. When he stood up again and looked at the attendant, he realized he had succeeded. The attendant hadn't noticed.

And thus, with the pages of Emily's letter attached to his body, and with a small smile on his lips whose full meaning he had yet to understand, he walked with a straight back, plane ticket in hand, and entered Gate 1, excited about his small rebellion, the last in his old life.

———

"If someday a white grand piano falls on you while you're walking down the street and you lose your memory, there's one thing that's still important for you to remember," the General said. "You can forget your name, the names of the stars in the solar system, and the ingredients in margarine, but please remember this. There are two types of people in the world: those who see in every choice the possibility to gain something, and those who see in every choice the concession they need to make.

"People are free, and they forget this all the time. People hope in different ways, people are afraid in different ways. There are people who warn themselves that if they do x then y will happen to them, and there are people who explain to themselves why y is a good reason to abstain from x. This is ostensibly the same thing, ostensibly the same decision, but there is always a difference between checking the possibilities and mapping the obstacles. Courage is indeed important; people don't understand what really constitutes courage. Every choice entails giving something up, and the courage required to make that sacrifice depends on how much you want something. Because, ultimately, you can't always be right in your choices. Occasionally you'll screw up, and not only occasionally.

"The difference is simple: happy people look at their lives and see a series of choices. Miserable people see only a series of sacrifices. Before every action you take when making a coincidence, you must confirm which type of person you're working with—the hopeful or the fearful. They look similar. They are not."

Eric exited the hospital and walked placidly along the street.

Upstairs, one of the doctors pronounced Guy's death.

Eric got what he needed.

In his pocket, warm and flashing, was Guy's last heartbeat. He decided he had time for a quick coffee before getting to the crosswalk.

And perhaps a piece of cake too.

He'd decide when he got there.

A bit of spontaneity, heh?

30

For every beginning, there is a beginning that preceded it.

That's the first rule.

That means that this rule also has a rule that preceded it, of course. But that's a different story.

When does life begin?

Is it the moment when the baby's head emerges into the world? Or perhaps his entire body has to come out?

Or perhaps it's only later, when he says his first word and becomes human in his own eyes?

And maybe it happens much earlier, the moment the sperm and the egg meet and get to know each other?

Every beginning has a beginning that preceded it. Life is a continuum, not a specific event.

But there is one point that is a bit problematic in this context.

The first heartbeat.

The first heartbeat generates the second one, and the second the third, but what generates the first heartbeat?

It happens somewhere during the fifth week, the doctors say. There are various and sundry explanations for how this occurs, but these explanations don't really make any difference to the heartbeats themselves. They still need something to get them started.

And thus, driven by the law that precedes the first law, another type of person roams the world. They aren't transparent, like imaginary friends, but neither do they exist like coincidence makers. They are seen and unseen, existent and nonexistent, imaginary and real exactly to the same extent, and they rove among us.

Occasionally they stand beside a pregnant woman, reach out a hand secretly and stealthily, and at precisely the right moment, grasp the new little heart between two fingers and give it one small squeeze. And that's it.

They are the igniters.

Quiet, covert, and very gentle (there aren't many things in the world as fragile as the heart of a five-week-old fetus), they are generally the best in their field when and if they decide to become coincidence makers.

Eric stands in the crosswalk. The red light lasted five seconds before surrendering to the passage of time and turning green, and people from both sides started to flow into the street.

This will be quick, so pay attention.

Here's the green-eyed woman; here's Eric.

He's walking slowly and with concentration; she's crossing the street opposite him, erect in posture and deep in thought.

Here, they're approaching each other.

Now we'll slow the world a bit. Pay attention.

Here, Eric is putting his hand into his pocket and pulling out Guy's last heartbeat.

Here, they're drawing closer and closer.

And now they're exactly next to each other.

And here, he's reaching his hand out sideways, and without even the birds noticing, he inserts the heartbeat in the small heart waiting inside the green-eyed woman. There's no need to squeeze. The last heartbeat is inserted in a smooth motion and becomes a first heartbeat.

And here, they're moving away from each other.

Eric smiles to himself. That was simpler than Emily's last heartbeat, he thought. He had also planted it in a small heart that longed for activity. It was so simple. Like riding a bike. You don't forget.

Once an igniter, always an igniter, he thought to himself.

On the other side of the street, life was beginning.

FROM *INTRODUCTION TO COINCIDENCES,*
PART I

Look at the line of time.

Of course, it is only an illusion. Time is a space, not a line.

But for our purposes, look at the line of time.

Watch it. Identify how each event on the line is both a cause and effect. Try to locate its starting point.

You will not succeed, of course.

Every now has a before.

This is probably the main—though not the most obvious—problem you will encounter as coincidence makers.

Therefore, before studying theory and practice, formulas and statistics, before you start to make coincidences, let's start with the simplest exercise.

Look again at the line of time.

Find the correct spot, place a finger on it, and simply decide: "This is the starting point."

1

Three hours before marking a small ✓ in his notebook, the man who had once called himself Eric and long ago stopped calling himself Pierre sat in a café and sipped from his cup with deliberate slowness.

Here too, like always, timing was everything, but he had a little more time, and he could actually allow himself to let the events happen on their own. That was the power of precise preparation. He had already fed the pigeon, plugged up the sewer, and even organized a rotten fish on the plate of the statistics professor yesterday, just to be sure.

He sat with his long body leaning back a bit from the table and reviewed the events in his mind again, the small cup of coffee gently held between his fingers. From the corner of his eye, he watched the progress of the second hand on the big clock hanging over the cash register. As always, in the final moments of implementation, he would enjoy going over the full picture of events in his mind, if only to confirm that there were no cracks in it.

"I thought it'd be simpler," he had said to Baum when they sat right here, at this café.

"I told you," Baum had said, "there's a reason five coincidence makers returned this mission uncompleted. The objective is not to get them to meet, but to make it so that the connection will last."

They sat and drank beer together. That was back when he had been Baum's personal assistant. Years of work alongside someone who was touted as the greatest coincidence maker of all time had helped him to see things in a much clearer way when he at last set off on an independent path. But this mission appeared to be very complex, even borderline impossible.

"The laws of imaginary friends are very strict in this matter," Baum told him. "From the beginning, I didn't understand why you took this mission. Everyone knows that one doesn't organize coincidences that include imaginary friends. That always complicates things."

"I thought there was no problem in remaining someone's imaginary friend over time," he said.

"Correct," said Baum, "but for that, one of them has to imagine the other. It's not called 'getting them together.' The first rule in love is that it can't exist only in the imagination of either person."

"I know." He remembered his heavy sigh. "I need to make them quit."

"It's impossible to quit being an imaginary friend," Baum noted offhandedly. "They have to be fired, or there has to be an official transfer request. And this must happen simultaneously, otherwise you'll have excessively large age differences in the next job. And even if you cause them to be fired, who knows which job they'll be transferred to? Forget it. Return the mission."

"But I've already started to move things."

"Submit a retroactive cancellation form."

"I don't return missions," he said. "When I start something, I finish it."

Baum shook his head. "Whatever you say. Principles are something I respect."

"So what am I supposed to do?"

Baum thought a bit. "That's a good question." He took another sip from his glass and said, "Honestly, I have no idea."

The moment Baum said this, it was clear to Eric that he had to find a way.

He would solve the problem for which Baum saw no solution. He would—and must—find a solution.

It had to be something that wouldn't occur only in the imagination, and which would be true and natural. And wouldn't break the rules. Ugh—he really couldn't stand that third rule.

He had called Baum and said, "I need your help with something."

And of course, Baum said, "I know."

"I need to organize a Coincidence Makers Course. We'll submit a request to transfer my two clients."

"Yes, yes."

"The course will be quite small, just three people."

"I said I know."

"You enjoy knowing in advance what people are going to say, huh?"

"You have no idea how much."

———

And now he was about to witness the final chord in a symphony of coincidences.

Or the opening one—depending on how you looked at it.

He got up from his chair and signaled to the waitress that he had left a tip, folded under the empty cup. As he went out into the hot sun, he took a deep breath. It was time to go to the park.

1

The moment she left the house, she felt today would be a good day. Perhaps it was the way the light poured onto the sidewalk; perhaps it was that new and strange aroma from the balcony of her neighbor on the first floor; perhaps it was because her shift had been canceled again and she had at least one whole day to be by herself. In any case, today would be a good day.

Something white, semiliquid, and indescribably disgusting landed on her right shoulder, and she looked up just in time to see the flash of a fast, rude pigeon with now-empty bowels. Without saying a word, she went back in to change her clothes.

When she emerged from the house again, this time wearing a red dress with white stripes, she decided that the good day would actually start *n-o-w.*

"Your book still hasn't arrived," the bookseller told her.

He was a pimpled, indifferent young man who was playing a game on his telephone while, all around him, the world's treasures waited patiently for him to take a break and consider reading them.

"Do you have any idea when it will arrive?" she asked. "Because these coupons are only good until tomorrow."

"It won't come tomorrow," he said. "It'd be best for you to look for something else instead. There are new books in the corner that I haven't arranged yet."

He gestured with his head toward the corner of the small store and immediately refocused on his telephone. Priorities.

It wasn't the first time this had happened. She had a plan for situations like this.

Someone watching from the side would probably see a dreamy student browsing the shelves while humming an unfamiliar tune to herself. From her perspective, it was a simple lottery in which the lucky book would be the one her eyes fell upon the moment she finished the song.

She approached the seller and placed what fate had chosen in front of him.

She had never heard of this poet, and she usually read prose, but you didn't get to new places when you followed the same path every day.

On the way back to her apartment, she almost fell into an open manhole. Of course. That's how it was on good days—the sewer was open in the middle of the street.

She lifted her eyes from the open book a moment before the worker in the yellow hat ran toward her and stopped her.

"Working . . . Dangerous." He panted at her. "Go around." He pointed toward the park.

"Why don't you just put up a barrier or something?" she asked.

The worker shrugged his shoulders. It seemed he didn't speak English very well. "Dangerous," he said. "Go around."

Something in this book of poetry had grabbed her. Almost without thinking, she sat down on a small bench in the park, opposite the lake, in the shade of a large tree. She read and felt that the curiosity from the pages was seeping into her. The text seemed childish and very secretive, which obliged her to stop demanding answers from the world and to allow herself to experience it in silent amazement.

She lifted her eyes from the book, closed them, and felt that the wind was again blowing the scent of a good day toward her. The tree above her made light rustling sounds. She opened her eyes and let the world enter.

The green of the park, the sparkle of the water, the changing colors of the balls that a young man was tossing into the air on the other side of the lake.

Today would be a good day.

1

The park was quite empty at this hour of the morning.

He came here, occasionally, when he could no longer bear sitting in the lecture hall, no longer stomach the incessant babble. With all due respect for the term "student," the human spirit wasn't designed to be shut in a classroom for such a long time. He needed some space.

So he would come here occasionally, mainly at the expense of statistics class and similar courses, run around the lake a bit, stare at the growing grass or at the gardener who was always around, who glanced back at him with an amused look. He would contemplate life and practice his juggling. Today, he was outside before the end of the sentence announcing the lecturer's flu.

The gardener was there today too, on the far side of the park, on a small hill, his knees planted in a bed of miniature roses. Not far from him sat a long-legged guy who was immersed in thought, an open notebook in his hand.

He was up to four balls.

It had been very easy to learn this. The main rule, he reminded himself each time, was not to look at your hands. You needed to watch the balls in the air and not try to see how you caught them.

It was strange, but he never really practiced juggling. The movements flowed almost naturally from the start.

He stood opposite the lake in the center of the park and started to toss the balls in the air, trying to get into a steady rhythm, which would enable him to continue to juggle with his hands while sailing off to a different place in his mind.

When he saw her looking at him from the other side of the lake, something happened.

His hands unwittingly stopped, allowing the balls to fall around him, and her look (perhaps curious, perhaps amused) pierced his soul.

She sat there, her hands resting on a book, her red and white dress fluttering in the wind in rhythm with her red hair.

He was used to having women around him. He was used to trying to charm them, trying to get them to look at him or trying to excite them with his wit, but none of them made him feel—how did you say?—that he really cared. It was a sort of game. He didn't understand why, but it always seemed to him that someone was whispering to him that the time had not yet come.

But here was this young woman on the other side of the lake, and he felt something starting to blaze near his heart.

Like a small, strong flame; like another heart beating; like an old love letter that had just awakened and was burning under the skin, one line after another, thanks to her eyes.

She curled her hands around her mouth and called to him: "Why did you stop? It was quite nice."

He tried to regain his composure and quickly picked up the balls.

"What are you reading?" he called to her.

She raised the book so he could see. "It's called *Humanityism*," she called. "By someone named Eddie Levy."

"What's it about?" he yelled back.

"You know, poems . . . I just started . . . I was busy watching you. I haven't delved into it yet."

"Wait a minute," he yelled, and started to circle the lake.

In a small suitcase somewhere, several memories moved around, like children turning over in their sleep.

He'd never remember this, but it really wasn't easy to find that butterfly.

He felt a bit idiotic flying all the way to the rain forest, roaming around the jungle for a week in order to find the home of the right species. He'd been stung by mosquitoes, nearly eaten by a leopard, and then had conducted exhausting negotiations with a butterfly for three days.

Though he finished the course with honors following this test, he always wondered why it was necessary. A simple movement of a wing that was supposed to happen precisely at a specific second— what good would come from it?

He was familiar with the theory behind "small actions and large repercussions," but let's be honest: this butterfly wing would not generate world peace or a technological revolution. A bit of air moves and, at most, makes a lot of air move in the end. That's the extent of it, right?

As talented as this butterfly might be, nothing would come of this beyond . . .

⁂

An errant breeze tossed her hair when he finally reached her, making him think that this was probably the single most beautiful picture he had ever seen in his life.

She sat and waited for him, her hands still resting on the book, and that same breeze carried to her nostrils a nearly familiar scent that made her eyebrows arch a bit in surprise.

Too many words ran through his mind at that moment. The pages by his heart, under his skin, were almost glowing with heat.

At last the one who was no longer Guy said, "Hi."

"Hi," said the one who was no longer Emily.

The tall man on the opposite bank of the lake made a small, decisive check mark in his notebook.

The gardener on the hill stroked a delicate petal with his finger.

And the four of them smiled, each one for a slightly different reason.